UNBOUND

Steel and Desire - Book Two

KENDRA GREENWOOD

Published by Blushing Books
An Imprint of
ABCD Graphics and Design, Inc.
A Virginia Corporation
977 Seminole Trail #233
Charlottesville, VA 22901

Kendra Greenwood
Unbound

EBook ISBN: 978-1-61258-781-3
Print ISBN: 978-1-63954-039-6
v1

Chapter 1

Giggles. Shoes clacking on the cobblestone driveway. Viktor Aristov tugged at the hairs on his bushy black eyebrows as he waited, then smiled. Wearing high heels, the three teens came into view, the full moon illuminating them in an eerie blue. He aimed and fired, three quick shots. Startled, the girls momentarily hung suspended before gravity took over and they plunged to the pavement.

The tranquilizer gun proved one of his best purchases. No fuss, no muss.

He rushed forward to retrieve his merchandise when another figure marched down the driveway. He'd only expected three females. Who was this?

A tall woman appeared. "Alyssa?" she said. "Louise? Brenda?" The heap of bodies stopped her short. She gasped. "Holy Mother."

Viktor reacted. The tiny barb hit the woman squarely in the chest. She slumped, lying atop an unconscious teen. Viktor squatted beside the pile of bodies. Dumb broad. She probably discovered the girls sneaking out for a night of fun and intended to stop them. Well, she wasn't part of the plan, but, hell, what a bonus.

Loading the four bodies into the van, he secured each with leg shackles bolted to the vehicle's floor. He turned the key in the ignition and gripped the steering wheel so hard his fingers went numb. Heart pounding, he blew out a long breath. The thrill of the hunt! Best part.

The van traversed the bumpy driveway, his foot heavy on the accelerator. He'd scored big time. The crew had taunted him about not meeting his quota after the cache of women from his homeland mysteriously vanished from the container ship. He'd show them. Not only had he grabbed three prime females, but an extra bitch to boot. And Americans fetched a higher price than Slavic women. Fifty-thousand U.S. dollars would fill his coffer with a little over three million rubles. Then he could afford to rescue his mother from that horrible institution and make her comfortable—enough food, clean bedding and fresh country air. He grinned with satisfaction. His brother was somewhere in a Siberian prison, unable to help the family, and his sister languished in a labor camp. Unemployment there had hit the population hard, half were out of work and only a quarter of those employed got paid on a regular basis. He'd found his way out, and living in America had blessed him with many bounties. He kissed the rosary beads he kept around his neck for good fortune.

The targets had been easy prey. Chatrooms provided the perfect vehicle to find lonely teenage girls searching for love. Create a fake profile, add a pic of a hot guy, tell each what she wanted to hear and boom—the fish bit the hook, begging to be reeled in.

Viktor turned onto the long dirt road leading to the Sound Avenue Nature Preserve. The county park was mostly deserted at night, especially at this time of year. Perhaps a few bird watchers and hikers during the day, but with winter approaching the boating and swimming festivities had ended. The cabins were empty because they had no heat, electricity or water. A perfect hideout for his operation.

Two colleagues met him and helped unload the merchandise. "Brother, where have you been?" Iosif said, hiking up the waistband of his trousers on his too-thin frame. "We worried."

"Picking up the final product," Viktor answered.

"Thought you lost it when the ship arrived empty last week," Mikhail said, twirling one end of his villainous dark moustache.

"I improvised." He unlocked the van's side door, sliding it open. The four females remained unconscious. "Those tranq darts work like a charm. Worth every penny."

Iosif jumped inside and unlocked the manacles on the three young girls. Each man slung a body over his shoulder and headed inside, leaving the woman for last.

Viktor returned to find her awake, her back against the sidewall, her head leaning precariously to one side. He climbed inside and squatted. Upon closer inspection, tears streamed down her face and she was mumbling.

Praying?

Chapter 2

Special Agent Laura Logan glanced at the readout on the dash of her black government-issued sedan: 4:12. Well, she'd almost made it home. The strobing array of blue and red flashing lights distorted the terrain. She grimaced at the squish of her boot heel into mud. These weren't her shit-kicker boots, those she stashed in her car's trunk. These were her *good* ones. She should've switched them up before arriving; it'd been bucketing rain all day.

She turned up the collar of her navy trench coat against the frigid drizzle and fished in her pocket for her ID and badge. A tall, well-built man in a khaki raincoat stood about twenty feet away, his head down, scribbling on a small notepad as he spoke to a uniformed officer. He glanced up as she approached and waited for her. He stuffed the notebook into his coat pocket. The officer excused herself.

"Laura Logan, FBI," she said, flashing her credentials. He sported dark stubble, like he hadn't shaved in a day or two. Laura assessed his features. *Italian stallion* came to mind. On second thought, he probably could grow that facial hair in about an hour.

"You got here quick," he said, grinning widely. Laura found this odd. At a crime scene, what could he possibly find to smile about? He extended his hand. "Detective Lieutenant Steve Moretti, Suffolk County PD." They shook, his grip forceful and warm. No, *hot*. His other hand opened his coat to reveal a gold shield hooked onto his belt.

"You the guy that made the call?"

"Yep. That would be me. So, how'd you make it from the city so fast? Screaming sirens, doing ninety?" He smiled again. So annoying.

"I was on my way home. Just finished for the day. I'm only about thirty minutes from here."

"Sorry to drag you away from getting into your PJs."

Seriously? "Are we gonna stand here and banter back and forth like two teenagers or can we get to work?"

Steve Moretti's levity vanished. He sighed. "Right." He retrieved his notebook and opened it, scanning his notes as he spoke. "The call came in around nine this morning. One of the nuns here reported that three females, each seventeen, plus an employee, a Sister Mary Katherine, went missing. She feared the teens had run away, but couldn't explain the disappearance of the good Sister."

"And you called us because you think this might be a sex trafficking abduction?"

Detective Steve Moretti was at the end of a twelve-hour shift and wanted nothing more than to go home, take a hot shower, imbibe a few cold ones and watch the NY Rangers hopefully humiliate the Penguins. The black sedan swerved into the driveway too fast, the driver slamming on the brakes. As she approached, he inexplicably held his breath, like she was walking in slow-mo. A movie goddess. She strode toward him

—regal—shoulders squared, chin tilted upward. The stridency of flashing police lights lit her up like a dancer onstage, the image surreal, features blinking in and out of clarity, until she stood before him. Although the afternoon was gray and dismal, her strawberry-blonde hair and violet eyes stood out as if she was the only thing of color in a black and white movie.

Her handshake was firm, even with that petite hand, with no gold band on her ring finger. They presented their credentials. He found her prickly, like she wished he wasn't here and could work the case alone.

He cleared his throat. "Been hearing rumors about a new sex-trafficking ring tied to the Russian mob. I think it's worth looking into."

Special Agent Laura Logan shoved her hands into the pockets of her coat, staring at her feet. She hesitated, then said, "How reliable is your intel?"

That didn't take long. Steve had no intention of confessing that he'd heard these rumors at the exclusive sex club where he moonlighted a couple nights a week. He couldn't afford the dues so in exchange worked as a dungeon master, bartender and since he carried off-duty, security on occasion. His duties included supervising the training of new submissives, a task he found incredibly satisfying. But this would be revealing way too much about his personal life. And he never talked about his involvement in *the lifestyle* with a vanilla. Never, ever.

He phrased his answer carefully. "I have some contacts at a sex club. Guys I know well. There are feelers out asking if anyone is interested in buying a slave."

Laura Logan shook her head, lips taut. "I still can't wrap my mind around the fact that men do shit like this. Although, I should know better by now."

A silver SUV pulled in behind Laura Logan's car and a short, round, bearded man disembarked wearing a priestly collar. He walked directly toward them. "I'm Father Flanagan, the director here."

"Hello, Father," Steve Moretti said. "Detective Moretti, Suffolk County PD." They shook hands.

"Laura Logan, FBI." Laura flipped open her ID again.

Steve chuckled and said to the priest, "Don't you run a school for wayward boys?"

Father Flanagan frowned. "Like I haven't heard that a million times."

When Laura's eyebrows scrunched together, Detective Moretti smirked. "It's an old movie... *Boys Town*. Spencer Tracy, Mickey Rooney?"

"How old are you?" Laura declared.

"I'm not *that* old. Soon to be thirty-four. You?"

"Thirty-two.

"My mom's a classic movie buff. She raised me on this stuff."

As the temperature plummeted, snowflakes spiraled downward, a few exceptionally large ones landed on Steve Moretti's long dark eyelashes. Laura involuntarily shuddered. Father Flanagan touched her elbow. "Why don't we take this inside? Looks like you're catching a chill." He guided her toward the front door.

The two-story colonial with wrap-around porch needed a paint job and one shutter leaned precariously sideways. Steve Moretti held the screen door open, allowing her entry, the familiar slap of the rickety wood reminiscent of her childhood home. Father Flanagan ushered them toward seats: an overstuffed floral couch opposite two upholstered chairs, surrounding a whitewashed coffee table. Textbooks and notebooks littered the tabletop, along with a few empty glasses and a crumb-laden paper plate. Laura's well-trained eye scanned the room on the lookout for clues. A blaring noise punctuated the air. They all reached for their phones.

Steve announced, "Amber alert. At my direction."

Laura studied the photos of the vics: a pair of auburn-haired teens, one onyx-coiffed, thin faces, a picture of the Sister—a plain woman with pale skin and short blonde hair—indicating that they may be in her company. Laura grimaced. It made it seem like the Sister was the kidnapper.

Slipping off her coat, Laura draped it over the sofa's arm and settled on the end cushion. Lieutenant Moretti sat across from her and Father Flanagan beside him. The priest eyed her intently. "Have we met?" he asked Laura. "You look familiar."

"Not officially, or even casually. I've seen you on the soccer field. I coach youth soccer, a twelve-and-under team. I think you coach one division up."

"That's it. The Rockets, right? I do the stats for the league. Your team is kicking some soccer ass."

Laura beamed, although she was a little taken aback at the Father's language.

"I've got a great bunch of kids. They play hard."

Chapter 3

I bet she plays hard. And boy, would Steve love to play with her. When he realized he was inappropriately smiling, he pressed his lips into a hard line and refocused, asking the Father, "Do you reside here?"

"I don't. I stay at the parish in Bellport. Wouldn't be smart to live in a residence with four nuns and a dozen troubled girls, if you get my drift."

"Of course." Detective Moretti had his pad out again and jotted notes. "What's your role here? How often are you here?"

"I manage the finances, pay the bills and tutor math on Tuesday and Thursday mornings. I was due in this morning."

"So, when did you get the call that something was amiss?"

"Sister Constance called me at seven. She expressed her concerns, said she'd questioned the other residents and established that the missing girls intended to sneak out to a party after lights out."

Special Agent Laura Logan said, "Do you have any idea how the teens made arrangements for a rendezvous?"

"No. We only have a landline and they don't have cell phones."

Laura said to Steve, "Burner phone?"

"More likely online."

"I assume the girls have computer access?" Laura said.

"Yes, but we block a lot of stuff and try to monitor their use. Of course, teens are pretty savvy these days and I wouldn't be surprised if they found ways around us."

"What about video surveillance?" Laura said.

"This is a residence and we strive to make it like a home. Our girls are runaways, throwaways; they've been incarcerated in juvenile detention centers. We start with an expectation of trust, although we clearly outline the rules and the consequences of violating them. Besides, we can't afford video surveillance. Nor do we have someone to monitor it."

"You can't afford a nanny cam?" Laura said. Steve glared at her. Okay, he was being the good cop.

A patrolman approached Steve. "Excuse me, Lieutenant, but I think you need to see this."

"I'll be right back," Steve said and followed the officer out the front door.

Laura Logan settled back into the comfy couch and crossed her legs and arms. When Steve vacated the space, she felt compelled to establish her authority, territory. "I understand the girls might want to sneak out for some fun, Father, but how do you explain the disappearance of Sister Mary Katherine?"

"I can't." Father Flanagan shifted uncomfortably in his seat and exhaled noisily. "Do you think they were kidnapped? I mean... a ransom is unlikely as there's no money here. They've been abandoned by their families, who have no money either."

"I'm loathe to project a theory at this time, Father. Too early. However, young girls, especially troubled ones, are prime targets for sex trafficking. I hope that's not the case."

Father Flanagan's wide eyes betrayed his shock. "What about Sister Mary Katherine? You can't mean? Mary, Mother of God, that's a terrifying thought."

Steve Moretti reappeared, towering over them. "Let's not get ahead of ourselves," he said to Father Flanagan, apparently having heard their last remarks. "Hopefully, there's a more innocent explanation for their disappearance. Agent, can I speak to you outside, please?"

Laura grabbed her coat and shrugged into it, trailing Detective Moretti.

Teeth clenched, Steve Moretti opened the screen door and let Laura pass as they stepped onto the front porch. "What the fuck?" he said as the door slammed behind them. "Why freak out the poor Father before we have any credible evidence to support a sex trafficking case?"

"It was your frigging theory. You made the call, remember?"

"Yeah, to Alyx Cameron and she sent you. She said you were the best. I thought you'd use a little more discretion."

Laura buried her cold hands in the pockets of her dark trousers, her eyes cast downward. She shuffled her feet, toeing a loose board. Her violet eyes met his. "How do you know my boss?" she said.

"I worked a case with her a while back. Before she was put in charge of the task force."

"You said you have connections at a sex club. Is that where you met her? When she did that training? The case where she broke that sex ring?"

Oh boy. How had they gotten here so fast? He was hoping to avoid this line of questioning. He could lie, but lying never panned out if you spent any amount of time with someone. Eventually you'd trip up. But then again, why should he? He wasn't ashamed of himself. If she had hang-ups about sex that was her problem.

"Yeah, I met her there."

"So you, what do they call it, *play* there?"

"That's none of your business."

Laura's eyes didn't leave his and he gritted his teeth again. An image of her sprawled across a spanking bench vaulted into this mind. He swallowed hard and redeployed his brain waves. "There are signs of a struggle at the end of the driveway. CSI has taken pics and are making imprints of the tire tracks. The tires look industrial, probably a commercial van. My guess is the girls came out here to meet up with someone, not sure how the nun got involved."

Laura faced forward, fixated on the snowflakes plummeting to the ground. "God, we have young girls possibly sold into sex slavery, along with a nun."

"The worst kind of horrible," Steve said, running his hand down his face in frustration.

Laura sighed loudly. "I know. I didn't mean to make a distinction. It doesn't matter who it is. It's despicable."

Steve stood alongside Laura, their breath wisps of gray smoke in the frosty air. "Let's finish interviewing the rest of the residents and we'll compare notes later."

"Agreed," Laura said, her arm brushing against his.

Close enough to smell her perfume, an intoxicating invitation of patchouli and smoky cream. Steve couldn't banish the images of Laura Logan naked. In bed. With him.

Chapter 4

Laura pulled into the potholed parking lot of the Triangle Pub, constructed on a three-sided plot formed by intersecting roads. One space in front was vacant. Although Steve had entered ahead—she'd followed him to the unfamiliar bar—he took a spot farther away, leaving the closer one for her. She should have gone directly back to the office, but convinced herself a quick bite, mostly to debrief with Steve would prove beneficial.

They walked to the front entrance together and this time Laura held the door for Steve. "After you," she said, outstretching her hand as if the hostess.

Steve smiled playfully and a wave of warmth spread through her.

The bar was more of a restaurant, definitely a local hangout, filled with photos of male camaraderie, patrons sporting prize fish hanging from hooks—a giant tuna and a shark—the bar's softball team, and kids' soccer and baseball teams emblazoned with the tavern's name. In honor of the upcoming Thanksgiving Day holiday, posters challenged patrons to sign up for the turkey shoot. The prize: $500 for the biggest bird.

"There are wild turkeys around here?" Laura said.

"Herds of them." Steve frowned. "Or are they called flocks?"

"Wild turkeys are called a gang, if they were domestic they'd be a rafter." Steve's eyebrows arched. She went on, "I was a bio major for a hot minute. Botany took me down."

"Anyway," Steve said, "my backyard is a hangout apparently. Not much sport in killing a turkey. They're dumb as shit."

Nearing the bar, a burly redheaded dude approached Steve, slapping him on the back. "Hey, bud, how ya doing? Long time."

"Hey, Cal, I'm good. You?"

"Ah, ya know, living the life, the daily grind, nothing new." Ogling Laura, Cal kept banging his hand on Steve's back. "Introduce me to your sweet lady, buddy."

"She's a colleague," Steve corrected. "Laura, this is Cal, my landscaper." Laura considered her landscaper, a kind-hearted, demure Mexican. And how she'd thoroughly checked his citizenship, not wanting to make any mistakes that might jeopardize her security clearance.

"Pleasure," she said.

Steve Moretti placed his hand on her lower back and ushered her forward. "Later," he said to Cal.

The hostess seated them in a corner booth. She deposited menus on the table, saying their server would be right over.

"Sorry about Cal. He's a bit crude," Steve said.

"I've dealt with way worse." Laura perused the menu. Hunger pangs pinched her gut, not having eaten since her morning yogurt, plus the five cups of coffee she'd sipped throughout the day.

Though this was a working dinner, guilt consumed her. She should grab some fast food and head back to the office. Who knew what abuse the teens and the sweet nun were enduring at this moment? The knot in her stomach threatened to undo any thoughts of eating. "Let's get a quick bite and agree on our approach. Then get to work."

"Sounds like a plan," Steve said. "This place has the best burgers in the county."

Laura hadn't eaten a burger in probably three years. She fit the stereotype of the abused child. Overweight as a teen, hoping to camouflage her body with fat, denying her sexuality. Safe. But when the FBI came calling, she hired a personal trainer who whipped her into shape and taught her how to kick her own ass. Often, she still felt like the fat girl in the crowd even though she got plenty of stares at the gym. At least she was confident in her athletic abilities.

Should she order a burger? "I don't usually eat red meat."

"You're not a vegetarian, are you?" Steve's saucer eyes betrayed his horror.

"No." She chuckled. "I'll take your recommendation and go for it."

"Cheddar cheese and onions? Mushrooms? Whatever you like. It comes with French fries and pickle."

"Cheddar is fine. That's enough."

The waiter arrived and Steve placed the order.

"You got it," the waiter said. "How do you like the patties?"

"Medium," Steve said.

The waiter focused on Laura.

"Same."

"Beverages?"

"Unsweetened iced tea, please," Laura said.

"Make it two."

Laura sighed. "I feel incredibly guilty stuffing my face when four women are in danger."

"You have to eat, maintain your energy or you'll be no good to anyone. Let's decide where we go from here."

Steve Moretti wished he sat across from this magnificent woman for a different reason. He tried not to engage in too much eye worship, because she took his breath away with every beat, each interlude.

He desperately wanted to order a beer. Eating a burger without a beer was tantamount to sacrilege, but they were on the job. Back to business. "I've got most of my division out canvassing the neighborhood to see if anyone saw or heard anything. The Amber Alert is out. There are no cell phones to track. My IT guys are scouring the residence's computers and hopefully something will turn up. Steve's mobile rang. "Moretti." Listening, his brow furrowed. "Uh-huh," he said several times. "Thanks, Jeff." He ended the call. "Something came up on the computers. Looks to us like catfishing but we're having trouble tracing the IP address. Probably used a VPN or proxy. Definitely a message about a party invite."

"No way of tracing it?" Laura said. "What if I put my guys on it? We might have better luck."

Steve tried not to be insulted. The Feds regarded themselves as superior, and maybe they possessed more resources. What the heck, he'd put his pride aside to do whatever necessary to get the women home safely. "Have at it," he said. "I'll have my guys send their stuff to you."

"Great. I'll make the call."

"By the way," Steve said, "you're not working with a partner?"

"She's on maternity leave. Back in a few weeks. I've been rotating through a bunch of NATs for the past few months.

"NATs?"

"New agent trainees." She rolled her eyes. "I won't lie, it's exhausting."

"I get that."

"What about you? Working solo too?"

Steve Moretti played with his napkin, folding it into a triangle. Did he want to go there? It was still too painful and he rarely spoke of it. "I don't have a partner any longer."

"He retire or something?"

"The latter."

Laura's violet eyes studied him as if she already grasped the truth but feigned ignorance. The story had made the papers so maybe she did know. Their drinks arrived and Steve took a long draught, stalling. "Besides, I've just been named Chief of Detectives and technically don't have a partner anymore," he said hoping to avoid fessing up.

"Congratulations, but doesn't that mean you're in more of a supervisory role than working on scene?"

"We're a small department so I often work cases myself and with any number of guys based upon the profile." It was the truth; he could work with whomever he chose these days. Not like years past when Tony had been his partner and best friend.

Laura sipped her tea, replacing the glass gently on the paper placemat. "He died." It wasn't a question.

"I would've taken that bullet for him in a heartbeat."

"I believe you." Laura laced her fingers together, laying her hands on the table. She lowered her head briefly, then glanced up. "I see it on your face."

Steve had become an expert at burying his pain. In some ways he was a different person after the shooting. He'd always been generous with his emotions, a gregarious and loving man. But then his girlfriend of three years had cheated on him and his partner got killed. All in the same week. Grieving wasn't something he was good at. His family worried about him and had no problem expressing their concerns every Sunday at the weekly family dinner. Some weeks he didn't go, not wanting to face their constant pep talks. He came from one of those big happy clans. The kind that didn't exist much anymore. His mother, a high school principal, was the eternal optimist, upbeat and caring, although not overly sympathetic.

When he was four, she'd sent him out three times to play after he complained he'd hurt his shoulder romping on the ground with friends. Eventually she figured out something was actually wrong and when the doctor diagnosed a broken collarbone she told him he was her big boy, strong enough to power forward. Her attitude was pretty much just suck it up and be grateful. Because it could always be worse.

"I'd rather not talk about it," Steve said, taking a long drink.

The waiter placed their meals in front of them. "Holy shit," Laura exclaimed. "This is more food than I eat in a week."

"Looks like you can afford a few pounds," Steve said, glad to be off the topic of his deceased partner.

"Careful. I spent my entire teen years overweight. Food and I have a funny relationship."

He wiped his mouth with the napkin and tilted his head. "I'll remember to be very careful with my compliments."

Laura wanted to be mad at Steve but for some reason she couldn't and he obviously had no desire to talk about his late partner. Was he killed in the line of duty, was it a heart attack, a car accident? She needed to know, because if his partner was killed on the job that could affect how Steve handled himself in the field. She bit into her burger, which was *fucking delicious*, and chewed slowly, savoring every second. "Wow, you're right this burger is amazing."

Steve raised an eyebrow. "A man never lies about a burger."

"What about video surveillance?" she said. "Do you have someone checking traffic cams?"

"This is a pretty rural area, not many cameras. My guys are on it, but not much is under surveillance."

"So what's our next move? Seventy-two hours and our chances of finding them decrease dramatically."

"I'll head back to the precinct and review everything that's come in. Hopefully there's a lead."

Steve had finished half his burger already. Laura took another bite and chewed carefully, not wanting to talk with her mouth full, then washed it down with tea. "I'll head into the office too. Let's touch base later tonight."

"Give me your number." He had his phone out and she recited the digits. When her phone rang, he said, "Okay, you've got mine too."

Laura's curiosity got the best of her and she blurted, "You said you met Alyx at that sex club where you work, or whatever."

"Or whatever? I bartend, work security sometimes and I play there."

"Not the relationship type, I take it."

"Been there, done that and it's not for me."

"I hear you. I'm married to the job and I like it that way. No drama, at least not of my own making."

"On the same page."

Laura offered to split the check but Steve adamantly refused and wouldn't allow her to leave the tip either. "I'd never let a woman pay the check."

"Pretty archaic," Laura said. "Very cave man of you."

Steve smirked. "You have no idea." Her pulse spiked again. He certainly was bossy.

Entering the Long Island Expressway, Laura dialed Alyx Cameron on the car phone. "Get me up to speed," Alyx said. Laura related the details of the case and Alyx responded, "So you think it's a trafficking case?"

"My gut says absolutely."

"You think Steve was on the mark?"

"I do. And we'll work the case together."

"Great. Let me know if you need me. You've got carte blanche at the office."

"Will do."

"By the way, good job finding those women on that container ship. Nice save."

"Thanks. That tip paid off. We got there just in time. They were in pretty bad shape."

"I know it's frustrating sometimes. It seems like progress is slow, but we are having an impact, even if it's just a few women at a time."

"True that."

"I've alerted everybody on shift to give you whatever you need. Daniel and I are at the Hamptons Shores house for the weekend, but if you need me, let me know and I'm there."

"Thanks, Alyx."

Laura was a little jealous of Alyx Cameron. Daniel, an eminent heart surgeon and a *hunk*, was quite the catch. But a long-term relationship wasn't for her. She didn't trust any man and had never had a serious boyfriend. She was pretty much a 'wham, bam, thank you, sir' kind of girl. Tina Turner was so right. What did love have to do with anything?

Alyx had met Daniel when he was her trainer for an undercover assignment in a sex club, the same club where Steve apparently worked too. Laura had to admit that her imaginings of what went on in a sex club gave her a tingle or two, not that she'd ever engage in such kinky activities. The stuff of fantasies, not reality.

Alyx wound up breaking a huge sex trafficking ring, rescuing seventy battered women before they could be sold into slavery. Big case, and Alyx had received wide acclaim from everyone, even the Bureau, who put her in charge of a new task force targeting human trafficking. She'd recruited

Laura in the first week, having been fellow recruits at Quantico, plus they'd worked a few cases together in the early days.

Navigating into the parking garage at 26 Federal Plaza, she parked and headed for the office. Why couldn't she quit thinking of Steve Moretti? Naked.

Chapter 5

S teve turned the knob to hot. A quick shower and shave then back to his office. Facing a marathon, he wouldn't be able to sleep until he'd overturned every rock and goddamned boulder in this hunt. His throat tightened at the thought of these women enduring horror upon terror, his niece the same age as the vics. The bomb kept ticking but there was one saving grace: when women were up for sale the perps would often leave them alone, understanding the better shape they were in fetched a much higher price. Not that they wouldn't be tempted to 'sample the merchandise' but hopefully the lure of more money would deter their more lascivious inclinations.

The fervent streams pounded him from every direction. The money he'd spent on the thermostatic shower system with six body jets and handheld attachment had been worth every penny. More than one lady had enjoyed his adeptness at facilitating an orgasm with that attachment. And, there she was again. Dogging him, like an itch he couldn't scratch. Special Agent Laura Logan. In his shower. Screaming in the throes of ecstasy.

He stopped at the local deli for a cup of coffee; the meh office brew was only in case of emergency. Parking in his reserved spot, he entered the precinct house, making a beeline for his desk. Images of Laura Logan, soapsuds covering her slick skin, lingered in his mind. Another hard on. Down boy, down. Jesus.

He passed by his secretary, giving a cursory hello, hung his coat on the hook, and settled into his squeaky chair. The coffee tasted good, no, great. He should have gotten two, one for later when he would still be shackled to the paperwork.

"Boss," Alice Lovely said, handing him a stack of papers. "I've got the reports from the officers on scene, plus the one from the tech department. No video surveillance found yet. Anything else you need before I go?"

Alice could be a Lilly Pulitzer model. Vivid prints in technicolors that probably existed outside of known frequencies and made his eyes hurt. Fronds and palm trees in neon hues. Like she was always a tourist on vacation. He wouldn't have known who Lilly Pulitzer was if his sister wasn't such a fan. And coupled with Alice's blonde Shirley Temple locks, it made it difficult to take her seriously if you never saw her in action. But she was a true gem, with a sharp mind, and her personality perfectly matched her last name. "This is great, Alice. Thanks. What would I do without you?"

"If things get crazy and you need me just call. Mike is at the Ranger Game tonight so I'm on my own. Glad to come back in. Anything I can do to help get those girls home safely, I'm in."

Steve wished he was home watching the game, his plan for the evening derailed. "I've got you on speed dial."

"Promise?"

"Promise." As she made her exit, his cell rang. *Unknown Caller.* "Moretti."

"Detective, I don't know what to do. The place is besieged

by reporters." He and Laura had given Father Flanagan their cards.

"Sorry, that can be a nightmare. Just tell them 'no comment' and give them my contact info. I'll handle it from here."

"Thanks, Detective. Any news?"

"Not yet, but we're working round the clock."

Within thirty minutes, reporters swarmed the precinct. The watch officer informed Steve they wanted a statement.

"I'll handle it. Tell them I need a few minutes."

"Yes, sir."

He dialed Laura Logan from his cell phone but it went to voicemail. "Shit. Where are you?" He didn't want to talk to reporters until after discussing it with the FBI. He wouldn't reveal any info that would compromise the investigation yet he wanted to make sure they were not just on the same page, but the same paragraph and sentence. Every consonant and vowel must fucking match. Not a second later she was on the line. He related the onslaught of the media. "I'm just about to make a statement but I wanted to run it by you first."

"We've got a lead," she said, ignoring his concerns about the reporters staking out his front door. "We've tracked down that IP address from the invite on one of the computers. It was sent using a hotspot. It's registered to a Joe Blow, obviously a fake identity. We haven't been able to trace the user. We've pinged a location. I have a street address. Heading there now."

Damn, she'd been right. Those FBI tech nerds had done it. "Give me the address, I can get there faster than you."

"I don't want anybody going in with guns blazing before I get there."

"I've been to many, many rodeos, ma'am." Steve huffed. He was definitely insulted this time.

"I didn't mean you, but there's always the possibility that someone will try to be a hero."

Which is exactly what his partner had done. He didn't wait for backup and had gotten shot. He too had a lead and called Steve to meet him there because they hadn't started their shift yet. But he couldn't wait and the outcome turned tragic.

"I don't want you going in by yourself," Steve said.

"I won't. I'm bringing back up."

"I'll bring my SWAT team."

Laura Logan's speedometer read ninety-five as she traveled the Long Island Expressway, sirens blazing, two additional vehicles in her wake. A trainee sat beside her, a bit pale. The heat of the chase somehow humbled you. All that bravado and confidence, questionable when you were about to face a life and death situation. Luckily, adrenaline kept you in hunt-and-fight mode, hopefully no flight needed.

"Fast thinking," she said to Steve. "I'm texting you the address but you wait for me. Promise?"

"Yes, ma'am. You're the boss."

Laura smirked. "I am not. We're sharing jurisdiction on this. I just don't want to do this without you."

"All right, but I have to ditch the press first. I'll make a brief statement then I'm like the wind."

"Whoever gets there first, let the other one know. Stay on the perimeter. I don't want them tipped off."

"Agreed."

Laura handed her phone to the newbie agent sitting beside her. "Text Detective Moretti the address."

"Yes, ma'am." Geez, what was with all the 'yes, ma'ams' and 'yes, bosses'?

The caravan took Exit 71, screeching left onto county

Route 24. The road had no streetlights and Laura kept her eyes focused, alert to the possibility of a deer darting across the rural road. A right turn onto Sound Avenue and almost there. No lights illuminated the Nature Preserve. In fact, most of the East End of Long Island consisted of country roads that could be treacherous at night. And during the daytime farm vehicles littered the path, traveling at ridiculously slow speeds. People often considered Long Island a suburb of New York City, which it was, but once you got past Exit 71 on the Expressway, the whole landscape morphed into acres of farmland and forest, dotted with a few strip malls and disturbed somewhat by the pretentious towns of the Hamptons. Bordered by the Long Island Sound to the north and the Great South Bay and Atlantic Ocean to the south, the area was known for beachfront property and some of the most beautiful stretches of pristine shoreline in the world. Fire Island had its own culture, much of it being a hot spot for the gay community.

The Park Police had been notified and the gate stood open upon arrival. Laura nixed the sirens and lights a mile back so as not to alert the perps.

Well, damn. *You're the boss?* Those words had never crossed Steve Moretti's lips. And he'd like to boss *her* around. In his bedroom. Jesus, Steve. You've got to get that woman off your brain.

Donning his trench coat, he buttoned the top button on his white shirt and straightened his tie, running his fingers through his dark, wavy hair. Which was getting a little long and he made a mental note to get a haircut. He inhaled deeply and slowly let it out. Talking to the press was worse than getting a prostate exam. "Let's do the circus," he said to the cadre of officers filling the precinct. "Stand behind me. I want a show of force, but everyone keeps his or her mouth shut. Got it?" A chorus of "Yes, sirs" filled the air.

The snow had stopped, only a few inches coating the grassy areas around the stationhouse. The ten-foot wide stone slab in front of the doublewide glass doors descended downward in five wide steps. The layered cement was covered with a sea of reporters holding microphones, and cellphones snapping pictures. Questions zapped through the air like stray bullets.

"Can you tell us more about the Amber Alert? Is it true that a nun was abducted? Do you have any leads? Is Father Flanagan a suspect? Is this a sex-trafficking case?"

Steve Moretti cleared his throat, his troupe of officers bolstering his back. "I have a brief statement to make but I will not take questions at this time." He paused briefly. "Three seventeen-year-old females are missing. They reside at the Sisters of Mercy residential site for teens. In addition, one of the nuns is also missing. That's all the information I can provide at this time. No one at the residence is currently a suspect. The investigation is progressing rapidly and I don't have the time or inclination to comment at length. I'm sure you will respect our need to maintain the integrity of the investigation until we make an arrest or deem it necessary to alert the public further."

Reporters barked more questions, ignoring his words completely. A tenacious group, as always. Were journalists as obnoxious in their personal lives? He reminded himself not to date a reporter.

"At this time we are pursuing several leads with the help of the FBI and hope to have some news in the upcoming hours. In that event, I will alert you and provide additional information."

More ricocheted questions.

"Thank you," Steve said, pivoting on his heels, leading the parade of blues back into the precinct. "I hate that shit," Steve said to the room. He sighed, shaking his head.

The SWAT commander arrived. "We're suited up and ready, Lieutenant."

"Okay, let's move out. Everybody on night shift is with me except for the desk sergeant. I've got other precincts covering for us if necessary. We're heading to the Sound Avenue Nature Preserve off Route 24. The FBI is en route and we're to rendezvous with them. No one makes a move without FBI direction."

Steve said a silent prayer. Please, let us be in time.

Chapter 6

Laura disembarked from her black sedan and unholstered her service revolver. She dialed Steve Moretti. "We're on site. How far out are you?"

"About five minutes."

"Cut your lights and sirens but be careful. It's pitch black out here."

A momentary silence and then, "Again, I'm not an idiot."

Why did he keep thinking she was insulting him? She was *protecting* him, which confused her. She'd never had the urge to protect a man before. Okay, she'd always protected her partners in the field, but she'd only known Steve for a day and didn't understand her need to safeguard him so intensely.

Her voice came out too high, screechy. "I don't think you're an idiot. I already told you that. I just want you safe." Oh my God. Had she actually said that out loud? She glanced at her newbie partner who sported a grimace. She sounded like a complete jerk and he obviously agreed. The heat of embarrassment temporarily warmed her yet ended in a shudder.

Gathering the team of agents around, she instructed, "Suffolk County PD is almost here. We need to approach carefully. I don't want to spook these guys."

———

Steve Moretti's convoy passed through the open gate and crept down the dirt road until they spied the FBI vehicles. The collective team of agents and police surrounded Laura. "I've got EMT on standby down the road," Steve said.

"Excellent. Who's in command?" Laura asked Steve. "Only one person should be giving orders."

"You're the boss," he said. *Again?* He'd said it, *again.*

"Well, technically, this is your jurisdiction, so you're the boss. But I'm happy to step in if you want."

Steve liked being in charge. Not only in his sex life as a Dom, which went without saying, but also on the job. Becoming chief of detectives had finally validated him and running the show elated him. Under his leadership the department had taken great strides. He'd upgraded the forensic tech unit and purchased state-of-the-art crime scene equipment. But for some reason he wanted to surrender to this woman.

He had no idea why.

———

Viktor viewed the oil lamp's glimmer from the cabin as he returned from the lake with two plastic gallon containers of water. The preserve shut off the water in the cold months and of course, the electricity too. Cold water would suffice to clean the females as well as perk them up. The sharp crack of a twig caught his attention, halting his forward motion. He crouched low, ducking behind a large oak and gently rested the containers on the soft pine needle carpet. His breath sat still in his chest.

Spidey senses raised the hair on Viktor's nape.

He had to deliver the merchandise by midnight and always got a little jumpy before the handoff. Keeping Iosif and Mikhail from abusing the merchandise had sapped him. Both were brutal with women. They insisted nobody would be able to tell but he doubted that. Not that he wasn't the same, but he knew when and where to unleash his inner beast. Once he had his money, he might even be able to get out of the business. He'd gotten too old for this anyway, hitting the half-century mark next month. He'd saved every penny, living in cheap motels and eating crap food. A quiet life with a slave of his own would be his pay off.

His uneasiness escalated into anxiety. They needed to load the merchandise into the van but they couldn't drug them. They had to look good for the buyers. The area was deserted, so it didn't matter if they screamed yet for some reason the woods proved unnaturally silent. No hoot of owls or rustling of leaves as skittish creatures scurried about, searching for food, preying on the weaker.

About two dozen shadowy figures came in from both sides of the cabin, guns drawn, stealthily approaching the backside of the bungalow. Damn Iosif. He'd probably been watching porn again and the cops had found their location because of his idiocy.

The officers closed in on the back entrance. If this many cops were at the back, there had to be more out front. They were surrounding the place. He considered his options. Outnumbered and he only had a handgun on him. Not enough to wage battle against law enforcement.

His blood surged, fueled by rage. All that money—gone. Thoughts of retirement—questionable. He had a considerable amount of cash saved. But would it be enough to last a life-time? To take care of his mother? Maybe he needed a break, some time to regroup. He'd had a bad string of luck lately.

First losing the merchandise on the cargo ship. How had they simply vanished into thin air? Now this. Was there an informant somewhere? Their sister organization, the 6X Society, had been thwarted by some fucking FBI agent over a year ago and there was a hit out on her. Dangerous to target an FBI agent, however. But the bounty was big. Maybe he should make that his next assignment. But she spent too much time in that office of hers. And when she wasn't working, she was with that rich dude, the one she'd just married. Maybe he'd snatch her and ask for ransom. Play that against the bounty to see who'd pay more.

Abandoning the water vessels, Viktor crept around the perimeter of the cabin to further assess the level of danger and get a bead on Iosif and Mikhail. Were they aware of the cops? Were the women still secured? He gave a wide berth, peering intently at the police troops circling the cabin. A female in a black suit and protective vest stood at the front door, two cops at her side. FBI, he figured. They bashed in the front door. Gunfire erupted. Using the noise as cover, Viktor headed toward what he hoped was the FBI chick's car. He found her purse in the back seat and checked her driver's license, memorizing her name and address, then crept back into the woods, circling back to where he'd left the water.

Doomed. No alternative but to escape and live to fight another day. Thank God for the boats at the lake.

Laura silently directed the group with two fingers, pointing right, then left. The officers spread out, Steve and several of his SWAT team hurtled toward the back of the cabin, a contingent of others flanking both sides. Laura approached the front door with two policemen carrying a battering ram. She tried the doorknob. Locked.

Laura nodded the order. The heavy metal log hit the front door, splintering the wood. A second ram and they were in. "FBI," Laura yelled. She aimed her Glock, finger on the trigger, primed to fire.

She surveyed the room. The women weren't there and two brutes faced her. Their comically stretched expressions told her they'd been caught off guard. The men hit the ground and rolled, pulling handguns from their underarm holsters. The back door flew open and Steve, with his contingent of law enforcers, entered. The two slavers pointed their guns at Steve.

"Freeze," Steve said. "Drop your weapons."

Shots rang out, hitting Steve in the chest. He flew backward and collapsed. Laura fired twice in rapid succession hitting both perps in the back of the head before anyone else got off a shot. They twitched and thrashed, then stilled. She ran to Steve's side and crouched. Steve moaned. "Shit, motherfucker, that hurts."

"Damn, she's fast," a voice behind her said, "none of us even got off a shot."

"You okay?" Laura said.

"Yeah. Just in the vest, I think."

"Search the premises," she ordered the remaining officers. She ran her hands over the hard steel of Steve's body, searching for injury. "Angels watching over you."

"You part of the garrison? You're a damn good shot."

Laura smiled and Steve grimaced, struggling for breath. Helping Steve to his feet, she secured his broad shoulders with her arm. "You sure you're okay? EMT should check you out."

"I'm fine. Don't worry about me."

"Agent, in here," an officer called out.

Laura, with Steve hobbling beside her, trod toward the side hall of the small cabin. Inside, the three teens and the Sister were shackled to the beds. Tears streaked their faces, a cascade of sobs escaped. "Check the perps' pockets for keys," Laura directed. She squatted, telling the victims, "You're safe. We've got you."

"My prayers were answered," Sister Mary Katherine said. "I knew you'd come." Laura was glad the Sister had faith. She, however, hadn't been as sure they'd find the females in time.

"Are you hurt?" Laura said.

"No," the Sister said, "a little battered, hungry and thirsty. Cold."

Steve questioned the teens, "Are you injured?"

"We're okay," the black-haired teen responded. "You came just in time. We overheard them saying they were about to move us out."

"Sell us as sex slaves," one of the redheads said. "We were so scared we wouldn't be saved in time."

Seconds later, the handcuffs were removed. The EMT crews invaded the tiny room, checking vital signs and eventually escorting them into waiting ambulances.

On her way out, the Sister broke away from her escort, "Agent," she said to Laura. "What about the other guy?"

"There was a third guy?" Steve said.

"Yes, the other two called him Viktor. He went out back for water."

Laura and Steve exchanged worried glances. Laura said, "We need to search the property again, although the gunfire probably sent him scurrying."

"Yeah, but he's on foot, he can't get far," Steve added. They directed their teams to search the perimeter of the property as the women were shepherded to the local hospital. Laura hoped they hadn't suffered any serious maltreatment while in the hands of the slavers and would await the medical reports for confirmation.

Steve's chest hurt like a son-of-bitch. Maybe he'd cracked a rib. He'd get checked out later. Right now, he needed to do his job and he wanted that third guy bad. Real bad. The dusting of snow provided the information they sought, footprints leading down to the lake. They stumbled across the two water jugs, hopefully yielding fingerprints.

"Damn," Laura said. "I can't believe he escaped."

"Looks like he took a boat across the lake and hiked up to the road. I've got guys searching the neighborhood. But he could be anywhere by now." They backtracked to the cabin and their vehicles. Steve loosened the straps on his vest, his teeth clenched tightly, swallowing the urge to groan.

"We'll get a sketch done and put out an APB. Hopefully somebody knows him or sights him," Laura said. She stepped closer and reached for a strap. "Here, let me help you with that." Together they removed the heavy armor and Laura handed the vest to an adjacent officer. She removed hers as well.

"Let's go, I'm driving you to the ER."

"I'm fine. I've got to get back to the precinct and I'll need to give an updated briefing to the press in the morning." He inhaled deeply but a sharp pain forced a gasp.

"Yeah, right," Laura said, gripping his elbow. "I'm not taking no for an answer. Have one of your patrol guys take your car back to your house. We'll do the press conference after you get checked out. Hopefully we'll have a sketch by then and get prints."

Steve wanted to protest, but he feared Laura was right. Yet he wasn't used to a woman fussing over him, other than his mother, and she wasn't all that fussy. "You win," he said. But suddenly he felt uneasy, bereft, sad even. Laura Logan would walk out of his life.

Chapter 7

The perimeter secured, CSI scoured the cabin and woods for evidence. Laura finally dragged Steve to the hospital around 6 a.m. He smiled as Laura threw her weight around in the ER, getting him x-rayed and treated, in and out in less than forty-five minutes. Two cracked ribs. Damn. But, he reminded himself, it could have been worse. Permanently worse.

Taped and armed with a handful of painkillers, he settled into the passenger seat of Laura's car as she held the door open for him.

They returned to the precinct where a bevy of reporters surrounded the front entrance. "Shit," Steve said. "I hate this part."

"You and me both," Laura said. "Let's get it over with so I can get you home to rest."

Steve introduced Laura and let her take the reins. Again.

"I'll make a brief statement and then I'll take questions," she said.

She handled the reporters with aplomb, announcing the

females were rescued and two perpetrators where dead at the scene.

"The Suffolk County Police Department, under the direction of Detective Lieutenant Steven Moretti, was invaluable in this effort and I commend them on their professionalism and expertise." She paused and sighed. "Unfortunately, one of the suspects escaped. I will have an artist's rendering soon and implore the public to call the tip line at 1-800 CALL FBI if they know or see this man. He's about five-ten, one-eighty, with short, gray hair. He has a scar on his right cheek."

Laura answered their questions patiently and succinctly and after another ten minutes they excused themselves, referring further phone calls to the FBI.

"Seasoned pro," Steve said. "And thanks for routing future calls from the press and the public to your office. We don't have the manpower to handle it."

"No problem. Now, let's get you home."

They arrived at his driveway and Steve noticed his lawn buried under a carpet of leaves. Thankfully, the smattering of snowflakes had already melted. Damn Cal, the worst landscaper. He'd have to call him to remove them before a serious freeze hit. His car had been returned as directed, parked in front of his detached garage. "The keys are in the driver side visor," he told Laura.

She retrieved them and unlocked his front door. Steve shut off the alarm. "Nice place," Laura said. "Tidy. Especially since you weren't expecting a visitor. Most single guys I know live like slobs."

"Caught. I'm a little compulsive. I don't like clutter. And I work too much so I don't actually spend a lot of time hanging out here."

"Do you need me to do anything for you? Can I bring some food while you recuperate?"

"No, thanks. Once my family gets wind of this they'll

descend on me with plenty of carbs." Although Steve had every intention of keeping his injury a secret from his family, providing it didn't make the evening news. "Besides, I plan to be back at work by Monday." And damn, he needed to call in sick to the club tonight. Colin would have to take over training the submissives this weekend.

"Well, enjoy your weekend off. I'll let you know if we pick up a lead on that third guy."

"Great," Steve said. "Don't be a stranger."

And Special Agent Laura Logan walked out of his life. Likely forever.

Viktor docked the small rowboat on the other side of the pond, hiking up to the main road. A strip mall lay ahead, where he found a white Jeep Cherokee with the engine running and grinned at his change in luck. Speeding west on Sound Avenue, he headed for the storage facility to retrieve his emergency stockpile of fake IDs, satphone, cash, and car. Those FBI bitches were in his sights. They'd know what it felt like to be a slave. Maybe he'd build an underground bunker that no one would ever find. There, he could take his time and inflict untold torture on those two. How much fun would that be? He could ransom them, or sell them as slaves.

Did he want money or revenge? Both. He'd have to plan carefully and take his time. He purchased hair dye and found a motel he'd never frequented before, checking in under one of his many aliases.

Patience wasn't one of his virtues, but the payoff would be enormous if he tamed his impulsivity. He wanted to fuck those bitches up now, but he could wait. Just not too long, his inner beast needed to be fed.

Sia belted out *Hostage* on the car stereo and Laura increased the volume. Weird coincidence. Hopefully she could deliver the sketch of the third guy to the press by the end of the day and she'd spend all her resources getting the bastard. She'd settled Steve on the couch with his remote control, fluffed a few pillows behind him and left. For some reason she wanted to stay and take care of him, but that was just ridiculous. Again, she'd never had the urge to pamper a man. She sighed as Sia sang about being held hostage by your love, cuffed, kissed.

An image of Steve putting her in handcuffs flashed and her stomach lurched. Well, not her stomach, a few inches farther down. What the fuck was wrong with her? She needed a cold shower.

She parked her car in the garage, entering through the kitchen and deactivated the alarm. Something to eat, a few hours of sleep, then a shower and back to work. Her cell rang. Maybe it was Steve? She imagined him in pain, confined to his sofa. Perhaps he needed something. When Alyx's name showed, she saddened.

"Nice work," Alyx said.

"Thanks, but one of them got away. I won't rest until I find him."

"I know. But he won't be able to do much tonight so don't stress yourself out. I'm pretty sure he'll be on the outs with his organization. It's definitely a setback for them."

"If you say so," Laura said, squeezing her eyebrows together.

"I do. Take the weekend off. I'll be back on Monday and we'll get to work."

The weekend off? She didn't even have a soccer game as they had a bye this week. Laura didn't like having that much time on her hands. Alyx had often chastised her for her worka-holic weekends, saying it made the rest of them look bad. Alyx was gently chiding her, but still.

Laura pondered going to the gym but settled on a nap instead. She woke, threw in a load of laundry then made herself a salad and poured a glass of icy chardonnay. Surfing the channels she stumbled on *Unfaithful*. Man, that guy was one sexy son-of-a-bitch and she thought of Steve again.

She switched the laundry into the dryer then watched the late night news in bed and slept late, apparently more exhausted than she'd realized. Pouring a second cup of coffee, she tidied up, vacuumed the living room and cleaned the bath-rooms. Everything spic and span, she'd do a little shopping. Maybe buy a few things for her upcoming Thanksgiving trip to Virginia. She always spent either Thanksgiving or Christmas with her mom. Their relationship was still strained and her mother never recovered after the death of her stepfa-ther. Laura's mother couldn't forgive herself for what happened. But *she'd* forgiven her mother. Each time she visited, she was cheery and upbeat because her mother's life was miserable. Her tiny apartment was dark and dreary, her finances limited to her social security and the paltry sum she earned as a part-time RN at the local assisted living facility. Her stepfather's police pension had been voided due to the *circumstances* of his demise. So, yeah, Laura felt guilty. Even if she shouldn't.

Steve felt better than he had a right to as he poured himself a cup of coffee. Had Laura made any progress on finding the other perp? He wanted to call but that was a bad idea. The FBI could handle the case from here and if they needed him they'd call him, not the other way around. However, he wished he had an excuse to call her. It was only Saturday so calling and saying it was business would sound stupid and he couldn't think of any reasonable excuse to check in with her.

The whir of the leaf blower outside distracted him. Cal had said he'd be over first thing in the morning. Steve secretly thought Cal was a little afraid of him. Never good to be on the wrong side of a cop. He laughed. Old Cal was probably not the most law-abiding citizen.

His landline rang. Had to be either a telemarketer or his parents. They were the only ones who called him on it. He glanced at the readout, "Hi, Mom."

"Darling, are you okay? I saw you on the press conference and you looked a little peaked, like you were hurt." The guilt from that time she'd sent him out to play three times with a broken collarbone still lingered after all these years. Now, she sometimes overcompensated.

"I'm fine, Mom, just a couple cracked ribs. Nothing to worry about."

"Oh my God. Do you need me to come over? I'll make you soup."

Oh no, here comes the onslaught of forced feedings. "Mom, I don't need any help. I'm just going to take it easy this weekend and I'll be back on the job Monday."

"Are you sure? I'm busy this morning but I could send one of your sisters over."

"Absolutely not. I don't need anything."

"Well, I'm proud of you for catching those awful men and saving those girls."

"Thanks, Mom. Just doing my job."

"Will we see you tomorrow for Sunday dinner?"

"I don't think so. I'm just going to rest and watch the game. I'll try for next week."

"We could come to you?"

His parents, two sisters with their husbands and five kids at his house was too much to bear. "Not necessary. I'm tired, Mom," he lied. "I'll talk to you later."

"All right. Love you," his mother said.

"Love you too, Mom."

Steve spent the rest of the day on the couch watching college football, dozing from the effect of the painkillers, which he'd be done with by tomorrow morning. He'd switch to ibuprofen. He ate in front of the television, leftover Chinese from two days ago, hoping it was still good because puking with cracked ribs would be incredibly painful. His cell rang and he sat up too quickly, wincing, grabbing it off the side table. *Laura Logan.*

"Laura," he said.

"Hey. Just checking in to see how you're feeling." Something about the lilt of her voice sent his blood racing. For some reason he felt like he'd known her a long time. A ridiculous notion since they'd barely met. And he knew nothing about her. Her childhood, where she went to school? Whether she'd been married or divorced? What her favorite color was? Her favorite food? Did she like to dance or was she a wallflower... and the ultimate question: what was she like in bed? What did she taste like? Shit, he was getting a hard-on.

This was becoming a trend.

Laura stared at her phone for a full minute before getting up the nerve to dial Steve's number. She was fawning over him. No reason to call about the case since she had nothing new. Just ask how he's feeling. That would be okay.

"Feeling better than expected," Steve said. "Laying low, watching football and trying to avoid my family who would be more than happy to descend on me with enough food to last a month."

"That's nice of them. Do you have a big family?"

"My parents, two married sisters and their five kids. You?"

"Just my mom. My dad died when I was twelve and my mom had sort of a breakdown. My aunt took me in temporarily but I wound up living with her until she died last year."

"Sorry," Steve said. "Do you still see your mom?"

"Once a year. She's in Virginia." She hesitated. "I won't lie. It's kind of depressing." All of Laura's holidays were lonely. She had no relatives other than her mother now that her aunt had passed. Her partner, Molly, would probably invite her to spend Christmas with her and her husband and now the new baby. Her aunt hadn't been a big holiday person. They usually went out to dinner Christmas Eve and managed to cook something halfway decent on Christmas Day. That's if her aunt wasn't working a big case, then it was takeout, just like the Jews said. The restaurants were theirs to plunder on Christmas because all the Gentiles were home. Ha.

"I hope I'm not overstepping but it sounds like your holidays suck. You should come to my house this year."

Had he just invited her to Christmas dinner with his family?

Holy shit. If he showed up with Laura, his family would be all over him, thinking he was dating her. He'd insist she was just a colleague, a new friend, but they wouldn't let him off the hook easily. "I could use a buddy to stave off their constant questioning about when I'm going to find a nice girl and settle down. They're relentless."

"Oh. Sure, I get it."

"You'd be doing me a huge favor." Steve couldn't be digging a deeper hole for himself if he had a backhoe.

"Christmas is still six weeks away. We'll see," Laura said, giving him a reprieve.

Steve changed the subject in hopes of not burying himself completely. "So what are you doing home on a Saturday night? How come you're not out clubbing somewhere?"

"Seriously? I'm too old for clubbing. Besides, I live in Muttontown, there aren't any clubs around here."

Steve was glad Laura couldn't see his wide eyes. The Incorporated Village of Muttontown in Nassau County was one of the wealthiest towns in America and home to some of the most affluent families in New York. Ironic, since its name stemmed from its former use as pasturage for sheep. "You live on the Gold Coast?" Laura didn't respond. He added, "I didn't see that coming." Now, he'd offended her. First, he'd embarrassed her by inviting her for Christmas dinner and now this. He couldn't be fucking this up any better if he tried.

"It was my aunt's house. I told you she sort of adopted me. She was a bigtime attorney, never married and when she died she left the house to me. I'll probably sell it. It's too big for me and I often crash at my apartment in the city when I'm working a case. You know, traffic in and out of the city can make your life miserable."

"Yeah, I try to avoid going into the city at all costs. Traffic makes me a madman."

An awkward silence hung on the air. "Well", Laura finally said, "I just wanted to make sure you were okay. If you need anything let me know."

"You're not working the case this weekend?"

Steve's query amplified her guilt. "Alyx told me to take the weekend off and we'll pick things up on Monday. By her assessment, I work too many weekends."

"I hear you," Steve said. "Keep me updated on your progress. I'm there if you need anything."

"Will do. Take care."

"Thanks for checking on me, Laura. Talk soon."

Laura held her phone in her lap. What the hell just happened? Buddy? He called her his *buddy*. And doing *a favor.* She calmed. She'd misunderstood. It certainly wasn't a date. Besides who brings someone home to meet his or her family on a first date? Speaking of family, what had overcome her? She never talked about hers. Never talked about her father's death... either of them.

Chapter 8

Steve spent most of Sunday distracted from football. Members of his family had called a half dozen times, offering food and help, and he had to practically threaten them with his service revolver if they showed up uninvited.

He'd acted like a total jerk on the phone with Laura. How could he remedy the situation? Or maybe he should just forget about it, and her.

He couldn't. Grabbing his keys, he used his car's police computer to locate her address. An explanation in person would be best. Or perhaps he just wanted to see her one more time.

A three-story colonial constructed of white brick with black shutters, and two chimneys, sat at the end of the long driveway lined with tall oaks. The sun sat low on the horizon, a reddish-golden glow in a halo around the magnificent mansion.

"Geez, she lives in a fucking palace?" The house must have like ten bedrooms. And he'd like to fuck Laura in every one of them.

Gripping the steering wheel tightly, his vehicle crept up the drive. Steve contemplated what he would say to extricate himself from this mess. It reminded him of high school when he'd said something stupid to a girl he had a crush on. God, he was acting like a teenager and he felt like one. He rubbed his sweaty palms on his pant legs. Where had his Dom personality gone?

Just as he reached for the brass doorknocker, the door opened. "Steve?"

"I… I needed to talk to you."

"How did you know where I live?"

"I'm a cop."

"Oh, of course." She crossed her arms over her beautiful breasts, barely contained in a skin-tight black tee. "That's kind of illegal."

"Arrest me." Although, he had no interest in letting her handcuff him. The cuffs would be on her.

Laura laughed and opened the door wide. "Come in. Give me your coat. Any news on the case from your end?"

Steve shrugged out of his black leather bomber jacket and handed it to Laura. She hung it inside the carved wooden-door closet. He answered, "A report on a stolen car near the nature preserve. A white Jeep Cherokee. We found it abandoned about twenty miles away. Dusted for prints but nothing. Good chance it was this Viktor. I sent a report to your office."

"Thanks," Laura said. "Bummer that nothing turned up. He's a slippery dude."

Steve surveyed the massive two-story foyer, trying not to gawk. Shiny black marble beneath his feet, a six-foot round table with a vase of white daisies sat in the center. "Should I take off my shoes?"

Laura's eyes drifted downward. "What? No. Of course not. Come, let's sit in the den."

He followed her dutifully into a cozy room with brown

leather couches and a crackling blaze in the fireplace. Now this room he could get used to.

"Sit," she said as she curled into a big armchair beside the fireplace. "How are you feeling? You probably shouldn't be driving. Did the doctor say you could?"

"I'm not particularly good at following orders. But I don't recall her saying I couldn't."

"So, to what do I owe the honor of this visit?"

Steve hesitated. "I thought I made you uncomfortable on the phone yesterday. I probably overstepped, inviting you for Christmas." His phone rang. "Sorry," he said, gazing at the screen. "I have to take this, if you don't mind."

"Sure, I'll get us something to drink. Wine or a beer, soda?"

"Whatever you're having." Steve walked back to the foyer to answer the call. "Colin, what's up?"

Laura heard every word of Steve's conversation. The foyer had better acoustics than the Met.

"Yeah, I'm okay. Just banged up, two busted ribs." Silence, as Colin said something. "She's a new client. I interviewed her last week, some major abuse, so go easy, we need to build up her confidence."

Laura grabbed the last bottle of pinot noir from the kitchen wine cabinet. She'd have to go down to the wine cellar to replenish her upstairs stash, but she hated going down to that creepy-crawly basement. Tomorrow. In the daylight. She popped the cork and poured the claret liquid into two stemless wineglasses.

"That sounds like a good approach," Steve said. "Tell her I'll be there next weekend to work with her." More silence. "Catch you next weekend."

Steve returned to the den and apologized again.

Laura handed him the glass. "Well, I should apologize to you; I sort of overheard your conversation. Even a whisper travels far in this house."

Steve's eyes narrowed but he didn't say anything.

"Was that the club?" Laura said.

"Yes."

"And there's some woman there that suffered abuse and so now, what? You're going to handcuff her and whip her?" Laura slumped into the armchair again and pulled her knees up, her bare feet gripping the oxblood leather. She took a long sip of wine.

"Whoa, sister. Let's walk that remark back," Steve said, returning to the couch. He placed his glass on the sandstone coffee table. "This woman is sexually repressed for good reason. She's been to therapy. We provide a safe environment for her to regain her sexuality."

"So, you're a sex therapist? Come on."

"Sort of, yes. And I do have a master's degree in psychology. Besides I don't whip people. Maybe a flogging, but that's a different thing and many women find it quite exciting, stimulating." Steve swigged his wine. Laura remained silent. "You're being entirely too judgmental. There is great variety in sexual appetites. What turns one person on turns another off. It's like my mother used to say at the dinner table. You shouldn't say you don't like something until you've tried it "

Laura huffed. "We're not talking about a four-year-old eating his peas."

"We sort of are… people's tastes vary, but the rule is: safe, sane, and consensual. And we monitor everyone closely. Besides, I don't think you have any idea what you're talking about. You should come one night and have a drink. I'll give you the tour."

"What?" Laura said, shaking her head. She'd already

downed half her wine and put her glass on the side table, hugging her knees. *Restraint, Laura.*

"What are you afraid of?" Steve said, crossing his muscular arms over his chest.

Laura had to admit he looked damn fine in that fitted V-neck gray sweater. And his ass in those jeans, well...

Steve continued, "Apparently, your buddy, Alyx had a change of heart working with Daniel. I dare say she enjoyed herself more than she ever imagined. She married the dude."

He told the truth. Alyx confessed that Daniel was amazing in bed and again, Laura had been a tad jealous. Maybe this was just what she needed. "Do you ever have, what do you call it? Vanilla sex?"

"Sure. Actually, that's not entirely true. I'm pretty bossy in the bedroom. I don't think that will ever change. Let's say it's more like vanilla and chocolate swirl. Or vanilla ice cream with hot fudge." Steve smiled mischievously.

'Bossy in the bedroom' sounded... *hot.* Laura imagined Steve licking hot fudge off her body. She squeezed her thighs together to tamp down the tingle between her legs.

This conversation wasn't going the way Steve planned. Not even close. And how had they wound up talking about sex? Damn, Colin couldn't have called earlier, or later?

"Look, I came to apologize for making you uncomfortable on the phone the other day and now it seems I've done it again. I should probably go."

"No, don't. I'm sorry if I sounded judgmental...it's just well, I have a difficult time seeing why women, and men for that matter, get off on bondage and... stuff."

"Then you should definitely come to the club. Expand your horizons. Experiment. It's just for fun, adult playtime.

No strings attached." He chuckled to himself. Unless I tie you up.

"I don't know. I wouldn't want to have sex in public."

"There are private rooms to use with new clients. Some people get off on public sexual display, but others play only in private. That's the point of the club, to cater to each individual's needs and wants."

Excited about bringing Laura to the club, he ventured on. "Look, Laura, I'm not the relationship type——"

"Me either," she said too loudly.

"Besides, who needs a relationship to have some fun?"

It had been six months since Laura had sex. She'd hooked up with a guy she'd met at a conference Alyx sent her to. She could definitely see herself having a good time with Steve.

"No pressure," Steve said. "Just think about it."

He finished his wine and stood. "Until next time."

She ushered him to the door, helping him on with his coat. "Thanks for coming by, and as for Christmas? Let's just see how things play out. Very generous of you to invite me."

"Hey, I'm a generous kind of guy. You'll see if you come to the club." He winked and there was that mischievous grin again.

Steve leaned in and gave her a quick kiss on the lips. "Call me if anything new comes up with the case. I'll keep in touch."

He gave a wave before getting into his car and Laura waved back. As he drove away, she put her fingers on her lips, the feel of his soft, full lips lingering. Maybe this could work. A friend you could have sex with, no relationship complications, but the club?

She wasn't so sure about that.

Chapter 9

Steve's humongous smile might be plastered on his face forever. Man, had he really invited her to the club? And it sounded like there might be a chance she'd actually come. And he wanted to make her come. Explosively and often.

He stopped at the local pizzeria and picked up a few slices for dinner, after arriving home, he changed into sweats and secured his gun in the drawer next to his bed. Like all law enforcement officers, his department had a regulation that required him to carry off-duty, even being specific about times and locations. Steve had carried a weapon for so many years that he felt naked without one. Thankfully his department didn't stipulate that he carry one of his two issued weapons: a Glock 17 or the Glock 43. He was allowed to carry any handgun when off-duty, provided he qualified with it twice yearly and had the make, model, and serial number on file at the department with the firearms instructor/training officer. His favorite handgun was his Smith and Wesson M&P full-size 9 millimeter. He carried that, along with his badge, identification, and two additional 17 round magazines at all times.

What did Laura carry off-duty? She'd need something that could be concealed in a handbag.

Pouring a beer, he settled on the couch in front of the Giants game to eat his dinner. Back to work tomorrow.

Laura arrived at her office early, waking in a sweat after a torturous night of sleep where in her dreams Steve tied her up and did evil things to her. She should call them nightmares, but somehow they evoked pleasurable feelings, excitement rather than fear. But no way was she going to that club.

She drank several cups of coffee and nibbled on a granola bar as she reviewed the latest reports on the case. Fingerprints had been lifted from the water jugs but no hits on the database. They'd been through the two dead perp's phones and IDs, all fake and untraceable. The number listed for Viktor was a burner phone with no way of tracking him either. All dead ends.

"Morning, early bird," Alyx said. "I hope you weren't here all weekend." She slitted one eye suspiciously.

"No, I came in around seven. Need to make sure I'm up to speed for the press conference."

Alyx took the seat in front of Laura's desk and settled her coffee mug on the corner. "Anything new on the case?"

"Steve got a report of a stolen car, a white Jeep Cherokee at the strip mall near the nature preserve. The time frame fits. Suffolk County PD located it abandoned about twenty miles away. Good chance it was this Viktor. They took prints. No hits. We also ran the phones we found at the cabin. Nothing."

Alyx sighed. "That's their usual MO. They're expert at covering their tracks. We caught a good number of them on site for the auction last year. Nothing we found led us to any additional suspects."

Laura bit on a fingernail before saying, "Alyx, can I ask you something personal?"

"Sure. Shoot." Alyx grabbed her cup and sipped.

"I know we've talked a little about your experience with that training you got from Daniel. And your time visiting that erotic club."

"Uh-huh," Alyx said taking another swig of java.

"Steve works at that club, right? I mean, he... what do they call it? *Plays* at that club?"

"You're interested in Steve."

"What? No. Just curious, I guess. I mean he is pretty easy on the eyes and he's definitely intriguing."

"Okay, curious cat, what do you want to know?"

"Was it something you were interested in before? Had you ever done anything like that?"

"I'd done light bondage play with a couple of boyfriends, but nothing else. And that last guy I dated took it too far and honestly, I was turned off by the whole idea of anything kinky." Alyx sighed and settled against the backrest. "Truth-fully, when Rob asked for volunteers to go undercover on that case, I shot my mouth off without thinking. Once I committed I had to follow through."

Laura wanted to ask exactly what kinds of kinky behaviors Alyx had engaged in. She needed details but couldn't bring herself to ask for specifics.

Alyx let out a slow breath. "Steve is a great guy. My first night there I was supposed to scene with him... you know what that means?"

"No."

"Scening is when you put on a public sexual display. We were supposed to practice in a private room and then move to an open area if I—" Alyx laughed, "—if I passed his test."

"So you were going to have sex with a total stranger? In public?"

Alyx smirked. "And you've never hooked up with a total stranger before? I seem to remember some guy at that convention last year."

"Guilty. But it wasn't in public." Now it was Laura's turn to smirk.

Alyx continued, "I know it sounds perverted. It was complicated by my feelings for Daniel. But Steve was great with me. He made me feel at ease, as much as possible, considering the circumstances." She hesitated and added, "Of course it never happened because I got abducted before he could get me upstairs."

"I'll admit I find him attractive and sexy as hell."

"Has he invited you to the club?"

"Yeah…"

"And?"

"I don't know. We talked about maybe just being fuck buddies. Neither of us is interested in a relationship."

"Uh-huh," Alyx said, tightening her gaze.

"Do you guys go to the club?"

"Nah, we play at home. When all was said and done, neither of us wanted to have sex in public. But I'll admit I've never had a lover like Daniel. He knows his way around a woman's body." Alyx blushed. "You should give Steve a chance. I have no doubt he's an expert between the sheets."

Now, Laura blushed. "Okay, then…" She fanned her face. "Let's review before the press conference."

Laura faced the crowd of reporters and held up the sketch of the remaining suspect. "As you know, two of the suspects were killed at the scene, however one man escaped. This is an artist rendering based on the descriptions provided by the victims. He goes by the name Viktor. If you see this man, do not approach, but call the FBI at 1-800-CALL FBI or 911 to reach the local police department. We assume him to be armed and dangerous. In addition, I'd like to report that the four females rescued are doing well. They've been released from the hospital and with some time and assistance from family and social services we hope they will regain their lives. Please respect their privacy. Thank you."

———

Viktor sat on the edge of the lumpy mattress as Laura Logan held up the rendering of his face. He was in the process of dyeing his hair and had stopped shaving. His beard grew quickly and would help disguise him. The scar would be more difficult to camouflage. "Bitch," he said to the TV. "I'm gonna fuck you up so bad. You and that other FBI cunt."

Today he would begin surveillance. He'd plan carefully. No screw-ups this time. Both their neighborhoods housed the rich and famous so he must be discreet. His car wasn't high end and it might appear suspicious on their streets. He'd do most of his reconnaissance at night, under the cloak of darkness.

Viktor checked the time, anxious to wash the black dye from his hair, the noxious stink unbearable. Showered, he packed his meager possessions into the gray duffle, kissed the rosary around his neck for good luck and vacated the seedy motel.

———

Steve hadn't been at his desk long, when his secretary, Alice, burst in. "The press conference is on now," she announced, grabbing the remote and switching on the wall-mounted television. Steve studied the screen. Laura wore a navy-blue tailored suit with a crisp, white, collared shirt. Her reddish-blonde hair reflected the sunlight, her cheeks pink and the barest hint of color glossing her full lips. She looked downright edible. The press hurled questions and Laura answered each with patience and fortitude. Steve admired her confident persona.

A week passed and Steve hadn't heard from Laura. Originally confident that Laura might visit the club, he wasn't so sure now. Had he come on too strong? His enthusiasm for most things in life often overwhelmed others. He was a big guy with a loud personality. At least he used to be, until that week when his partner got killed and then he caught Jillian cheating on him with that actor guy. They'd dated for three years. He'd even bought a ring. The sting of being such a dupe still pained his ego.

Maybe his family was right. He'd lost his verve, his optimism, a vision for his future. The prospect of dating random women had lost its appeal. Playing at the club would mollify his sexual appetite, but he needed a friend. Most of his guy friends were married and, between jobs and family, didn't have much time to hang. Consequently, he worked too much to fill the dead space.

Steve maneuvered into the parking lot at Stony Brook University's soccer field. He'd promised a dozen times to attend one of his nephew's games and today was the day. His family met him with a flurry of hugs and kisses and manly pats on the back, reminding him he should stop blowing them off. He was lucky to have such a big loving family.

"How are you feeling?" his mother asked.

"Better, as long as I don't make any sudden moves. Getting in and out of bed is the worst part."

Impressed at his nephew's athletic talent, he hooted and hollered along with the crowd as their team soundly trounced their opponent. The beautiful fall day, warm for November, stood in sharp contrast to last week when several inches of snow had blanketed Long Island.

"Will we see you tomorrow for family dinner?" his father inquired.

"Yeah, I'll be there. The usual time?"

"Yep," his father said, smacking him on the back. "It'll be good to see you with everyone around the table." A sharp pain nipped Steve's insides and he groaned. "Oh, so sorry, son. I forgot about your ribs."

"I'm fine," Steve said. "Don't worry about it."

He kissed and hugged his family goodbye, complementing Joey on a well-played game with a tussle of his longish dark hair. The kid beamed. He made his way through the throng of soccer fans toward his car. Digging the keys out of his pocket, he stopped when he heard her voice.

"Steve?"

Chapter 10

Surprised seeing Steve at the soccer field, Laura contemplated approaching. He said he'd call her in a week if she hadn't called first. The week was up. Almost. Maybe he hadn't really wanted her to come to the club, he was just being polite. Or perhaps he felt sorry for her. Was she broadcasting her membership in the 'no friends' club? Other than Alyx, and her partner, Molly, she didn't really have any other gal pals, one of the repercussions of attending boarding school in Connecticut—no local friends. And Molly and Alyx were both married, and now Molly had a baby. She always felt like a third wheel when invited to either of their houses. Those thirty-something years, which would eventually give way to her forties, could be devastatingly isolating once everyone you knew paired off. But Laura could never have that life. She was irrevocably damaged by her parents' dysfunctional relationship. Emotionally scarred, all the therapy in the world couldn't erase the loathsome hatred she had for her stepfather.

She shouted Steve's name.

Steve shielded his eyes with his hand to get a better view. Even with his sunglasses the sun was too bright to make out… *Laura?* Then he remembered, she and Father Flanagan agreed they'd met on the soccer field where they both coached youth teams.

"Hey, Laura, how are you?"

"Great. My team won." She smiled brightly as she rested the netted bag carrying a half dozen soccer balls on the macadam. Dressed in a powder blue tracksuit and her hair in a sleek ponytail, she looked like a kid herself. Flushed cheeks, dazzling smile.

"Well done," he said.

"Thanks. They're a great bunch of kids. What are you doing here?"

"My nephew had a game. I've been promising to come, so here I am. The kid is pretty talented."

"What division is he in?"

"Twelve and under."

"Awesome. It's nice that you take an interest. I have some kids whose parents never come. It's sad."

Laura's face darkened. Had Laura been one of those kids? She'd hinted that her home life wasn't exactly like the *Brady Bunch*, her father dying when she was just twelve, and how she'd spent her high school years away at boarding school under her aunt's supervision. And, she'd mentioned she was a chubby teen. Best not to follow that line of questioning.

He switched gears. "So, I saw you on the press conference Monday morning. Nice job."

"Yeah, it's never fun talking to the media."

"You're preaching to the choir," Steve said. "Nothing new on the case?"

"Nope."

An awkward pause rustled the space between them. Should he ask if she was interested in coming to the club? "I planned on calling you when I got home. I gave you a week to accept my invitation." Steve held his breath in anticipation.

Laura focused on her white Nike sneakers, making him wait. "I'll admit to curiosity. But I'm only interested in coming for a drink. I'd like to see the place before I commit to anything."

"Of course, whatever your comfort level is. No pressure."

"I definitely do not want to have sex in public. You can take that to the bank."

"No expectations. Promise. Just come. See."

"I hope I don't end up regretting this."

"Tonight? Meet at my house and let's go together. Or if you prefer, meet me there. It's a bit of a drive, though. A long lonely stretch of rural roads."

Holy shit. Tonight? It was two o'clock. Was there enough time to shower, shave her legs and do her hair? She could lie and say she had plans. On the other hand, she might as well just get it over with. Overthinking made her anxious. "Uh, sure. Tonight's fine. Your house. What time?"

"I need to be there by eight so let's say six-thirty at my place in case there's traffic. Although it's pretty safe at this time of year."

"Dress code?"

Steve laughed. "I'd say more of an undress code. A skirt and no underwear for easy access."

Steve shaved close, his skin as smooth as a baby's butt. He donned his black polo with the club's crest on the pocket and tucked it into his black belted jeans. Damn, he'd forgotten to get a haircut this week, his thick dark locks unruly, he resorted to fingering a dab of gel through it. He took a deep cleansing breath and let it out slowly. He winced, pain lingering from the cracked ribs. Why was he nervous?

The end of the UConn vs. Holy Cross game played on the 60" screen bolted to his living room wall. He'd attended Holy Cross on a football scholarship and prayed they'd win. The score was close, his alma mater leading by a field goal. Ten minutes left in the game.

He whooped and hollered as they ran out the clock, the score: Holy Cross 24, UConn 21. The doorbell rang. His pulse quickened as he approached the front door.

She wore a bone-hued leather jacket over a fitted, short white dress with a low neckline—not enough to show much cleavage—and black patent leather heels.

Steve whistled. "Wow, you clean up nice."

Laura grimaced. "Seriously? I look that shitty the rest of the time?"

"No," Steve said, finding himself in the proverbial shithole once more. "I just meant you look amazing." Why did he always say something stupid when he was around her?

"Underwear?" he asked.

"Not admitting to anything. You'll have to find out for yourself."

"Hmm… I do love a challenge."

Steve held open the door to his government-issued black Ford Explorer and Laura settled into the passenger seat. They headed east on Sunrise Highway, the speedometer hovering around eighty-five. Law enforcement officers never adhered to speed limits. Never got tickets either. Once, a driver tailgated him when he was seriously exceeding the speed limit. Eventually the guy passed him on the right and Steve called it in. Turned out the driver was also a cop, both of them in unmarked vehicles.

Steve had a Pandora jazz station on. "We're making good time," he said after a bit, decreasing the volume. "Let's go over a few things before we arrive. I don't want you getting yourself into any trouble."

Trouble? Already worried about the evening's festivities, Laura's anxiety increased. "Do tell," she said.

"When you arrive you'll be required to sign a disclosure stating you are a willing participant and understand the rules."

"Rules?"

"Read everything carefully. A common mistake for a newbie is interfering with a scene. It may appear that someone is being hurt or abused but it's not your call. We have dungeon monitors for that."

"Understood."

"Someone like you, who is accustomed to saving people, might misread the situation and act inappropriately. If that were to happen the Dom in the scene has the right to punish you."

"Let me guess. I'll get a spanking?"

"Dom's choice. Anything from a spanking to removing clothing and putting you on display naked." Laura gulped, wringing her hands. Steve reached over and clasped one. "Don't worry, I'll make sure that doesn't happen. I just don't want any misunderstandings."

Laura gazed into his big brown eyes. "Breathe, baby." She hadn't realized she'd been holding her breath. "While we're on the topic of honesty it's important for you to understand that complete openness between a Dom and sub is vital. You need to express how you feel when asked, or you could get hurt."

"Is that what I would be? A submissive?"

"Technically yes, and protocol requires that you address each Dom as sir or master. If it's a female go with mistress or ma'am."

"Steve, I'm not sure about this."

"Maybe I've said too much. Tonight you needn't worry. Protocol dictates that a submissive must be with a Dom, which is me. No one can touch you without my permission and I won't allow it."

Now, he'd frightened her. What was wrong with him? He was trying to put her mind at ease and instead he'd freaked her out. "Don't overthink this, darling. Just keep an open mind and enjoy. The people are nice and nothing sexual will happen tonight. If you're interested we'll talk about it and plan it out carefully so you are comfortable." He still had Laura's hand in his and he gave a squeeze. A frown marred her face. "You okay? If you've changed your mind, I'll turn the car around right this second."

"But you have to work."

"Doesn't matter. I'll get someone to cover for me."

The lines on her forehead vanished and she smiled. "No, I'm fine. I'll behave appropriately." She rubbed her thumb back and forth over the back of his hand. "I trust you, Steve. I know you'll have my back. Just like you do on the job." His chest expanded, his heart threatening to pop out. Just like his cock.

Steve pulled into his assigned space in the parking lot. "Okay then," he said. "Let's have a little fun. Maybe you'll let me cop a feel." He winked and her violet irises brightened.

Opening the massive wooden door with a large brass door-knocker, Laura entered the sizable foyer ahead of him. A huge man dressed in a simple black suit, white shirt and no tie, sat behind a mahogany Queen Ann style desk. He rose upon seeing Steve.

"Master Steve," he said. "Good to see you, how ya feeling?"

"Evening, Zach, much better. You?"

"Very well, Sir. You were missed last week. The ladies got lonely."

Steve enlarged his gaze in warning, yet didn't respond.

Zach cleared his throat, message received. "Who's your guest?"

"This is Laura Logan. She'll need to fill out the appropriate paperwork. She will be an observer. No play."

"Of course." Zach opened the top desk drawer and retrieved a three-page document, setting it on the tabletop. He plucked a feathered pen from the holder and placed it alongside the paperwork.

Steve touched Laura's shoulder, garnering her attention. "Read and sign the disclaimer and wait for me. I'll be back in ten minutes. Zach, do not let her in without me. Understood?"

"Absolutely, Sir."

He gave Laura a quick peck on the lips. "See you in a few." Then he vanished through the ominous dark door leading into the club, leaving her alone with Zach.

Chapter 11

"Have a seat," Zach instructed. A crooked smile softened his acne-scarred face, which on first-impression made him scary. His nose had definitely been broken more than once.

Laura settled into the dark upholstered chair beside Zach's desk. The shiny black marble floor along with the onyx and white striped wallpaper screamed elegance, the complete opposite of Laura's imaginings. So Steve was popular with the ladies, according to Zach. Laura figured a fine-looking man like Steve could get his fill of carnal activities for the entire weekend.

Zach placed the document and pen in front of Laura. "Make sure you read carefully. The last chick got herself into some serious shit. There are punishments for breaking the rules and take my word for it, it's something you want to avoid."

"Yes, Sir," Laura mumbled. "Steve made that clear."

"You needn't address me as Sir, I'm not a Dom," Zach explained.

"I didn't realize…"

"Nah, not my thing. I just work here part-time. I work bank security as my day job."

Laura read the words painfully slowly. She found it difficult to concentrate as her minded drifted to what happened on the other side of that black door. Finally finished, she signed her name. *Was she really going through with this?*

"Great," Zach said, taking the document and filing it in the cabinet behind his desk.

While Laura waited for Steve's return, several members arrived, signed in, and entered into the chamber of horrors. Everyone acted jovial, as if going to a party. She needed to focus on that notion. Pleasure. Playtime for grownups.

"Hey, Steve," came Colin's booming voice from behind the bar. "All better?"

Steve shook Colin's outstretched hand. "Mostly."

Jack, the owner, exited his office door and waylaid Steve. "Glad to see you're back. The submissive trainees missed you last weekend. Although Colin handled them well. Maybe a little harder on them than you."

Colin smiled and stretched out his hands. "Come on, they love me."

"Well, thanks for covering for me. You did me a solid."

"Happy to help."

"How did Lori do?"

"I read your notes carefully. She's been through some bad shit. I think we made progress. She was skittish at first, but calmed as the night went on. I didn't leave her on her own at all. If I wasn't with her, I made damn sure one of the other masters was."

"Good. Listen guys, I've brought a guest. She'll only be an

observer and I don't want to leave her on her own. I'll probably need help with the trainees again tonight."

"No prob," Colin said. "Whatever you need."

"I think they're all ready to be assigned to a Dom we trust tonight. Can you make sure that happens?" Steve said to Colin and Jack. They nodded. "I can still help monitor and step in if necessary."

Jack said, "Who's your guest?"

"Laura Logan. We worked a case together recently. She's part of Alyx Cameron's FBI taskforce. It didn't take long for her to figure out I worked at the club, something I wouldn't normally fess up to. She's major-league hot and curious about the goings-on here so I'm giving her the tour."

"Anxious to meet her," Jack said. "How's Alyx?"

"Good. She and Daniel seem absurdly happy."

"Haven't seen them here," Colin said.

"They play at home. I don't think Daniel wants to share an inch of her with anyone else."

"Don't blame him," Colin said, shaking his head.

"I better go back for Laura. She's filling out the paperwork with Zach."

The club entry door opened and Steve marched his exquisite body in her direction. "Ready?"

"Aim. Fire," she said with a wan smile.

Steve threaded his fingers through hers and tugged her toward the inner sanctum of carnal pain.

"Break a leg," Zach exclaimed to her back.

Heavy metal music played over the sound system, luckily not so loud that you couldn't hear yourself think. Human musk filled the air. Bodies, scantily clad in leather and latex, or nothing at all, moved to the pounding beat of an old Metallica song. Flesh pressed flesh in erotic gyrations. Studded collars attached to leashes around both men's and women's necks, and many had piercings in places that made Laura cringe.

The place was humongous, with a second floor guarded by black wrought-iron railings. Lighted display windows lined the far wall. Laura glimpsed what was on exhibition yet the crowd blocked her view. Crossing the dance floor, they came upon a bar constructed entirely of glass.

Two large men conversed behind the counter, both obviously having spent copious amounts of time at the gym. The one on the left appeared older, maybe in his fifties, while the other seemed closer to Steve's age. They wore the black polo shirt with club insignia. Other masters? Or what did Steve call them? Dungeon monitors? A vision of a medieval torture chamber flashed behind Laura's eyes. Maybe she should run.

"Laura, this is Jack, the club owner," Steve said of the older guy.

Jack extended his hand and Laura took it. "Pleasure, pet," he said.

"Nice to meet you, Sir," she said, choking on the salutation.

Continuing introductions, Steve said, "And this is Colin, one of the club's masters."

"Hello, Sir," Laura said.

Colin grinned widely. "Excellent, little subbie. Already on board with the protocol."

Laura blanched at being called a subbie. She was considering the idea of some kinky play, but no way, no how, would she ever consider herself a submissive. The term flipped her stomach. Although, she did like the idea of Steve bossing her around in the bedroom. But then... if he was the boss then by default she'd be the sub... *ordinate*. Ugh. Maybe she needed to stay away from naming anything.

"Speaking of protocol," Steve said. "A pair of red handcuffs, please, Master Colin."

"You got it." Colin reached under the counter and pulled out a pair of fur-lined scarlet leather handcuffs. "Wrists, please, little pet," he said to Laura.

Laura's beckoning eyes found Steve. "All subs wear handcuffs," he explained. "We attach charms indicating what behaviors they are willing to participate in. Blue for bondage, green for intercourse, yellow for mild pain and a few others that we won't discuss at this time."

Laura drew her bottom lip between her teeth at the notion of Steve doing anything like that to her in public. Although, privately, well, it sounded kinda hot.

"Not to worry, darling," Colin said. "Red handcuffs signify you're only here to observe. No touching allowed."

She extended her wrists and Colin snapped a cuff around each, then hooked them together by the center clasp.

"There. Officially submissive," Colin said with a sly grin.

That word again. Ugh.

"Do you want to check in with the trainees?" Colin asked Steve. "They're in the locker room waiting to be inspected."

"Might as well," Steve said. "I don't want them to think I've abandoned them."

Colin led the way, and Laura, cuffed hands attached to Steve's, followed along obediently.

The locker room resembled a typical layout like her gym. Six women stood in a row, eyes focused on the floor, hands clasped behind their backs, probably handcuffed with the appropriate charms for consenting behaviors. Barely clothed, they wore micro-mini-skirts, skimpy midriff tops or camisoles. No jewelry, which Laura figured might be a liability during the festivities. And faces heavily made up, a little too garish for Laura's taste.

"Good evening, subbies," Steve said. "How is everyone doing tonight?"

Flurries of 'Fine, Sir', answered his query.

"Excellent." Steve released his hold on Laura and faced the first woman in the row. "Lovely outfit, Kate," he said, scanning her body. He slid his hand under her skirt, up the side of her hip. "No underwear. Good girl." She didn't respond and Laura wondered why. "And no speaking unless you are asked a direct question. Getting the protocol down. I'm pleased." And, she had her answer. The petite blonde stayed motionless and quiet, gaze still fixed on the gray tile beneath her feet, but a hint of satisfaction curved her lips.

Steve worked his way down the line, making a few adjustments in their attire, opening a button or removing an item and checking to insure the no underwear rule was adhered to. Laura studied the women. Who was the female Steve had referenced during his phone call with Colin last weekend, the one who'd suffered traumatic abuse?

"You'll be taking yourselves out for a spin tonight. We will pair you with a Dom of our choice. They are all experienced and excellent with new members. Of course, Colin will be keeping an eye on you, so if you need help, ask. Any of the dungeon monitors are also available if necessary."

The row of demure women remained silent.

"Eyes on me," Steve said, and five sets of orbs beamed his way. "Who can tell me the safe words and what they mean?" They all raised their hands and Steve called on Kate.

"Green means everything is fine, yellow means you're getting uncomfortable and you need to slow down, and red means stop… Sir."

"Excellent. If you tap out with the word red, your Dom will sit and talk with you to understand what's distressing. But don't wimp out either. You need to let your Dom take you where he thinks you need to go. To test your limits. What you want and what you need aren't necessarily the same." Steve paused. "Any questions before I set you loose?"

"No, Sir," came the collective response.

"Master Colin," he said, "will you make the assignments while I show our guest around?"

Colin clapped his hands together as if he was about to embark on something exciting. "They're ready and waiting. I'll make the intros." He escorted the line of new submissives out to the main chamber.

"Laura, you're carrying, right?"

"Of course."

"No firearms on the floor. I'll lock yours up with mine."

Laura handed over her pocketbook and Steve disappeared behind a door to the right. Gone less than a minute, he returned and said, "Our weapons are secured in the safe in Jack's office. If there's an emergency and you need to get into it, the code is 696969."

Steve escorted Laura to the bar, picking her up by the waist and plopping her on a barstool. "What would you like to drink?"

"Scotch, rocks and a splash of water." She leaned over, gripping his right biceps with her shackled hands and whispered, "Do I have to call you master?" Her warm breath near his ear quickened his pulse.

Steve whispered back, "You do not."

"Thanks. I'm having trouble with the whole master thing. Makes it sound like there's a slave on the other end."

Steve chuckled. "You're not far from the truth. Many people enjoy being a slave. The definition varies, mostly it means the Dom is in complete control. He tells her what to wear, what to eat, he may even feed her."

Madge was tending bar as Colin busied himself pairing the new trainees with Doms. "What can I get ya?" Madge said, interrupting their discussion on slaves.

"Dewar's on the rocks with a splash of water for both of us."

Laura gaped at Steve, then said, "Are you fucking kidding me? I find it hard to believe that any woman with a brain would choose that kind of relationship."

"You'd be surprised. Many are powerful in the workforce, but in their personal lives they want something entirely opposite."

"Not gonna happen," Laura said. "Not in this lifetime."

"I'm with you. Not the type of relationship I'd ever be interested in. Not that I'm interested in a relationship at all." After a string of unsatisfying couplings, culminating in the horrible breakup with Jillian, he'd committed to eternal bachelorhood. His definition of marriage: Betting half your shit that you'd love somebody forever. Terrible odds.

Chapter 12

Viktor spent a week following Laura from home to work and back, the gym, running errands, and a soccer field just that morning. Surveilling both Laura and Alyx became impossible so he set his sights on his most recent nemesis. Maybe he'd luck out and find them together.

He tailed Laura from her house to an address in Rocky Point, a sleepy little hamlet on the North Shore of Suffolk County. A midsized cape covered in Beechwood siding sat back from the road on a well-manicured lawn. Laura's dark sedan spun into the driveway and Viktor parked near the end of the street, behind a green minivan. He skulked down low in the driver's seat and waited. Ten minutes later a black Ford Explorer exited the driveway, Laura in the passenger seat and that other cop from the raid behind the wheel. Was she dating this guy? That could complicate things. Perhaps he needed to do something about that.

The car sped by and Viktor quickly made a U-turn in pursuit. On the highway he realized it would be impossible to keep up with them. They were doing almost ninety and he couldn't risk getting pulled over by highway patrol. Good thing he'd planted that tracking device on Laura's car.

Steve unhooked the clasp binding Laura's cuffs together. "Easier to drink."

"Why thank you, Sir." Somehow, calling him sir suddenly rolled off her lips too easily.

Laura sipped her drink, resisting the urge to swallow it in a few quick gulps. Liquid courage. Steve chatted with Madge, who lamented about her most recent client, a teen arrested for DUI. His father was a prominent judge and Madge was doing her best to get the kid a light sentence, as long as counseling and community service were involved. Madge apparently had her own law firm.

Laura figured she must be a Domme and someone she had no interest in engaging on any level. Her thick body wasn't obscured by cellulite, instead was all muscle, and her dark spiky hair and smoky eye makeup made her downright menacing. Not to mention the numerous piercings in her lips, ears, and nose, and possibly other places. How did that play out in court, in front of a judge? Maybe she removed them for work.

"Let's take a stroll," Steve said to Laura, downing the last of his drink. "Bottoms up, darling."

Laura sucked the last drops of scotch off the ice cubes.

"He's not kidding," Madge interjected, leaning her tattooed forearms on the bar top. "There will be plenty of subbies strapped to benches with butts exposed for their Dom's pleasure." The formidable Madge grinned from ear to ear. Laura didn't want to see anyone doing anything to anyone's butt.

Steve picked her up by the waist and landed her on her feet. He took her hand and led her into the bowels of the club. Laura blanched at the number of naked women collared and leashed to their Doms and also a good number of men equally engaged with either male or female Doms/Dommes.

The majority of space surrounding the dance floor was dedicated to intimate seating areas with black leather couches and chairs separated by large potted plants. Even with dim lighting, no doubt existed as to what body parts were touched and penetrated. Women and men alike shrieked upon climax, making Laura squirm.

Steve pointed to subs wrapped in soft blankets where Doms fed them assorted juices and chocolate. "Doms provide aftercare," he explained. "The goal is to get your submissive to what we call *subspace*. It's sort of like your orgasm takes you outside of your body. The experience is overwhelming and exhausting, intense, and often disorienting."

Laura saddened, although she'd had plenty of sex, she'd never actually achieved orgasm. She'd contemplated purchasing a vibrator, she'd read they could help you get in touch with your body, but truth? She was broken inside. Something snapped during years of abuse at the hands of her stepfather, something that could never be undone.

Her emotions, her heart, bound by abuse. Never to be unbound.

But she liked sex well enough, and was a willing participant, even if she never reached nirvana.

"I'm confused. I thought this was all about sex and no feelings came into play. It looks like they really care for each other."

Steve landed both hands on her shoulders. "They do. The relationship between a Dom and sub is special, even though many do not extend their engagement beyond the club. They each go home and lead separate lives. Sometimes a Dom will take a sub home for the weekend, but when it's over they find someone new. Of course, occasionally the relationship turns to love and then the rules change."

"Like Daniel and Alyx?"

"Exactly, although their relationship wasn't a true Dom/sub one. They were kind of play-acting the roles. But I think Alyx liked it more than she wanted to admit."

Steve eyed Laura carefully, trying to judge her comfort level. They hadn't gotten to the hardcore stuff yet and he pondered how much he should show her. It could be too much for a newbie. He pointed to the second floor. "Upstairs are the private playrooms for those who don't care to play in public. Each has a particular piece of equipment and a bed with restraints. Doms reserve them for a set time."

"Can I see one?"

"Possibly. I'd have to look at the schedule to see which are in use."

They reached the rear of the enormous room. Behind the lighted display windows, all kinds of apparatus were being used. People, some in stocks, were secured by their appendages and necks into demeaning positions while their naked bodies were flagellated by all manners of whips, canes, paddles, leather straps and floggers. One guy dripped hot wax onto the tender parts of his submissive strapped to a bondage bench. Threesomes and foursomes abounded, varied combinations of men and women engaged in oral, anal and vaginal sex.

"This is called *scening*," Steve explained. "Doms sign up to use the space, then put on a 'scene' with their sub while others watch. When done, they clean the equipment before others take their turn."

"I've never seen anything like this," Laura said. "Not even in a porno flick."

"You watch porn?" Steve said, his gaze expanding.

"Not now. When I was away at boarding school there was a DVD that got passed around."

Steve smiled, imagining Laura's gigantic teenage eyes as she viewed forbidden footage.

Laura edged closer to a glass pane where a Dom's meaty paw soundly spanked a petite redhead's bottom. Strapped to a bench, immobile, she shrieked loudly. The Dom paused, tweaking the plug in her butt. The woman cried out with pure joy.

"She seems to be enjoying that," Laura said.

"Spanking is one of the favorite activities here. I'd daresay it's even popular in the vanilla world."

"I thought it was considered kind of perverted."

Steve slipped an arm around Laura's narrow waist. Close to her ear, he said, "I think many more people engage in it than are willing to admit. Most women I've been with are into it."

"What's that thing in her butt that he keeps twisting?"

Impressed by Laura's openness and willingness to learn, Steve explained, "An anal plug. It stimulates nerve endings and intensifies an orgasm."

"Geez," Laura said, "I don't know."

Steve escorted Laura through a dark hallway toward the theme rooms. "Scenes are also acted out here. These are more like role-playing."

He studied Laura's reaction as a Dom and sub pretended to be a boss and secretary, the secretary having obviously misbehaved, was being paddled.

"Here's some serious sexual harassment," Laura said. "Somebody contact HR."

Steve laughed. "It's only a game, darling. Power exchange

is a sexual fantasy for many people; however, they would never act that way in the workplace."

They moved on from the office scene, to one that resembled the inside of an Arabian tent, and yet another replicating a medical examining room. The hallway ended in a massive door similar to the gothic front entrance of the club and Steve explained that this was the dungeon. Screams penetrated the thick wood.

"Perhaps we should avoid the dungeon at this point."

"Good call," Laura said. "I'm trying to convince myself that those screams are 'safe, sane and consensual'. But you were right, the urge to dash in there and rescue someone is nudging me."

Steve pulled her by the hand, returning to the main room. They ambled toward the front and Steve identified what he called the submissives' pen, a roped off area where about twenty women sat together and chatted. Some sipped on a cocktail, all were outfitted in fetish gear and a few were manacled with chains hooked to the floor.

"When a Dom wants to leave his sub unattended for a few minutes he will chain her to the floor in the submissives' waiting area. As an unattached sub, this is where you wait to be approached by a Dom."

"So, it's not like a regular club where you walk around trying to pick someone up?"

"Nope. The procedures are well outlined and it's only a Dom that initiates an encounter. Submissives are to be silent and obedient, totally under the Dom's control."

"I'm not sure I like that part, but I'll admit some stuff was hot."

"Excellent," Steve said. "That's what I'd hoped, that maybe you'd find ways to stretch your sexual appetite."

Laura leaned into him and in a low voice said, "Can you show me one of the private rooms now?"

"Sure, give me a minute. I'll be right back."

Upon his return Laura was engaged in conversation with Mark, one of the dungeon monitors.

"Steve, talking with your lovely lady. I see she's come for the tour." He extended his hand and Steve took it in greeting.

"She has."

"Red handcuffs?" Mark said.

"Yes, she's only here to observe."

His dark eyes focused on Laura. "Well, little pet, I hope you enjoy yourself and that you'll return for some playtime."

Laura blushed crimson. Steve put his arm around her. "Not too much too fast, Mark. We're going easy here."

"Understood," Mark said. "Slow and easy, just the way I like it." He smirked. To Laura he said, "But remember, no pain no gain."

Steve noticed Laura holding her breath as Mark said his goodbye. "Breathe, baby."

Laura exhaled forcefully. "He's pretty intense."

"You have no idea. He's a wizard with a whip."

"Yikes."

"Exactly."

Steve clasped Laura's elbow, ushering her toward the spiral staircase to the second floor. "There's an open room. Come on."

Steve drew a key from his pocket, unlocking the door to the erotic chamber. Laura stood transfixed in front of the king-sized bondage bed with the red quilted canopy. A spanking horse took up the left side of the room and a plethora of *toys* were stashed in the armoire. Oh, the fun they could have in here.

He let the ambiance settle over her, waiting for her reaction.

Laura wandered the layout, running her hand over the red satin quilt, pressing on the mattress for firmness. She fondled the leather straps hanging from the headboard, a matching set secured to the footboard and spied the tethers hanging from the canopy. "You know how to tie a woman up?"

"Of course. I tie a mean knot."

Laura narrowed her eyes. Opening the armoire, she gasped. Steve smiled inwardly knowing that lashes, floggers, handcuffs and other items of delectable torture hung from the rack. He hoped she didn't look in a drawer. Shutting the doors forcefully she stood motionless for a moment before ambling over to the other side of the room. She faced the bench, tugging on the black straps that could secure a willing woman into submission.

Returning to Steve's side, she said, "It's quite romantic, the recessed lighting, the furniture. It feels like a high-end hotel room, except for the straps and *that thing*." She pointed toward the restraining bench, then crossed her arms over her chest. "I was thinking it would be more like a workout room in a gym."

"Well, you would get a workout. Just not the type you're used to."

Laura laughed. "I guess."

"Would you like to give it a try? Not tonight, when you're ready."

Laura gave a crinkled expression. "Perhaps."

Steve hardened. Thoughts of what he could do to her sent his pulse zigzagging.

"Just so you know, before you play at the club your doctor has to complete a form saying you're healthy. Since I work here, I'm tested every month so I'm good to go. Also, there's the matter of birth control. Everyone uses condoms in the public areas. Whatever happens in the private room is left to the participants."

"I've just had my yearly physical for the Bureau, so that shouldn't be a problem. And I'm on the pill."

"Excellent," Steve said, securing her hand. "Let's head back to the bar. I bet you could use a second drink."

He settled onto the barstool and perched her sideways on his lap, his erection pressing against her firm ass. She gave him a knowing glance but said nothing. He hugged her and gave her a kiss on the cheek, then his tongue touched her lips.

Chapter 13

S afely strapped into the front seat, Laura's mind whirred with a series of carnal images as Steve barreled down the expressway. Not to mention the kiss. The man sure could kiss.

She hadn't anticipated how thrilling this outing would be. Definitely not into anything brutal, but the bondage and spanking got her pulse racing. And Steve would be the guy to experiment with. She felt protected around him. He'd never hurt her and maybe, just maybe, she'd tap into a new sensuality. Too often it had been fast and furious, a blur of body parts moving in synchronicity. The guy always left satisfied because she was good at giving, just not so good at receiving. And most guys were more than fine with that. Steve might be different.

"You're quiet," Steve said, dragging her from her musings. "You okay? I didn't traumatize you too much, did I?"

"No, not at all. Some of it is outrageous. I could never see myself getting whipped or caned. And blood and knife play? Well, that's just insane from my perspective."

"Agreed. Not into any of that stuff. Sometimes a sub is

into pain, but I can't deliver on that. I mean, to each his or her own, and if they get off on that, so be it. I'll hand them off to someone like Mark."

"Yeah, I'm definitely not a sadist or a masochist."

"That makes two of us."

"So did you find anything you would like to try? I think the spanking scenes had your undivided attention."

Laura imagined Steve's hand against her bare backside and a wave of heat rushed through her. She peered at him in the darkness, oncoming headlights illuminating his face in rhythmic flickers. Could she fess up? Tell him that spanking was a turn on?

"Well?" he prompted.

"I liked it. I did. But part of me thinks that's deviant."

Steve bellowed a laugh. "Honey, there's a lot that goes on at the club and in the privacy of people's homes that could be considered deviant. Spanking doesn't qualify."

"Time to expand my horizons, perhaps."

"It's only eleven. We could fool around at my house tonight."

Laura's heart rate sped up. The man moved at lightning speed. This morning, bumping into him at the soccer field, he'd talked her into coming to the club in like a nanosecond. Now? He'd propositioned her and they'd be back at his place in about fifteen minutes. What the hell? No time like the present.

Laura studied Steve's profile in the dimness. He was a damn fine-looking man. He was safe in so many ways. A cop, a protective Dom, and not interested in a relationship. What more could she ask for?

"Before I change my mind, the answer is yes."

Steve unlocked the door and Laura entered ahead of him. She slipped out of her coat and he hung it in the front hall closet. He was psyched to show Laura a good time. He hadn't had sex in weeks and honestly, no one had excited him this much in a long damn time.

"Cocktail?" he said. "I have scotch, or beer and wine."

"Scotch it is," Laura said as she settled on the couch and crossed her long legs. Steve went behind the bar and mixed drinks, then returned and sat beside her. They clinked glasses.

"Here's to pain and bondage," he said, "just a *little* pain."

Their gazes locked in a bondage game of their own. Steve couldn't look away, mesmerized by those brilliant violet irises. "You're an incredibly beautiful woman, Laura. I'm glad I met you."

"Thank you." One corner of her lip quirked up and she batted her eyelashes. "You're not so bad yourself."

They sipped slowly, making mindless chatter until their glasses emptied. "Time to take your first step into protocol," Steve announced. "Ready?" Laura nodded. "Say the word," Steve ordered.

"Yes... Sir."

"Eyes on me and stay perfectly still." Steve plucked an ice cube from his glass, laying it against Laura's mouth, he rubbed it back and forth across her bottom lip. He slowly dragged it down her chin and neck, nearing the cleavage that peeked out from under her dress. Drawing tiny circles on her warm flesh, the melting liquid trickled into her bra.

Laura shuddered, licking the moisture off her lips and swallowing hard.

He returned the dripping cube to his glass and pulled her from the couch, securing her in an embrace. Her eyes never left his. "You're going to love this."

It took a few seconds for her to speak. He definitely had

her attention. "Are… are we doing this in your bedroom or do you have a secret sex chamber in the basement?"

Steve huffed a laugh. "Tonight we're in the bedroom. I'll leave my other secrets for next time." He wagged his eyebrows playfully. "Like Mark said, slow and easy."

Reaching down, he caught Laura behind the knees, swooping her into his arms. She yelped, her arms reflexively circling his neck. He carried her into his bedroom and threw her on the bed with enough force that she bounced. Laura squealed again. He set about dimming the lights and lit the candles on the bedside tables, then stepped out of his shoes and socks.

Laura clambered backward, leaning against the gray pillow shams that partially hid the filigreed iron headboard. Jillian had picked out the charcoal and gray bedding, which he still liked, although he'd ditched the hundred other pillows she had decorating the quilt. He pulled his phone from his pocket and plugged it into the speaker on his nightstand, selecting his favorite jazz station.

Standing at the foot of the bed he announced, "Here are the rules." He tucked his hands into his armpits. "You must keep still until I say you may move. You are not to speak unless I ask for a response. You will remember the safe words: green, yellow and red. You recall what they mean?"

"Yes, Sir." Laura whispered. She was already on edge. Perfect.

"But don't be a wimp. Don't use red unless you want everything to stop."

Laura nodded. "When I ask a question I want a verbal response. Communication is paramount or I won't be able to safely test your limits."

"Yes," she said. "Yes, Sir."

"Good girl."

He reached over the low footboard, the spindles on the corners being the important parts, grabbed Laura by the ankles and yanked her toward him, flattening her to the mattress. Her sharp intake of breath excited him and although desperate to be inside her, he reminded himself to take her slow.

Her skirt had hiked up, revealing the crotch of her lacey white panties. "Mystery solved," he said. The no underwear rule at the club was for ease and convenience but truthfully, he liked removing a woman's lingerie himself.

Confiscating her shoes, he dropped them at his feet. "I intend to fuck you in these sexy heels eventually. But tonight you won't be wearing anything."

Laura bit her lip and stayed quiet.

"I'm going to get you naked and restrain you to the headboard. You okay with that?"

Laura nodded.

Steve frowned.

"Oh, sorry. I mean, yes. Yes, Sir."

He reached under her skirt and pulled down her silky panties, sliding them over her delicate pedicured feet polished in a fuchsia hue, and tossed them over his shoulder. "Turn over," he instructed, and Laura rolled onto her stomach. Straddling her thighs, he eased down the zipper of her white dress, revealing flawless porcelain skin. He slipped both hands inside, running them up and down her back, then sought out her breasts. He repeated the motion several times, warming her to his touch.

Steve studied her profile, eyes closed, long lashes touching her cheek. He nimbly unhooked her bra and massaged her upper back and neck. She purred softly.

He knelt up and flipped her over in one quick motion. A faraway gaze unnerved him and he wasn't sure what emotion fueled that look. "Eyes on me," he ordered and she sluggishly complied. "Color?"

"Ah, green," she said.

"Sure?"

"Yes, Sir."

Gliding the dress off her shoulders, he jerked it down over her hips and legs, discarding it on the nearby chair. The bra, straps already dangling, followed, exposing her inviting breasts. Round and high, with dark pink nipples fully erect.

"You have a magnificent body, Laura. I'm privileged to have you in my bed."

"Thank—"

He pressed two fingers to her lips. "No talking, pet."

Steve ran his vision over her sumptuous body. "You're shaved. I like that very much."

"Doesn't everybody—"

He pressed a hand over her mouth. "Quiet." Her smile spread under his palm. If this were a true Dom/sub relationship he'd probably punish her. Maybe he should? "If you keep this up I just might have to leave welts on your ass."

"You wouldn't," she mumbled under his hand, ignoring his directive.

"Ah, there you go, you've just earned five swats on your adorable cheeks."

He reached under her and wrenched down the covers, letting her back lean into the cool sheets. Standing at the foot of the bed, he yanked his black polo shirt over his head, tossing it on the bedside chair. Unbuckling his belt he pulled it from the loops and laid it beside her. "We might need this later," he said with a lascivious grin. He unbuttoned his fly but left his jeans on.

Naked and at Steve's mercy. Human flesh wasn't spontaneously combustible. But, oh God, she just might be the first human to ignite. Now she knew for sure. She liked being bossed around in the bedroom.

No, she fucking *loved* it.

Chapter 14

S teve's commanding presence kindled something in Laura that she'd never experienced. His thighs bestrode her hips, and he bent to kiss her. His full firm lips pressed against hers as his tongue plundered her mouth, leaving her with the palpable heat of passion. Responding eagerly, she wanted those lips everywhere. The kiss ended too quickly.

"We're in no hurry," Steve said near her ear. "Easy." He knelt up and she noticed the healthy bulge in his pants.

Looming over her, hips pinned beneath his muscular thighs, she gaped at his massive chest. A smattering of dark hair on pecs hard as steel, biceps bulging, and he wasn't even doing anything strenuous. His dark eyes pierced her wantonly, as if he could eat her alive. Her heart hammered so forcefully she feared he'd hear it. His dark brown hair fell over one eye and he ran his fingers through his longish locks to put it back in place, which only served to emphasize his biceps even more.

"I'm going to tie you down," he announced.

Oh God, yes. But she kept her lips tight, obeying.

Her eyes followed as he rose from the bed and retrieved items from the nightstand's bottom drawer. Green satin scarves, sashes?

"On your stomach, we're starting backwards."

Laura complied. What did *backwards* mean?

He tethered her right wrist, wrapping the sash around three times before securing it to the headboard. "How does that feel? Not too tight?"

"No, Sir."

He repeated the motion with the second scarf, leaving her arms stretched out. She tugged both several times, then wrapped her hands around the spindles. Yep, secured and immobilized. Just like he promised. Goosebumps prickled her skin. Her anxiety rose a few degrees, which was probably the point. A shuddering fire coursed through her. *Hot.*

He twisted her hair into a makeshift ponytail and laid it on the pillow. His mouth found her shoulder. Bites peppered the back of her neck. She moaned, and unknown sensations trembled up and down her spine. "Shush," he whispered near her ear, as his lips trailed down her back, his gnawing teeth enflaming her sensitive skin.

Spreading her legs wide, he knelt between them, rubbing her buttocks, caressing, bending to kiss each tenderly. His fingers slid inside her, ever so gradually, plunging, prodding, massaging. His other hand squeezed her bottom. And then he slapped her ass, lightly. Then again, harder. The sting surprised her.

He slid his warm palm over her bottom, rubbing away the pain. Keeping his fingers inside her, he alternated, a swat and a thrust with his fingers. Two more quick swats, followed by a soothing stroke. Then two more.

He leaned over and kissed her buttocks again, his tongue laving away the burn.

"Pain can transform into pleasure, excitement," he said. "Give me a color."

It took a second to get her lips to form the word. "Green."

"Good girl," he said, his voice deep and gruff.

Laura's response to his spanking emboldened him. Time to turn her over and soothe her before ratcheting up the stimulation. He deftly untied the restraints, repositioning her on her back and secured her slender wrists to the headboard a second time. "Next time we'll play with an anal plug."

"I don't know."

He shushed her again. "I'm in charge and you'll do what I say until you tap out."

A sheen of sweat on Laura's skin hinted at her excitement. Unless it wasn't excitement, but anxiety, and Steve wasn't sure it was the *right kind* of anxiety. He tugged her knees up, exposing her fully. "Stay like that. Do not move." He rose and stepped out of his jeans, tossing them atop his shirt. His boxer briefs followed, freeing his erection, and he crept back onto the bed. A lion stalking his prey.

The weight of him pressed her into the semi-firm mattress, his cock at her entrance. He sought a breast, kissing, gently biting. Laura gasped. Rolling a nipple between his fingers, he massaged it into a stiff peak, then assaulted her other breast, kissing, sucking. God, he could do this for hours. "I love these," he said. "And they're all mine, for now."

He kissed her mouth, deeper, wetter, until her lips were engorged, his tongue probing, tangling with hers. Rubbing her arms, he kneaded the flesh, feeling her skin warm to his touch. "The restraints still okay?" he said.

"Yes," she whispered.

Laura had her eyelids closed. Her body suddenly went rigid, her hands yanked at the scarves.

Alarmed at her change in body language, Steve commanded, "Laura, eyes on me." When she didn't respond he raised his voice. "Laura, open your eyes. Look at me. Give me a color."

Steve's voice was so far away. And then she was back in her childhood bedroom. Steve's hands were *his* hands. Laura couldn't get her breath. Gasping for air, she whimpered, which transformed into sobs, the ugly cry. She couldn't stop.

"Red! Red!" she finally yelled. "Untie me, I don't want to do this."

Steve instantly released the restraints. "What's wrong? Did I hurt you?"

She broke into sobs, her chest heaving with the terror that had seized her.

Steve wrapped his arms around her tightly. "Laura," he whispered, "tell me what's wrong."

She turned away from him, positioning her knees like a fetus. "If I tell you, you won't want to be with me anymore."

He pushed her flat onto her back, resting one hand on her stomach and his head on his other hand. "Nothing you say will make that happen. Never."

Unable to make eye contact with him, nausea sickened her. He grabbed her chin and forced her to face him. "Open your eyes, damn it, and talk to me."

"I can't," she sputtered.

"I won't take no for an answer, Laura. We'll stay here all night until you fess up."

It took forever until she finally said, "I've never had an orgasm before."

Steve studied her face for too long. Why had she agreed to this? Everything was ruined; he'd be disgusted with her. He'd never want to see her again. They should have just stayed friends. She attempted sitting up, to flee, but Steve kept her firmly in his loving embrace, holding on to her so she didn't disappear into her past.

Steve's stomach knotted. What had happened to her to cause this reaction? "I don't understand. You're not a virgin, are you?" Good Lord, if she was, then he'd misjudged *every*thing.

Steve forced her to face him. They lay on the gray sheets, nose to nose. He studied her sad eyes, wiping away the tears from her cheek. She hiccupped a sob.

"No, I've had plenty of sex. It's just that I can't let myself go, to just feel. I'm good at giving but not so hot at receiving."

He hesitated briefly, then: "You've been raped."

Laura narrowed her eyes. Twenty seconds might've passed. "Worse."

"I'm here. Tell me. I want to know." He caressed her cheek with his thumb. "Please."

She inhaled deeply and released a long slow breath. "My stepfather. He worked days. My mother did the graveyard shift at the hospital. It started one night when I had a nightmare and woke up screaming. He crawled into bed with me and his hands were in places they shouldn't have been. I was terrified, but he was saying such loving things to me, I was... well, confused. He said it was a secret way that dad's loved their daughters and no one could know about our special time together."

"Oh, God, Laura, how old were you?"

"Ten."

"Your mother didn't know?"

"No, I tried to tell her many times, but I just couldn't."

Steve fell back onto the bed and covered his eyes with his forearm for a few seconds, he sighed heavily and then he was back facing her, slinging his arm over her waist. "How long did this go on?"

"Until I was twelve and I got my period. I knew about getting pregnant and I understood that this was wrong, abnormal."

"How could he do that to you? Jesus, I'd like to kill that motherfucker."

"You're too late."

Then Steve remembered Laura had said her stepfather was dead.

"The day I finally mustered the strength to tell my mother, I found her in the kitchen. She was dressed for work and my dad was due home any minute. I couldn't risk it happening one more time. My mother got hysterical, but managed to compose herself before my dad came home. Well, barely."

"How did he react?"

"Did I mention that he was the town sheriff?"

"Jesus, no."

So, she'd resolved to tell Steve. Everything.

The faded floral wallpaper, the stale smell of coffee, the faint odor of bleach—her mother cleaned incessantly— brought the horrid day back. Even if she could only remember it in black and white.

Laura grabbed her mother by the shoulders and shook her. "Mom, stop screaming and listen. He'll be home soon."

"He and the mayor run this town, Laura. No one will believe us."

"Then we should leave. Aunt Teri is a lawyer. She'll help us."

"I don't know. She's very busy."

"We're family, Mom, she'll help."

Her stepfather walked in from the garage through the kitchen door and unbuckled his holster, laying it on the kitchen table... of all days to get home early. He grabbed a beer like he did every day before heading toward the bedroom to change and lock up his service revolver. Her mother charged, pounding his chest. "How could you? You're a fucking pervert. She's our daughter." The beer bottle fell, spewing its contents.

Her father seized her mother's wrists and pushed her against the wall, her head hitting the shelf that held her collection of ceramic cows. They fell to the tile floor, splintering into shards. Exactly the way she felt.

His face was so close to her that the spittle flying from his mouth peppered her face. "What's wrong with you, woman? What are you saying?"

"You're having sex with a twelve-year-old? What? I'm not enough for you?"

He slapped her face. "Get a grip, Sarah. You're stark raving mad."

He'd kill her if Laura didn't stop him. He had her neck in a death grip, choking, strangling. Laura charged him in an attempt to free her mom. He backhanded Laura and she went flying across the room. At that instant something snapped, and a great sense of calmness possessed her. Unfortunately for her dad, he'd schooled her in gun basics.

She removed the weapon from his holster, released the safety and aimed, ordering him to let her mother go. When he saw Laura, he released her mom, she fell to the floor, smashing her head on the baseboard. He charged Laura and she pulled the trigger. The bullet hit him in the chest and he went down hard. Laura stood over him for several minutes, watching him gurgling, struggling to breathe. "You'll never hurt another child. In fact, you'll never hurt anyone again." The calm confidence wrapping her in false security. Blood poured from his chest and mouth. His body went limp and his eyes rolled backwards. He was dead.

But a part of him stayed alive. Terrorizing her. Forever.

Laura didn't miss a beat and her words washed over Steve like sewage. Steve grabbed Laura's hand and squeezed. "Oh, Laura. I... I'm so sorry."

The dam had opened and her words were an unrelenting storm, spewing ugliness into her world.

"My mother freaked. I told her to call 911." Laura paused, sucking in a bottomless breath. "My mother was paralyzed; I'll never forget her hands stuck on her mouth. I almost made the call myself. But as I reached for the phone my mother said his cop buddies would never believe us. We called Aunt Teri and she came so fast. Thank God, she was a lawyer. Convinced me not to talk to anyone. She made it all go away, made everything okay. At least on the outside."

Steve moved the damp hair off her face, running his fingers through her long unruly locks.

"You can figure out the rest. The handcuffs, the police cruiser, the attempts to interrogate me. I guess I was in shock but I followed my aunt's advice to the letter. Stay quiet. Don't talk."

"I'm so grateful you had someone looking out for you."

"I wish you could have met my aunt. She was something. She came into that precinct with a vengeance. Those deputies didn't know what hit them. I was out in twenty-four hours and well, it took some time, but she got the charges dismissed and I went to live with her. My mother couldn't cope with any of it and wound up in a psych ward for a year."

"Geez, Laura, I don't know what to say." He continued stroking her hair lovingly.

"I still don't know what was wrong with me. Why I allowed it to happen in the first place, or why for so long. Years of therapy and few answers."

"It wasn't your fault."

Chapter 15

Goddammit. Steve had worked with several abused women at the club and considered himself well read on the subject. He'd taken plenty of in-service training too. He could help Laura. The idea of her living the rest of her life like this would haunt him for eternity. She deserved to learn to love herself again. And to trust.

Laura twisted out of his embrace and sat up, her feet dangling over the edge of the bed. "I need to go."

"No, wait, please. Let's talk a little longer." Steve stood and grabbed a t-shirt from the top drawer of his dresser. He returned to her side and slipped the collar over her head. Her hands found the armholes and she freed her hair and it flowed down her back in gentle golden waves.

Donning a shirt himself and a pair of gym shorts, he took her by the hand and led her back to the living room and perched her on the sofa. "Stay here," he instructed.

Returning with a glass of ice water, he made her drink half before resting the tumbler on the coffee table.

"There is clinical research on ways to overcome sexual trauma. I can cite the studies for you if you want to read them. And the bottom line is this is about vulnerability, pet. You'll never feel anything sexual if you don't let down your guard. You have to trust a man in order for him to give you real pleasure. He took both her hands in his, rubbing his thumbs over the backs. "Please, don't think I'm being trite but I've worked with other women who've suffered sexual trauma. Let me help you get there."

"Not women like me."

"Not exactly like you, but again it's about vulnerability, and trust. Do you trust me?"

"I do. At least I think I do."

"Good. Then we should try again. Not tonight, but soon. It happened a long time ago, if it was recent then I wouldn't suggest this. But you'll have to give yourself over to me, wholly and unequivocally. Do you think you can?"

"I want to, I do." She shook her head. "God knows I've tried so many times to just let go, but there always comes a point when that trigger gets pulled and I'm dead on the floor. Just like my stepdad."

"I'll find that trigger for you and we'll neutralize it. You can get past this."

"I appreciate your…"

"Laura, let me help you."

She sighed.

"There's no way I'm letting you go home tonight. We'll get some sleep. I'm a bum on Sunday mornings anyway and we can lounge around and talk things through over coffee."

Laura wanted to stay, wanted to let Steve help her, but it was futile. And she desired his friendship more than an orgasm. If he failed, she'd never be able to look him in the eye. *Cut and run.*

Steve smirked. "I'm still the Dom and I give the orders while you're under my roof. So, I say sleep, pet. Let's go." He yanked her up and marched her back to his bedroom.

Now. Now. Now. Cut and run.

She couldn't.

He let her wear the shirt to bed. Last thing she saw was those blue numbers on the bedside clock announcing 2:07.

Laura awoke disoriented, gazing at the unfamiliar clock: 8:37. Last night's debacle hit her like a runaway train. *Oh, God.* She'd screwed up royally. After telling Steve she was in for some kinky sex she'd fumbled at the five-yard line. *Shit. Shit. Shit.*

Steve's leg rested heavily on her hips, an arm across her waist, securing her tightly to his warm body. He never should have made her drink all that water because now she was about to burst. Slowly, she inched his leg downward, over her thigh and calf until she freed herself. He roused but didn't wake. She tiptoed toward the bathroom, hoping he'd stay asleep. *Cut and run.* But he'd catch her, she'd never make a clean escape. Did she want to?

"Hey," came Steve's sultry, sleepy voice. "You're not bolting, are you?"

Geez, he could read her mind. Downright scary. She returned to the bed and stared at his sumptuous chest. A muscular thigh peeked out from under the sheet, his hair a messy tousle. "Still here," she said, crossing her arms over her chest.

Steve reached up and grabbed an arm, rolling her onto the mattress. That's it! She should thank him for last night. Sliding a leg between his, she wrapped it around his calf and pushed with her hips, forcing him onto his back. She straddled him, pining his muscular shoulders to the sheets.

He bellowed a laugh. "Nice move, little miss FBI agent."

She pulled the over-sized t-shirt over her head and threw it on the floor. Emboldened by the daylight—the encounters with her stepfather having occurred under the cloak of darkness—she reached for his cock, bringing it toward her lips.

"Whoa. What the hell are you doing?" He grabbed both her wrists and yanked her up so they were face to face. Her breasts smashed against his solid pecs.

"I think they call it a blow job, mister."

"Why?"

"Did I do something wrong?" Laura couldn't figure out if Steve was bemused or... angry. She'd never met a guy who'd turned down oral sex. Never. Ever.

"No way, pet. I call the shots and I won't be taking any pleasure other than the pleasure I can give you. Then I'll take my turn."

"What? That's ridiculous. Guys don't think that way."

"This guy does. The lady always comes first. And I mean that literally and figuratively."

Alas, she'd screwed up again.

"You're a dick."

"That's rude. Most people just call me *detective*."

He settled her on her back, centering her head on the pillow. Resting his head on his elbow he said, "I've been thinking and I have a few ideas. First, you need to tell me in detail what types of behaviors were forced on you. Then we'll flip the script. Introducing new things to distract you from your expectations. If it's something you've never experienced before, those old triggers can be avoided."

"Like what?"

"I intend to surprise you." He tweaked her nose with his index finger as if she were a child. "That's half the fun, pet. There are ways to release emotional pain and provide new stimulation and pleasure in places you're not familiar with."

Egads. Sounded scary. But kinda good scary.

"I think a new environment might help also. What do you

think about going to the club and using one of the private rooms?"

Viktor spent the entire night dozing in his car while his target languished in that detective's house. She definitely had to be dating him or she wouldn't have spent the night. Luckily he had the alarm set on her car tracker so if she left he'd be alerted.

The blaring noise jerked him out of his dream, whipping the little FBI agent with a cat o' nine tails, the perfect pink skin on her back adorned with bloody stripes. Hand inside his pants he tugged on his erection, which popped up every time he thought of the little bitch.

He slunk lower in the driver's seat as she drove past.

Viktor was basically squatting in the abandoned duck-hunting cabin. Careful not to arouse suspicion, he brought in equipment and supplies under the cover of night. The sleepy east-end town was mostly quiet during the week, compared to the weekends when city dwellers arrived in droves, in search of pumpkins and homemade pies. The Nature Preserve was mostly a summer hangout and abandoned at this time of year. But still, he couldn't arouse the interest of the locals, mostly farmers and shop and motel owners. A generator could provide limited electricity, and hot water with the aid of a propane tank. Hopefully he'd soon have her under his control, secured for her punishment and his pleasure.

One last bit of sleuthing to be done: cracking her alarm code. She used a remote device to allow her car access, but used the keypad by the kitchen door to arm and deactivate the house alarm once inside. The keypad was visible through an adjacent window. Today he'd brought binoculars in the hopes of catching her inputting the numbers. Once he had the code he'd test it out while she was at work, casing the house and planning the kidnapping.

Viktor parked down the street as Laura turned into her long driveway. He hustled through the woods with his binoculars hidden under his black pea coat. He arrived just as the garage door closed. Running to the side of the house he peered through the window as Laura punched in the numbers. 0709.

Laura sat behind her desk Monday morning sifting through a mound of paperwork. She tried not to gulp her coffee. If she didn't know better she'd swear she had a hangover. Emotionally hung over, that might be why she felt as though she hadn't slept for a week. The night with Steve haunted her. He hadn't called, and she certainly hadn't contacted him. Why had she been compelled to confess her deepest darkest secrets to that man? Seriously, she'd met him what... two weeks ago? She'd known other guys for months and never mentioned her sordid past. And she'd faked plenty of orgasms without being detected. Why hadn't she done that with Steve? Taken the easy way out. Instead, she blurted out her inability to climax. Geez.

Leaning back in her chair she chewed on her pen, shaking her head slowly. *You're hopeless, Laura Logan.*

"You look like crap," Alyx said, closing the door behind her and taking the seat in front of Laura's desk. Her boss smiled, sipping her required dose of caffeine.

"Good morning to you too."

"Tough weekend? You go to the club?"

"Maybe." Laura had fully intended to put Steve and the club in her rearview mirror for the time being. She'd be on a plane to Virginia on Wednesday to visit her mother for

Thanksgiving. No decisions would be made until she'd taken a serious time out.

"Don't be coy, darling. Fess up. You know all my dirt." Alyx crossed her legs and settled back as if she intended to be there for a while. "And I want to hear yours."

She knew enough. Alyx was the only one Laura had told about her past. Laura had feared a background check would eventually discover that she'd killed her stepfather and so she'd told Alyx about it while they were at Quantico. Apparently, her Aunt Teri had kept her word and the record ceased to exist.

Laura sunk back into her chair. "I didn't do anything at the club."

"Too bad for you."

"Look who's talking? You didn't want to play there either and I believe you still don't."

"Honestly, I see it a little differently now. Daniel and I still don't want to play at the club, but if I was single I might."

Laura studied Alyx's face. There was no reason to lie. "I'll admit some of it was tantalizing. I might consider a private room with Steve."

"So you didn't have sex with him this weekend?"

"You're asking me to kiss and tell?"

Alyx sat up and placed her coffee mug on Laura's desk. "I'm ordering you to. Need I remind you that I'm expertly trained in the art of interrogation?"

Laura momentarily averted her gaze, lacing her fingers together atop the desk.

"Don't make me put you in a room and shine a bright light in your face."

"I believe that technique is outdated and illegal, my dear."

They both laughed. "All right, we tried some stuff in his bedroom but I panicked and tapped out."

"Hmm, what do you think happened?"

"I'm not exactly sure but I found myself back in my childhood bedroom and Steve's hands were *his* hands."

"Yikes."

"Tell me. Steve was great though. He thinks he can help me, that breaking those old patterns will avoid the trigger that shuts me down."

"I don't understand. You've had plenty of sex. What was different this time?"

Okay, now she was trapped. Did she want to confess that she'd never had an orgasm? That she was unable to let herself go? To fully trust a guy? But Alyx was one of her best friends and maybe confession was good.

Laura wrung her hands and bit her bottom lip.

"Okay, that body language tells me you're in serious distress here. What is it, Laura? You can trust me. No judgments. I'll just listen."

"I-I've never climaxed with a man, or by myself either."

Alyx kept silent.

"I almost get there but I fade at the last minute. Some trigger gets pulled and I'm locked up so tight I can barely breathe."

"And no other guy has ever noticed this?"

"Not until Steve. Apparently I should have pursued acting instead of law enforcement."

"Then I say, thank your lucky stars. Let him help you."

"He thinks he can. He says we need to flip the script. Avoid those old behaviors. Try new things, new environments, other forms of pleasure."

"I think he's right. Or at least it's worth a shot."

"He wants to know the details of my abuse because he thinks there are some triggers there. If we identify them then perhaps we can avoid or eventually banish them."

"Makes sense to me."

"I'm not making any decisions until after the holiday. I'm

going to visit my mom for Thanksgiving. It'll give me time to think."

"Good, but don't overthink it, Laura. One thing Daniel taught me is that overthinking is an antidote to enjoying sex. You just need to let yourself go, be in the moment and allow yourself to be vulnerable with a man you trust."

"Wow, those are the exact words Steve used."

"You do trust him, don't you?"

"Perhaps. But for the life of me, I don't know why. I've only known him for like two weeks."

"Same thing happened to me with Daniel. Something about these Doms makes them… I don't know what to call it, but just easy to be vulnerable with. Maybe it's because they break down all kinds of barriers you never knew were there. And they're confident, they know what they're doing."

Laura had to agree that Steve's confidence and expertise were a huge turn on. "I'll agree with you there. It's strange, but I feel the same."

A knock on her office door abruptly stopped the conversation. "You need to sign for a package," Rich, the latest NAT said.

"Coming," Laura said.

And she hoped maybe, some day, she would.

Chapter 16

Steve's phone rang as he headed to work via Sunrise Highway. He answered without checking the screen. "Moretti."

"Hi bunnie." His mother had used this moniker for as long as he could remember. His high school and college buddies chided him about it, especially his football teammates. But secretly, he kind of liked it.

"Hi, Mom."

"Just making sure you're coming for Thanksgiving dinner."

"I'll be there. I'll bring the wine as usual."

"Wonderful. Two o'clock." His mother hesitated and he waited for the routine grilling. "Are you bringing anyone?"

"No, Ma, just me."

"You should have a woman in your life."

"Not for me."

"Hmm," his mother said, hesitating a little too long. "What about a man, then?"

Steve laughed. "I'm not gay. I prefer going solo. It's not complicated."

She sighed. "Honestly, Steven, you were always such a happy child, kind and generous, and I know women have thrown themselves at you since you were in middle school. I can't believe none of them stuck."

Me either. But he'd tried and lost too many times. Not everyone needed to settle down. "Can we stop this line of questioning? I'm pulling into the precinct."

"Of course, dear. See you Thursday. Bye, bunnie."

He shut off the car, which ended the call. Leaning his forehead on the steering wheel he let out a long slow breath, then smiled. He loved his mom to death. He wished he could make her happy by bringing home a woman he loved, it was the only thing left on her bucket list, she'd all but told him. No pressure, she'd said. Yeah, right.

"Morning, boss." Alice wore a neon pink shift decorated with giant multi-hued fronds. He winced. The brilliance made his teeth hurt.

"Morning," he said. She helped him off with his coat and hung it on the hook behind his door. He took his phone from the pocket and placed it on his desk. He desperately wanted to call Laura and struggled with it all day yesterday and into the night, but she needed some space.

Was this morning too soon?

Assured that his correspondence would be waiting for him on his desk, Steve settled into his creaky chair. As he scanned the top sheet, Alice reported, "Nothing new on the kidnapping of the nun and those girls. APB still out but no sighting of the missing subject."

"Thanks, Alice."

Alice was a true enigma. She wasn't a cop, but a senior clerk-typist off the civil service list. They'd stopped using police officers for secretarial work under his command, a waste of training in his mind.

A thoroughly modern, strong-willed woman, Alice proved

intelligent and savvy, yet, she often treated him like a secretary from the 1950s. He finally convinced her to not make him coffee in the morning since he preferred stopping to get his own on the way in.

"Anything else you need, boss?"

"No. Thank you, Alice."

"Don't forget the time sheets need to be signed before you leave today. We're also out of overtime by the end of the week unless you get approval from the higher ups."

"Got it, Alice."

"Door closed or open?" she asked, her hand on the knob.

"Closed, please."

After signing his name like a thousand times, he deposited the papers in his out basket. He stared at his phone. Should he call? Jesus, why was he stressing over this? Maybe because he'd opened his big mouth and promised Laura he could help her. What if he couldn't deliver? He had to stop doubting himself. Was his Dom personality shriveling up? *Get a grip, Steve.*

He finally texted, "You okay?" Then waited impatiently. What had become of society that a response to a text was expected within five seconds? If you didn't hear back immediately from someone it meant that you weren't important. Except he'd only met her two weeks ago and that barely qualified as friendship.

"Hey," his screen said. "I'm fine. Sorry I made a giant ass of myself Saturday night."

Okay, this wasn't a conversation for texting. He dialed her number. "Hey," she said again.

"Great to hear your voice. And you have to stop thinking like that. All your feelings and actions are justified. You just need to change those you don't want anymore."

"Sounds good, but I don't know if—"

He cut her off. "No more self-doubt. Let's focus on the positive."

"All right."

"Have you thought any more about coming to the club?"

"Well, I'm flying to Virginia to see my mom for Thanksgiving. Maybe the weekend after?"

Steve swallowed his disappointment with enormous difficulty. He'd hoped she'd come to the club with him this Saturday. "Sounds like a plan." He paused. "What's your itinerary?"

"Leaving Wednesday afternoon and returning Sunday. What about you? Are you spending Thanksgiving with your family?"

"Yep, no way I can avoid that, not that I'd want to. I'm lucky to have them."

"True that."

Geez, he'd stumbled into trouble again. He shouldn't be bragging about his family when Laura had virtually no one. She told him her mother was a broken woman, barely managing her life. The idea that Laura would become like her mother terrified him.

He moved away from further discussion of family. "Have a great trip and I'll see you when you get back. I'll reserve a room for the following Saturday."

"I guess," Laura said too quietly.

"No pressure, Laura. You can always change your mind. We'll go slow."

"I know, slow and easy, just like Mark says."

He could sense her smile through the phone. "Exactly."

"What do you have?" Laura asked Rich.

"A lead on Viktor's whereabouts." He consulted his notepad. "A guy named Ben Emerson owns a hardware store in Ridge. He saw the poster of the perp in the Post Office and thinks the guy has been in his store."

Laura jumped up from her desk chair. "Let's go."

It took an hour for them to arrive at the local hardware store to interview Ben Emerson. Laura and Rich offered their credentials and Rich presented the sketch of Viktor on his cell phone. "This the guy?"

Ben studied the photo, the lines between his eyes deepened. "Well, he's got a beard and dark hair, but the scar is the same. I think it's the same guy."

"Why was he here?" Laura said.

"Ropes, chains and padlocks. He's actually been in three times and he ordered a generator too. Bought duct tape and some basic tools, electric screwdriver, hammer, nails. Stuff like that. I joked with him, asking if he was building a fortress or something. He said he was just shoring up an old chicken coop, course no idea why he'd need a generator for that."

Desperate for this lead to pay off, Laura inquired, "Did he pay with a credit card?"

"No, always cash."

Rich said, "Did you notice what kind of car he drives?"

Ben leaned both hands on the wooden counter. "Yeah, it was an old junker. A black Toyota, four-door."

"Any chance you got a license plate?" Rich said.

"Yup, got that too." Ben reached into his cash register and lifted up the cash drawer, retrieving a slip of paper. "Here you go, agents."

"Call it in," Laura ordered Rich. He walked out onto the pavement to forward the plate number to the office.

"Your help has been invaluable in our investigation, Mr. Emerson. Could you show me the exact items he bought?"

"Sure." Ben walked her around the store and she snapped photos of the merchandise Viktor purchased.

Returning to Laura's side, Rich said, "The plates are

stolen." Laura gritted her teeth. Damn, the guy was good at covering his tracks.

"Probably a long shot but, any idea where he might be living?"

"Well, agent, it's a small town, and people keep to themselves around here. Lots of farmers who work long hours. The fall is tourist season, pumpkin and apple picking, farm stands selling fresh cider and homemade pies."

"I see." Laura handed Ben her card. "If you spot him again, call this number."

"Will do." Before they could exit he added, "One more thing, agent. He might be squatting on abandoned property. There are a lot of old farmhouses in the area. Foreclosures after the market crash."

"Thanks, Mr. Emerson. You've been a big help. I'll look into that."

Laura and Rich, along with three other agents went through all the property records for the small town. Several showed promise and Laura put a team on it, yet searching acres of property took time. Maybe she should call Steve, have him add his resources. She was tempted to work through the Thanksgiving holiday, but Alyx would probably nix that.

Viktor checked his gun, releasing the magazine and insuring the rounds were loaded properly. Satisfied, he shoved the magazine back into the grip and secured the weapon in the shoulder harness under his jacket. Tonight, was the night. Everything was ready to bring her back to his makeshift dungeon at the secluded cabin. The alarm test had been successful, allowing him access to her private domain. He hadn't fully grasped that she was a rich bitch. Maybe he'd steal her money, an unexpected windfall. Languishing in her lavish home, he drank her beer, stretched out on her bed, inhaling her scent on the sheets. Rummaging through her dresser drawers, he fingered her fine lingerie but eventually settled on a pair of lacy black panties from her hamper. Pressing the slinky garment against his face he breathed in her salty, sweet fragrance. He pocketed the bikini bottoms in the back pocket of his jeans, a souvenir to hold him until he had her to himself, bound and gagged.

Victor parked on a side street, waiting for Laura to exit the FBI parking garage, the tracking alarm announcing she was on the move. He started his car, anticipating her left turn, but she turned right and he had to make a quick U-turn. He expected she would head home, but instead she entered the Belt Parkway. *Fuck. Where was she going?* He often forgot about the American holidays. She might be leaving town for Thanksgiving. Was she on the way to an airport? You get to both LaGuardia and JFK airports by this road. *Shit.* He'd been pumped about finally having his little slave tied up and at his mercy. But he'd have to wait several more days. Viktor pounded the steering wheel as he drove. "Fuck, fuck, fuck. Fucking bitch!" he screamed. His vehicle swerved right, slightly crossing the dotted white line.

A horn blared and he glanced out the passenger-side window. Some guy gave him the finger and he returned it, double-fold. Laura entered the long-term parking lot at LaGuardia airport and Viktor despaired. Nothing left to do but go back to his stolen homestead and get drunk. He'd been saving the expensive bottle of vodka for a celebration once he had her. Well, he'd have to buy another bottle.

Chapter 17

Laura ubered to her mother's apartment in the fifty-five-and-over community. A pleasant enough complex, with a swimming pool and clubhouse, even a small gym. Not that her mother ever availed herself of these amenities. The unpleasantness came in the residents. Older, infirm, walkers and wheelchairs in abundance. Of course, her mother was probably numb to it all since she worked at the local assisted living center. Her mother had no joy in her life. Guilt still consumed her, even though Laura had told her countless times the bad days were in the past and should stay there.

They ordered Chinese takeout and ate in front of the TV watching reruns of *Friends* and *Seinfeld*. Laura finished her second glass of chardonnay as she helped her mother clear the dishes.

"I've got everything for tomorrow's dinner," her mother offered. "I bought a turkey breast since whole turkeys are for families. And sweet potatoes, stuffing mix, and makings for Caesar salad. I know that's your favorite. Oh, and some White House rolls and I bought a pumpkin pie."

Laura loaded the empty wineglasses into the dishwasher. Her mother's words: 'turkeys are for families' made Laura think of Steve and his big Italian family, which further depressed her.

Her mother rambled on, mindlessly placing the paper containers of leftovers in the fridge. "I know I should have baked a pie, but I've been working a lot of overtime hours since everyone else wanted time off for the holiday. The pay is good and I can use the money."

Laura stopped loading the dishwasher. "Mom, I have plenty of money. Let me help you."

"Absolutely not, Laura. I owe you everything. You owe me nothing. Less than nothing if that was possible."

Laura leaned her back against the counter, her hands gripping the edge. "Mom, please don't keep doing this to yourself. None of it was your fault."

Her mother faced her. "You're wrong, Laura. It's all my fault. I should have known, I should have seen the signs. I mean, what kind of mother doesn't know her child is being abused?"

"That's not true, Mom, and if you'd known you would have done something. Let it go. It's done. I'm fine."

Her mother's sad face infuriated Laura. Why couldn't they ever see each other without this recurring nightmare?

Her mother continued as if Laura hadn't said a word, retrieving her wineglass from the dishwasher, her mother poured another glass. "Your real father would be furious with me. I made a disgusting choice for a second husband and then I allowed him to abuse our daughter. If there hadn't been that accident, and he'd come home to us, none of this would have happened."

"Oh God, Mom. Stop. I can't keep listening to this." She took the wineglass from her mother's hand and rested it on the counter. "Maybe a third glass is unwise."

No stopping her. "It's terrible that you never even met your dad, getting deployed right after we found out we were expecting you."

"Mom. Enough."

Silence, finally. She pulled her mother in for a hug giving her all the warmth she could muster. "Shush. Let it go, Mom. Please."

Not tired, she spent the next few hours on her laptop. Curious, she Googled Sex Trafficking in Virginia and learned that Virginia ranked 15th in the U.S. for the most reported cases of human trafficking in 2016. Last year, the state reported 148 cases with 59 involving minors. In response, Virginia enacted a new law to help its youngest victims. House Bill 2282 required the Virginia Board of Education to develop guidelines for training school counselors, school nurses and other relevant staff on the prevention of trafficking children.

Laura reflected on her own abuse. Why didn't she tell? Why hadn't she confided in a teacher or counselor at school? Why didn't she resist, run away, fight back? Why... why... why? She slammed her computer shut and rested her forehead on her arms. Too much. Coming home was too hard. It forced her to remember things she'd vowed to forget.

Tears filled her eyes. She wished she could go home. God, how she missed her Aunt Teri. And... she missed Steve.

Steve carried the case of wine into his parents' house, his nephew, Joey, holding the door open wide. "Hey, buddy," he said. "When's your next game. I'll try to be there."

"Really, Uncle Steve? That'd be awesome."

"What's your record this season? Pretty good, right?"

His nephew followed him into the kitchen where the Moretti women were hard at work preparing the holiday feast.

The perfect perfume of freshly baked pies and turkey roasting in the oven panged his hunger, probably the best aroma on the planet. "We're undefeated. 10 and 0."

"Incredible. Good job," Steve said, resting the box on the counter. "Six bottles of pinot noir and six bottles of white Bordeaux as requested," he announced. "The white is chilled." The three women preferred the white and the men the red, with a few beers thrown in on occasion.

Joey was glued to his side, which was a fairly regular event. "Just like your football team, Uncle Steve, when you went undefeated and won the states."

"Exactly." Steve gave the boy's dark hair the usual ruffling. His nephew beamed.

"Maybe I'll get a scholarship just like you did for football."

Unfortunately professional soccer had never taken off in the U.S. He'd thought there'd be a chance when Beckham arrived but it never happened. Football still outranked soccer in popularity by about a zillion miles. Thus, scholarships weren't as prevalent as they were in football and the likelihood of his nephew scoring one was remote. The kid was small for his age and to play any type of college or pro sport you had to be on the larger side. Not that small guys couldn't make it in the pros, but they had to be fast, because if one of those bruisers nailed you it wouldn't be pretty. At eleven, the kid still had plenty of time to grow, but Steve's sister was petite and she'd married an accountant with not much bulk or height, and not much athletic ability either. His sister had been a talented soccer player in high school but Steve didn't think enough athletic DNA was in Joey to make the big leagues. Maybe he'd be surprised.

Wiping her hands on her apron, his mother rushed over and gave her only son a kiss on the cheek. She pulled a white thread off his black sweater and flicked it into the kitchen trashcan beside them. "Looking handsome as ever, bunnie."

"Thank you, Mom." His older sister, Vicky, and the next sibling in line, Mary, kissed opposite cheeks in tandem.

"Good to see you," Vicky said.

"Mr. Studly arrives on time. That's a new one," Mary said. Steve had suffered mercilessly under the care of his two older sisters. When he was little they dressed him in princess clothes and made him go to their tea parties. As he got older, they anointed him the prince and made him escort them to countless balls. Thankfully there were tons of boys in his neighborhood and as soon as he was allowed to play outside by himself, he spent every waking minute outdoors.

"I'm never late," he said. Close enough to grab them both, he secured their necks in his massive hands and squeezed until they yelped. "Be nice."

"Okay, okay," they both said. "Uncle!"

"That's better," he said. His nephew giggled to the side, covering his mouth with his hand. A flurry of pink entered the kitchen as his two little nieces whooshed past him, screaming in mock terror.

His father followed them, making monster hands. "I'm gonna getcha," he growled. The girls hid behind their mother, clutching her legs through the flouncy green skirt. They were the Lilly Pulitzer crowd and Alice came to mind.

His father continued his hunt and the girls ran from their mother to Steve, beseeching him with their outstretched arms. "Uncle Steve, save us, save us."

Steve laughed and scooped up the bustle of pink, clutching the girls tightly. "Go away you big bad wolf," he said to his father. "Be gone."

His dad dropped the scary persona and everyone had a good long laugh.

Steve helped make the salad while his dad, and brother-in-law, Sean, mixed cocktails. A bevy of martinis and manhattans and a few started early on the wine.

A delectable assortment of appetizers covered the coffee table as the family sat around, friendly banter and chitchat filling the air. Vicky's oldest daughter, Maggie, the one he'd thought of when the kidnapping occurred, pouted in a side chair, unhappy at the no-phone rule her mother enforced when they were all together. Eventually, she'd forget about it. Yet it always took a while. Maggie's younger brother was the same age as Joey, but the two had nothing in common. Ironically, his other nephew was twice Joey's size but had no interest in athletics, instead favoring more intellectual pursuits. The kid was a computer whiz.

The sumptuous feast came to an end and Steve had to open the button on his jeans. "I overdid it again," he lamented. "You're cooking talents are just too much for me, ladies."

They turned on the football game and Steve would have preferred to sack out on the couch and watch the game, but he'd been trained better. He did the dirty work, washing the baking and roasting pans and the delicate stemware banned from the dishwasher. His dad dried, while his sisters and their husbands finished clearing the table and stowing the leftovers.

Drying his hands, intent on heading home, his phone rang. He'd placed it on the center island and the screen announced *Laura Logan*.

"Who's that?" his mother said.

"Oh, a girl is calling Stevie," Mary said.

"A girl?" Vicky said. "Do tell?"

"Jesus, stop it. All of you. It's work." Steve grabbed the phone and marched into the dining room and down the hall to his old room, still enshrined with the mementos of his young life. Inside, he shut the door and sunk onto the bed. "Hey."

"I hope I'm not getting you at a bad time."

"No. Not at all. I was planning on calling you when I got home. Besides, I was in dire need of a rescue."

"From your lovely family?"

Steve's whining wouldn't make any sense to Laura, and he loved his family to death, but sometimes they could be overwhelming. He eyed his football trophies, the scholar athlete award being the crowning glory, as he furthered his explanation. "They're great, but when you live alone, a crowd wears you down pretty quickly. How was your Thanksgiving?"

"Good. We cooked a nice meal and Mom is dozing in the recliner. I worry about her. She's frail and drinks too much wine."

"I'm sorry, it must be tough."

"And she always has to bring up our worst days. I keep telling her to let the past die, but she just can't. Sometimes I think her death certificate will say 'Died of Overwhelming Guilt.'" Laura laughed.

"I can't imagine how she must feel. Gotta be hard."

"Yeah, well anyway, I called to wish you Happy Thanksgiving, but I also wanted to tell you that we got a lead on Viktor just before I left. A guy that owns the hardware store in Ridge says he thinks the perp was in several times."

"You mean Ben Emerson?"

"You know him?"

"Sure, been in his store lots of times. He's Cal's father. You remember my landscaper, the guy we met at the Triangle Pub?"

"I do. Well, Mr. Emerson saw the sketch in the post office and the scar on the guy's face looked familiar, even though it seems he dyed his hair black and grew a beard."

Steve sighed in frustration. "You should have called me. I could have followed up while you were away."

"I've got a team on it. The guy bought some curious items: chains, rope, padlocks, duct tape, even a generator. Ben suggested we check out abandoned properties in the area. He might be hiding out in an old homestead. Apparently there are a lot of them nearby."

"Yeah, right after the mortgage crisis." Steve remembered how the crime rate spiked during the recession when so many people lost their homes. He'd just graduated the police academy. "You sure you don't need my help? I can put a bunch of guys on it right away?"

"No, got it covered. Just going to take some time to check out all the properties."

"If you need backup let me know."

"The other reason I called is to tell you I'm definitely in for the club next Saturday."

Steve sat up abruptly, heat radiated through his chest. He answered too quickly. "Awesome! I'm looking forward to it."

"I won't lie, I'm nervous."

"Don't be, I've got this," he said. "I've got you."

Steve's nephew didn't have a soccer game the Saturday after Thanksgiving so he set out to interview Ben Emerson. Laura said she didn't need his help but he was determined to be of assistance anyway. He understood that she wasn't good at asking for anything, even if she was in danger. Based on what Laura reported, he feared Viktor was up to no good again. Sounded like he was building something that could be used to secure new merchandise. On the other hand, the guy would be stupid to still be working in the area when he'd recently had his operation thwarted. It would've made more sense to set up a new ring elsewhere.

The tinkle of the bell mounted on Ben's entry door announced his arrival. Ben was behind the counter. "Morning," Steve said.

"Steve Moretti. How's it hanging, buddy?" Cal and Ben, your basic everyday guys, no sophistication. No class. But also no bullshit.

"I'm good, Ben. How's the family?"

"All good. Cal's business is doing well. Josh and Elliot are on his payroll and off mine, thank goodness. And little Sally is off to college. At least one of my kids will have a degree."

"That's great."

"Lynn is up to her ears in pies. 'Tis the season." Ben's wife baked the best pies on the east end and she garnered a tidy sum during the fall season as city people, *cidiots* as the locals nicknamed them, visited nearby farms stands, buying apples and pumpkins and assorted fall sundries. Ben patted his rotund belly. "Of course, I'm still on quality control. Making sure the goods are up to par."

They both laughed. Steve rested his hands on the counter. "I hear the FBI visited a few days back."

"Yeah. I think I identified that guy they're looking for, the one that kidnapped the nun and those girls." Ben frowned. "Hey, weren't you working that case too? I saw you give the first press conference."

"I was, but the case was handed off to the FBI. I'm here if they need me."

"That FBI chick is one hot lady," Ben offered. "Sorry, don't mean no disrespect."

"No problem. I can't argue with your observation."

"So, what can I do you for? I take it this isn't a social visit."

"Can you go over what you told the FBI the other day? I want to help out if I can, and since I know the area pretty well, I might come up with something they'd miss."

"Makes sense."

Steve noted Ben's observations in his notepad as he followed the owner around the store, pointing out the items Viktor purchased.

"The FBI said the plates on the car were stolen, so I wasn't much help there."

"No, you've been tremendous help," Steve said. "I have a lot to go on. And here's my card also. If the guy shows up again call me."

"You got it," Ben said.

Home, Steve dressed for the club, his enthusiasm seriously lacking, consumed with thoughts of Laura—lashed to the king-sized bed, the restraining bench—his cock deep inside her. It promised to be a very long night.

Monday morning, Laura sat at her desk going over the reports left by her team regarding property searches near Ben Emerson's hardware store. Her cell rang and Steve's name popped up. "Hey," she said.

"Home safe and sound?"

"Yup. For once, no delays or cancellations. We actually landed early."

"How's your mom?"

"Doing okay. Sad to see me go."

"Can't blame her." He paused. "Listen, Laura, I hope you don't mind but I've been working on the case in your absence. I have my patrol guys showing Viktor's sketch around town. I didn't go into property records officially since you said you're on that. I have been putting out feelers and I'm hoping someone will notice something."

"Thanks, Steve, much appreciated. We're working our tails off too. I'm gonna get this guy if it's the last thing I do."

"That sounds ominous. Like it will be the death of you."

Laura laughed. "It's just an expression. Don't overthink it."

"Just be careful. I don't want you taking any unnecessary

risks." Laura stayed silent. Why was Steve being so protective? However, she had to admit she had been doing the same. "I'll let you know if anything turns up," Steve said. "It's still your case."

"I appreciate it, Steve. Thanks."

"Still planning on coming my way Saturday?"

Laura winced at his word choice. Although she hoped she'd come, literally.

Had he gone to the club Saturday night? How many women had he had sex with? Her stomach knotted. Did she dare ask him? "Yes, see you Saturday."

"I'm looking forward to it."

"Did you work at the club Saturday?" She grimaced, instantly regretting the query.

"Ah… yeah, but it was quiet because of the holiday. Lots of people out of town. I mostly did paperwork."

Why was she so relieved?

"Gotta run," Steve said. "A call just came in on dispatch. Talk soon."

Laura stared at the phone screen as the red button vanished. She slumped against her office chair's backrest and exhaled. Guilt pinged her chest. She'd put Steve in an untenable situation. No way could he reverse the damage done at the hands of her stepfather. No one could.

Chapter 18

One more day until they'd get to play at the club and Steve was about to burst. Every time he envisioned Laura strapped to the bondage bed, in the private room he'd reserved at the club, he got a hard on. He distracted himself at work and luckily it had been a busy week and he found himself out in the field most days, other times he needed a cold shower or some other form of relief.

They hadn't been in contact since Monday morning and he'd purposefully avoided calling her for two reasons. One, keeping her on edge was part of the plan and second, he feared she might chicken out, so if he didn't talk to her maybe she'd just follow through without resistance.

Noon, and it was time to check in and confirm tomorrow night's rendezvous. Two hours later and she hadn't answered his texts or calls. He'd even tried Alyx, to no avail. Odd, he couldn't reach either. Maybe he should call FBI headquarters and ask where they were, but this wasn't a business call and that might be a bad idea. Calls at the FBI were probably logged.

Frantic and desperate, he dialed Daniel Taylor's number. "Hey, Steve," Daniel said.

"Hey, sorry to bother you."

"No problem. Just finished up a catheterization, heading home from the hospital in a few minutes. What's up?"

"I've been trying to reach Laura Logan all day but I can't find her. She hasn't answered my texts or calls. I tried Alyx but I couldn't get her either."

"If they're working a case, it's hard to get through. I can't always reach Alyx when she's at work."

"Okay, I'm sure it's nothing. Just let Alyx know I'm trying to reach Laura."

"Sure."

"Thanks."

Steve picked at the last of the Thanksgiving dinner leftovers, then dumped the rest in the trash. He had no appetite, his worry about Laura consuming him. Where the hell could she be? Maybe she was planning on standing him up tomorrow. She'd changed her mind. Of course, who did he think he was? Not a sex therapist, not a therapist of any kind. Perhaps his ego was getting the best of him. He should leave her be, let her figure out her life on her own. Over the years he'd self-analyzed enough to accept that he was a hopeless fixer. Which made him a good cop, but not necessarily a good partner in a relationship. More than one woman had explained that they just needed him to listen when they were upset, and not offer criticism or a solution. God knows he'd tried but his inner voice always broke through.

He finished loading the dishwasher, then grabbed a beer, sank heavily onto the couch and propped his bare feet on the coffee table. ESPN dissected the weekend games, who was favored to win, who had players on the injured list and the possibility that an early winter storm would make the NY Giants suffer in Green Bay.

He couldn't focus on the announcers, his mind drifting through horrible possibilities, foretelling Laura's demise. A car accident? She'd slipped in the shower and hit her head, lying unconscious on her bathroom floor?

The ring of his cell phone startled him and he spilled his beer as he lunged for the device on the side table. "Alyx," he said.

"Hi Steve. Daniel told me you called earlier. Sorry I didn't get back to you, I was up to my ears in interrogations today. We've busted a new arm of the 6X society."

The 6X society was the ring that had abducted Alyx. They rounded up about seventy percent of their clan at the raid but a good number of them were still out there trying to regroup.

"That's great. Good work."

"You looking for Laura?"

"Yes, she hasn't returned any of my texts or calls. I'm worried."

"Her mother died."

"What?"

"She got the call this morning. Her mother didn't turn up for work and someone went to check on her. She'd died in her sleep. Laura jumped on a plane."

"Oh God, that's awful."

"I know, but in some ways I think it's a relief. For both of them."

"I understand. There's a lot of pain there."

"Exactly."

Steve pinched the bridge of his nose, his head pounded. "Thanks for letting me know. I wouldn't have slept a wink tonight."

"No problem."

"Listen, Alyx, if you talk to her, tell her I'm thinking of her."

After a pause, Alyx said, "You care for her. I mean, really care?"

Steve didn't know what to say. He did care, but how much? Was something else going on here that he hadn't anticipated? "Sure, I do. But we're just friends at the moment." He hoped Alyx would leave it at that.

"She could use one right about now."

He should go, be with her. No one should be alone at a time like this. "Alyx, what's her mother's name? You wouldn't know her address, would you?" He added, "I'd like to send flowers."

"Her mother's name is Sarah Chambers. I know she lives in Midlothian, but I don't have the exact address. You'll have to use your police skills to find it. But, I don't imagine there'll be a service. They're not religious and I think she'll probably cremate her."

"Thanks again for putting my mind at ease. Have a good night and tell Daniel I'm sorry I bothered him."

"No worries. All good here."

Steve vacantly stared at the TV screen. *The Bachelor* could be on, a show he detested, and he wouldn't have noticed. His mind was far away, imagining Laura viewing her mother's body, making arrangements, crying—lost. His heart was breaking.

An hour online and then the phone, he couldn't find a flight that would get him there in less than ten hours. Ridiculous, you couldn't find emergency transportation when you needed it. He tracked down her mother's address. Google maps said it was a six-and-a half-hour trip, he might as well drive.

He stopped for coffee, turned up the music and headed south. There'd be no traffic at night and he'd exceed the speed limit by twenty or thirty miles per hour. Hell, he'd probably make record time.

Foiled again. Viktor threw the red plastic cup into the fireplace, the few remaining drops of vodka accelerating the flames. He watched it twist and twirl in on itself, melting, spitting until it vanished into the ashes. Another trip to the airport. Where was the bitch going now?

Pounding his fist into the wooden beams framing the mantel, he screamed, a visceral growl. Why was his life so difficult? He'd worked hard, saving his money, living a crap life and now all he wanted was to reap the bounty of his labors.

His impatience had reached explosive proportions. He needed to vent his anger, and yet he couldn't risk taking it out on a woman, or any other human. But... perhaps... yes! That detective, the one she'd been screwing. He was a serious liability, he needed to be out of the picture.

Laura stared at the ceiling in the darkness, tears slipping past her ears and dribbling onto the pillow. The streetlight outside beamed through the windowpanes, casting square shadows on her sheets and the wall. She'd identified the body and signed all the paperwork. They wouldn't require an autopsy. Tomorrow she'd pick up the ashes and... then what? Should she take them home, or perhaps spread them somewhere in Virginia? She wracked her brain for a place that would be special for her mother. She couldn't think of anything. A park, or beach, or... Wait. Her father's grave? Her biological father. She didn't even know where it was. Or if he had one. How could she find out? Well, she was a trained investigator. She'd get the job done.

Pale sunlight illuminated the room. She glanced at the clock: 6:37, and slowly rose, like a zombie under a voodoo curse. God, how old was she, eighty? She padded toward the bathroom, switched on the light and peered at her face in the vanity mirror. Yeah, she looked eighty. Dark circles ringed her eyes, the whites' red from the flood of tears. Her messy hair would be appropriate if she'd had a mad night of sex, but, yeah, no. Then she remembered. She was supposed to go to the club with Steve tonight. He'd called and texted but between being incommunicado on the plane and busy making arrangements she had forgotten to call him back. Shit.

Steve should cut her loose. She was baggage he needed to lose. *Cut and run.*

She set the coffeemaker to brew and went into the living room and turned on the TV. Peering out the front window, she noticed a car in the driveway behind her rental. She frowned.

Oh God, Steve? She ran to the front door. He slept in the front seat. The sidewalk cement was freezing under her bare feet as she tiptoed around to the driver's side and gently tapped on the window.

He sat up quickly, running a hand down his face. His smile lit her up like a firecracker. She opened the door. "What in hell are you doing here?"

"I thought you might want company."

"And you drove all night?"

He shut the engine and lumbered out. "I couldn't get a flight. Why couldn't your mother have lived in Atlanta? There were plenty of flights there."

She pumped up and down on her frozen toes, her arms wrapped around her torso for warmth. "How long have you been sitting here? Why didn't you come to the door?"

"I only arrived about an hour ago. Didn't want to wake you."

She tugged on his arm, "Come, I have coffee on."

"Now you're talking."

He grabbed his bag from the backseat and followed her inside.

She tucked her hair behind her ears. "I know I look like shit."

"Not to me." He pulled her in for a hug. "How you holding up?"

Sinking into his solid embrace, she inhaled his clean scent. She wanted to stay like that forever, never having to be out there making adult decisions. Secure in the cocoon of his strong arms.

"Barely," she mumbled into his coat.

"I'm here now and we'll get everything done and then head home."

"I'm sorry I didn't answer you when you called and texted. I was on a plane a few hours, then the funeral home and—"

He shushed her with his forefinger. "No problem. Alyx finally told me what happened."

"I'm sorry about the club. And now you missed another night working because of me."

"Forget it."

"I'm too much trouble."

"Not in a million years."

They drank coffee and ate English muffins with peanut butter, then showered and dressed. She gave him her mother's bedroom because she just couldn't bear to be in there.

The day passed quickly as they busied themselves with picking up her mother's ashes and doing some sleuthing to find her father's grave. They stood at James Logan's gravesite and Laura broke into uncontrollable sobs. Steve comforted her with an arm around her heaving shoulders. "I—I've never seen his grave before. It's hitting me harder than I imagined."

"How old were you when he died?"

"In my mother's belly," Laura said, gazing up into his brown eyes. Steve drew his eyebrows together. "My mother was only three months pregnant when he was killed in a training accident overseas."

"Jesus, that's terrible."

"I wish I could have met him."

Steve rubbed her back soothingly. "Me too."

"You have his name," Steve said.

"And I'm so glad. Thankfully, my stepdad never asked to adopt me."

Steve helped Laura open the sturdy cardboard container encasing her mother's ashes. They sprinkled them around the gravesite.

Laura touched the top of her father's headstone. "Sorry I never met you, Daddy. I needed you to take care of me. To love me." Dizziness swarmed her and her legs turned to jelly. Everything went black and Steve caught her just before she hit the dirt.

Chapter 19

Steve asked Laura to accompany him back but she insisted there was still too much to be done. Heading home during the day seriously reduced Steve's drive time. He probably should have waited until that evening. Doing eighty on Sunrise Highway, he'd finally emerged from the city rush hour traffic around sunset and should be home imbibing a cold brew in about twenty minutes.

Traveling in the middle lane, headlights came up behind him, so fast that in a matter of seconds the bumper of his car hid the beams. *What the fuck?* Steve shifted into the left lane, his wheels catching the rough shoulder pavement. He clutched the steering wheel tightly, keeping the car straight. The car was beside him, an old clunker driven by a man wearing a hoodie. It plowed into the side of his car, forcing him onto the shoulder again. *Asshole! You have no idea who you're dealing with!*

This time Steve couldn't course-correct fast enough and he skimmed the guardrail, the side door scraping against the rigid gray metal. Sparks flew and he pumped the brakes gingerly until the car came to a stop. "Jesus fucking Christ," he bellowed. The car sped ahead and out of sight, the guy had to be doing ninety. Damn, he chastised himself, he'd been too frazzled to catch the license plate number. He called it in on the radio, hoping highway patrol would sight the car as it barreled down the highway.

Home, he took pictures of the damage, notified the insurance company, then popped the cap on his beer. He leaned his ass against the counter and took a long swig when it dawned on him: Motherfucker. Somebody was trying to kill me.

Laura had to get rid of her mother's car, cancel the lease and clear out the apartment, intending to donate everything to Goodwill. She found her father's military papers and death certificate among her mother's files, along with a diamond engagement ring and a matching gold band she'd never seen her mother wear. The ring was beautiful, dainty, nothing ostentatious. Had to be the one her father gave her mother. Her real father.

Emptying the bottom drawer of the double dresser, she shoved some ratty sweaters into a trash bag. Something wrapped in tissue paper lay in the drawer. Slowly opening the fragile wrapping, she gasped. A flag folded into a triangle mounted inside a wooden and glass frame read James J. Logan, U.S. Army. Laura fell from her knees, sitting heavily on the carpet. Her hands went to her mouth as a sob escaped. Why had she never seen this?

Tears flowed freely and she pressed her fingers against her lips. *Oh, Daddy, I wish I'd met you. I wish you were here.*

After several minutes she rose and tucked the treasured items away in her suitcase for safekeeping.

Returning home late Thursday night, she slept the entire next day. She woke at sunset and dragged her weary body downstairs to the kitchen. She should eat something. Her phone vibrated in the pocket of her fluffy pink robe, a gift from her mother and probably the girliest thing she owned. She had her phone on silent so she could get some uninterrupted sleep. The screen announced messages from Alyx, her partner, Molly, and Steve. His text read, "I hope you're home safe and sound. You're probably exhausted. I won't bug you, just call when you're able," followed by the heart emoji.

Hmm. Lots of people sent hearts in a text and it didn't mean anything. Not love, just a heartfelt message, right? They'd both agreed this was only a friendship, a friendship with benefits. That's all. And yet, Steve had come through for her when her mother died, arriving without her asking him to —she never would have. Dialing his number, she held her breath. Tomorrow night they'd be at the club and she was both excited and terrified. She reminded herself that she trusted him.

"Hey," he said. "You get home okay?"

"Late last night. I've been doing the vampire nap."

"You needed it."

"I guess." She laughed.

Steve wasn't entirely sure he wanted to tell Laura about his recent near-death experience. "I can't say I fared as well."

"What do you mean?"

"Some asshole side-swiped me on Sunrise Highway."

"Oh my God! Did you get hurt?"

"Just my car. I scraped the guardrail. Not too much damage."

"Do you think it was an impaired driver?"

Did he really want to confess his suspicions? "Not so much. I think it was intentional."

He pictured Laura slapping her hand over her mouth. "What? You mean somebody was trying to kill you?"

"Pretty much."

"Who?"

"As a cop I'd venture there are plenty of people who'd like to exact revenge."

"I guess. Have you been going over old cases? Trying to narrow down suspects?"

"I'm giving it some thought but I doubt I'll be able to get any credible evidence to act on."

"You called it in, right? Did you get a license plate, did highway patrol see the car?"

"Negatory on all counts. It was kind of a hot moment and it was dark, I didn't get the plate."

"Right. I get it. You're sure you're all right?"

"Fine, just frazzled my nerves."

"I can only imagine."

He hesitated, then said, "We still on for tomorrow night?"

"Sure."

"Have you got your medical form?"

"I do. Luckily, I asked my doctor to send it before I left for Virginia."

"Excellent. So you're ready to play."

"As I'll ever be."

"Why don't you get here at six? I want to go over the experience with your stepfather before we get to the club." Laura didn't respond. "You okay with that?"

Another pause, then, "With you, I am."

"Good."

"What should I wear? Do I have to follow the club rules for attire?"

"Doesn't matter to me. You won't be wearing anything for long and you won't be mixing with the clientele. No one else will touch you."

Laura dressed casually this time. Her intent wasn't to impress. She donned her favorite scoop-neck black cashmere sweater over skinny jeans. Even though she didn't think her undergarments mattered she'd wear her lacy black demi-bra and matching panties. However, she couldn't find the lacy bottoms anywhere. Even searching her sock drawer, thinking maybe she'd misplaced them when putting away her laundry, and then the hamper. Huh, nowhere to be found. She substituted another pair of black bikini bottoms. What the hell, Steve probably wouldn't notice anyway.

Having left her car parked in the driveway after returning from the gym, she clicked the fob to unlock her sedan when a creepy shiver crept across her skin. What did her mother call it? *Someone walking over your grave?* Her hand froze on the door handle and her eyes searched the area. The oddest sensation overtook her, like someone was watching. Scanning the woods surrounding the house a second time, she finally shook her head in disbelief and attributed her uneasiness to what lay ahead. A night of playtime at the club and maybe a breakthrough to ecstasy. Ha. Really? Probably not.

Exiting the driveway, she made the usual left turn onto the street then headed right onto the expressway. Force of habit had her checking the rearview mirror until she'd entered the highway. Again, she had the feeling someone was following her.

Steve barely focused on the Army/Navy game, one of his favorite sporting events of the year. But he couldn't keep his mind off Laura. He was determined to get the job done tonight. However, he had to admit that it might not happen. It could take more time, a lot more. He needed to prepare himself for that possibility. Patience, Steve, he reminded himself.

Headlight beams pierced his front window and he jumped up from the sofa. Over anxious? Before she could knock, he opened the door wide and met her bright smile. "Good evening, Sir," she said, giving a little curtsey and offering up a metal tin with a red bow atop. "Submissive reporting for duty."

Steve laughed out loud. "You're a regular riot."

"Why thank you, Sir. For you," she said of the gift.

He took the offering from her black leather gloved hands. "Thanks."

She put her palm on his chest and pushed him backward. "Now let me in, it's fucking freezing out here."

Steve bellowed another laugh as Laura brushed past him. He shut the door quickly, placing the tin on a nearby table, waiting to take her coat. She removed her gloves and stuffed them in the side pocket.

"What's in the tin?" he said as he hung the coat in the hall closet.

"I baked cookies. Peanut butter blossoms."

He picked up the box and cracked the cover and inhaled the fragrant aroma. "Oh man, I love these. My mom always made them for Christmas. Thanks."

"Good, I hoped you weren't allergic to peanuts, so many people are these days."

"Nope. And I will eat pretty much anything. You know, like any respectable bachelor."

Laura smiled. "I suspected as much. Any news on the car that sideswiped you?"

"Nothing. I'm really aggravated at myself for not getting the plate number."

"Probably stolen anyway."

"Have a seat," he said, gesturing toward the couch, securing the lid and resting the container on the coffee table. "Do you want a drink?"

"No thanks. I think we should do this part sober. Maybe a drink at the club."

"I agree." Steve sat beside her on the sofa and took both hands in his. "I need as much detail as you can manage. I don't want to upset you but remember this is a safe place. No judgments."

"I know. Honestly, Steve, I have no idea why I'm so comfortable around you. I just know I am."

"That makes me happy." He wanted Laura to be happy, too, and he intended to do everything in his power to achieve that goal.

Laura leaned her shoulder into the couch back, Steve's hands serving as her anchor.

"I'm ready," she said.

"Let's start by me asking you questions and you answer as honestly as you can, I'll ask for more detail as I see fit."

Laura nodded in consent.

"You said the first time was after you had a nightmare. Do you remember what the dream was about?"

"Not much. I was running down a dark street and someone was chasing me. I have no idea who or why."

"That's a fairly typical nightmare. What happened next?"

"My stepdad came in and sat on the side of my bed. He stroked the hair off my sweaty face and told me not to worry, he was there. I was still crying and he pulled back the covers and slid into bed. He pulled me close and rubbed my arm, soothing me."

"What was he wearing?"

"A pair of sweatpants and his undershirt."

"What happened next?"

"His hand moved from my shoulder to my ass. He continued rubbing in what I assumed was an attempt to calm me down, but it felt weird."

"What were you wearing?"

"A nightgown. No underwear. My mother always said to sleep without it, you know, to let everything breathe." Laura laughed. "That sounds pretty stupid now that I've said it aloud."

"I have heard Dr. Oz espouse such advice." Steve arched his eyebrows. "Anyway, go on. What happened next?"

"He pulled me on top of him and hugged me tightly. His erection pressed into my thigh, although I didn't understand that at the time. But again, it felt wrong. His hand crept under my nightgown and rubbed my bare ass. I finally told him he was squeezing me too tight and to let me go."

"Did he?"

"Yes, and that's when he told me he had a special love for me and that he would always protect me and take care of me. And that it was a secret between us."

Steve continued his patient questioning and the details poured forth in an unburdening avalanche Laura had never experienced before. Even with the countless therapists she'd worked with.

Painful as it was, Steve garnered valuable information from Laura's sordid tale. Her stepfather forced her to touch him in the early stages, which then progressed to him touching her, and eventually rape over a period of about eighteen months. Steve relished the fact that he'd discovered an important key. Everything happened in the dark. Often, the use of a blindfold helped a woman avoid visual distractions that would prevent her from feeling what she needed. That would be a huge mistake with Laura.

Steve marveled that Laura related her experience without much emotion. He figured she'd probably told it to plenty of counselors over the years and that much of it just came out as rote narrative. He had one more question and he hoped that Laura would be able to answer. "When we were together last time you tapped out. Can you tell me what you were feeling when you said red?" They faced each other on the couch and Steve held both Laura's hands in his.

Laura glanced down at their joined hands before returning his gaze, her eyes searching. "The feeling begins low in my belly, it's a good sensation at first, but then as the intensity builds it's like there's a rope leading upward, it starts to twist and tighten and then my heart starts pounding. I get a ringing in my ears and then I can't breathe. It's like the rope is strangling me, choking me and I think I'm going to die."

Shit. Sounded like a panic attack. That was probably an accurate assessment. He knew a little about those attacks. His roommate in college had them. The keys were relaxation, deep breathing and exposure therapy. Which was exactly what he had planned.

He rubbed his thumbs over the backs of her hands. "We're going to fix this Laura. I promise." She smiled weakly. "Bad things happen to good people and good things happen to bad people. You can't control what happens to you only how you react. Hopefully, there will come a moment when you realize that this abuse no longer has power over you."

Recognition dawned on her face. "I never thought about it like that before."

"I'm confident we have enough to go on. You still game for the club?"

She brightened. "Why not?"

Laura handed Zach her medical form and he added it to her file.

"Enjoy," Zach said as they headed toward the club's entrance. Many patrons greeted Steve as they sought the bar. He introduced Laura as he went along, denying several Doms 'permission to touch'.

Colin, the Dom who'd placed her in the red handcuffs last time, stood behind the bar, pouring drinks. Steve and Laura settled onto barstools and Colin came over to take their order. "Evening, Master Steve," he said and then to Laura, "Welcome back, little subbie."

"Thank you, Sir," Laura replied.

"The usual?" he said to Steve.

"Please, for both of us."

Colin poured scotch over ice into two crystal old-fashioned glasses and added a splash of water. He gave each a swizzle and perched them atop a napkin in front of his patrons. "Let me know when you're ready and I'll take you up."

"Just the one drink and we'll be primed," he said to Colin. Laura gulped a mouthful of the icy liquid, the slight burn down her throat a comfort, the strong elixir calming her nerves. She'd been somewhat confident when she left Steve's house and even for most of the ride, yet seeing and hearing the carnal screams echoing inside the massive chamber had her on edge.

They socialized with clients as they sipped their drinks, like patrons at any normal tavern, until the ice cubes sat alone. Steve gave Colin an upward chin nod, then grabbed Laura's hand and pulled her gently off the stool. Colin led the way down the dim narrow hallway to the circular staircase leading to the second floor. Halting at the first room at the top, he unlocked the door with an archaic key. Laura thought it would have been something more modern, like a keycard or keypad. But then again, the scary seventeenth century castle design was a theme, complete with dungeon and stocks. No dragons.

Colin pushed the door open, sweeping his arm in a welcoming gesture. Steve tugged Laura inside and Colin followed, shutting the door behind them.

This was a different room than the one Steve showed her at their last visit, bigger, grander, what she imagined a VIP room in an expensive hotel would be like, something she'd only seen on TV or movies. The recessed lighting was enhanced by candlelight emanating from candelabras on tall stands in the four corners. A huge arrangement of red roses and white baby's breath decorated the long table against the far wall. To the left stood what Steve called a restraining bench, just like the one in the room she visited last time. Was Steve planning on using the intimidating apparatus? Her belly did a little flip.

She ambled over to the king-sized bed and sat down, pumping up and down to test the firmness of the mattress, unsure why, it wasn't like she was going to purchase it. Just nerves, she figured. The restraints were in full view, black satin sashes tied to the four posts. Glancing up, dark tethers hung from the canopy. Yikes.

"I've taken care of everything on the list, Master Steve," Colin said.

"Thanks, Master Colin."

"Will you need me to assist?" Laura blanched. Two of them?

"Nope, I've got it covered," Steve said.

"If you need me you know where to find me." He came close to Laura, "Permission to touch?" Colin asked Steve.

"Yes. Nothing sexual."

Colin gripped both her hands, forcing her to stand. He kissed the back of one in a most chivalrous manner. "Remember, pet, we're masters at this. Steve will take excellent care of you."

Laura attempted to speak but the giant frog in her throat nixed that. Colin placed his large hand on the side of her face and rubbed her cheek with his thumb. "Remember, love, it's about trust. Let Steve set you free."

For such an imposing man—well over six feet tall and musculature akin to all the Doms, plus those piercing blue eyes, well—he said such sweet things. Even if his touch was unnerving, like all the masters.

Colin leaned in and kissed her on the mouth, his warm soft lips catching her off guard. "Later, pet," he said. He shut the door quietly and the lock clicked.

Laura's jaw dropped. "He would have stayed if you wanted him to?"

"Of course. We often double team."

"What? Two of you?"

Steve laughed. "Problem with that?"

"You do that? Have a ménage, or what, an orgy?"

"I used to. Not so much anymore. I prefer to have more focused and singular attention these days. Maybe I'm getting old."

Laura tugged on the bottom of her black sweater sleeve. "What was on *the list?*"

Steve came close, unbuttoning his tailored white shirt. He'd not worn the standard club garb tonight. "That's for me to know and you to find out," he said with an impish grin. "Are you stalling, little subbie?" He yanked out his shirttail, exposing his rock-hard chest.

Laura blinked several times. "Maybe."

He chucked her chin up with his knuckle. His brown gaze probed hers and she already felt naked. He kissed her deeply, plundering her mouth, then announced, "Time to lose the clothes."

Steve dropped his shirt on the chair near the door and returned to Laura. "Hands up," he ordered.

"Cops don't say that anymore. Besides, it's a cliché."

Steve put two fingers on her lips and tried not to laugh. She was a major smartass and he needed to shut that down fast. "We're in protocol now. That means you do not speak unless I ask for a response. Understood?"

Laura nodded. Steve still had his fingers pressed to her lips.

"And you will call me Sir, or master."

"But…" Laura mumbled under his fingers.

"No buts, unless it's your butt." Her face reddened, and she glanced downward.

This was going to be so much fun.

Chapter 20

Last chance to escape. Did she want this? Laura had to admit that thinking about having sex with Steve had her pumped. Something about knowing you were going to get fucked made it all the hotter. Guys were probably better at spontaneity but a woman needed a little warm-up. Although, in Laura's case, all the foreplay in the world wouldn't get her off. Maybe tonight would be different.

She threw her hands in the air and Steve yanked her black cashmere sweater over her head, then tossed it on the chair atop his shirt. His huge hands landed on her shoulders then drifted down her arms. He secured her wrists in his, his smile slow and unexpected. "We'll take all the time you need." Laura lowered her eyes.

"Okay, Houston, we have a problem."

He chucked her chin up again. "There is one important rule tonight. You are to have eyes on me at all times. Stay in the now."

Laura fixed her attention on his enormous brown irises, yet couldn't dispel the doubt that hung over her like the Sword of Damocles.

Steve ran his fingers up and down her arms in comforting strokes. "What is it, Laura? You may speak."

"I-I just don't want you to be angry or disappointed if this doesn't work. It won't be your fault."

Steve chuckled. "Let's opt for a positive attitude, pet. That's half the battle. Sexual pleasure is rooted in the brain, not the genitals."

Laura hadn't considered that. Her stepfather lurked in the deepest darkest corners of her brain, like the boogieman, with razor-sharp claws hiding under her bed. He waited for the exact moment she let down her guard and then he pounced.

Steve worried he was losing her. He better move this along.

Fuck, those transfixed violet eyes, so damn beautiful, difficult to keep his focus... and those magnificent breasts, full and high, threatening to tumble out of her lacy black bra. His chest pressed into her, thrusting his hands into the back of her jeans, the heat of passion threatening to consume him. Circling his hands frontward, he opened the button of her jeans and inched the zipper down, then walked her backward toward the bed until the mattress hit the back of her knees. He pushed her down flat then reached down and snatched away her jeans. "You remember the safe words right?"

"Yes, Sir."

"Give me a color."

"Green," she said without hesitation. But he wasn't so sure. Last time, she seemed perfectly fine and then like an ignited match, she zoned red. And he didn't want her tapping out before he had time to get her to nirvana.

"Laura, I want you to think carefully about the safe words. Honesty is paramount. Yellow is the safe word we should be most concerned with. If you're even getting close to uncomfortable you must let me know. If we hit red, we're done. Clear?"

"Yes, Sir."

He gazed down at her plush body sprawled across the black satin sheets, clad only in her bra and skimpy black bikini bottoms. The club insisted on satin bedding because it made for ease of movement. Steve thought it somewhat tacky, but it did the trick.

Steve unbuttoned his jeans but left them on. "Move up so your head is on the pillow." Laura quickly complied and he crawled onto the mattress and settled in beside her. One hand stroked over her belly and down a hip, then moved toward a breast. He sank his hand into the cup, seeking out a nipple, giving it a little tug. Laura gasped, her gaze fixed on his.

He secured her on top of him and released her bra clasp, then plundered her hair with his fingers and devoured her mouth. Laura responded eagerly to his kiss, but he needn't linger there long because her eyes were closed... the danger zone. Although, Laura indicated that her stepfather never kissed her, so that left kissing in the safe space as long as her eyes weren't shut for too long. He kissed her again tenderly, then took a hand and nibbled each finger.

Rolling her back on the mattress he skimmed the straps of the bra down her arms and off, throwing it over his shoulder.

Steve fondled her breast tenderly, teasing the nipple, almost a tickle. She smiled, keeping her eyes focused on his handsome face. His touch calmed her. The sensation different, tender, did she dare think it? *Loving.*

"You're an incredibly beautiful woman, Laura." Heat rose in her face, then surged everywhere. The urge to say thank-you sprang to mind, but protocol dictated she remain silent.

"We're going to focus on breathing and relaxation first," Steve said. "Slow and easy." He continued to massage her breast, then leaned in and kissed the lonely one. He took the nipple into his mouth and laved it in a circular motion. Laura held her breath, the sensation overwhelming, so arousing.

He set the nipple free, the cool air quelling the ardor. "Breathe, baby," Steve said as he trailed his fingers to her belly, her hips, finally resting atop the silky fabric covering the V between her legs. "Big cleansing breath in and let it out slowly, pet." Laura obeyed. "Again," he said. He made her do it three times.

"Do you ever self-pleasure?" His fingertips brushed down the tops of her thighs and returned to her mound. He tugged her panties down sliding them over her legs and pitched the flimsy garment toward the chair. It hitched on the back spindle.

"No, Sir."

"Why don't we start there?" He pushed her legs apart, then secured her hand in his, dragging it slowly downward. He trapped her middle finger between his and laid them against her soft folds. "Give me a color, Laura."

It took a second before she said, "Green."

"I want you to focus on who is with you in this bed. Say my name."

"Ah... Steve, Sir. I'm with Steve."

"Excellent. And these are my hands touching you. Our hands together."

Her eyes drifted toward the ceiling. Steve was beautiful in a terrifyingly lethal way, all coiled power harnessed by intimidating self-control. And yet his strength, his domination, made her feel safe. His confidence and sure hands robbed her of the will to resist.

"Eyes on me, baby," Steve said, garnering her attention and forcing her to face him. "Stay with me, pet. I don't want you wandering off." The fire in his gaze spiraled her higher as his hand guided her finger inside, gently stroking the sensitive nub. Their joined touch probed, a relentless rhythm that threatened to be her undoing. A shuddering lava flow coursed through her. A low moan erupted. Could this be it?

Everything stopped.

Steve loved playing with a woman's body. His lips sought out a breast. He took his time, sucking and licking the dark pearl, sucking it against the roof of his mouth. Their linked fingers stroked back and forth, the folds swelling under the gentle assault. Her clit engorged. Her hips wiggled. He met her eyes and edged his voice with command. "Stay still for me, Laura." Her eyes vibrated a stunned pleasure.

Time to change it up. This was his favorite. Getting a woman close and then backing off, delaying an orgasm as long as possible produced spectacular results. He'd make her want it. Bad.

He released her hand and retrieved the small packet of lube from the side table where Colin had stashed it. Laura's vision followed his every move and he knew she was dying to ask what he was up to. But she stayed in protocol. He was proud of her.

Spreading her legs wide, he knelt in the space between them. "Now for something completely different," he said. "Hold on to the spindles on the headboard. And do not move."

Laura obeyed. "Good girl," he said. "This will serve as a distraction from your usual expectations and also enhance your pleasure." Both hands grabbed a knee and he pushed them up and apart. "Stay still."

He lubed the soft ring of her anus, massaging the muscle

slowly before slipping a finger inside. Laura gasped. "Say my name," he ordered.

"Steve," she blurted.

"Give me a color."

"Green."

"You sure?"

"Yes, Sir."

He placed a dab of lube on the plug, then stroked her clit gently. She was so wet. He massaged her ass cheeks and parted them. His finger stretched her open, softening the tissues. Using the slick plug, he rimmed her anus a few times and slowly pushed in the small blue firefly plug.

Laura squeaked, her face petal pink.

"This wakes up the nerves," he instructed. "Nerves you're not familiar with."

He twisted it in a circular motion a few times and Laura inhaled sharply. "Oh my," she exclaimed.

"No talking," he ordered. "Just breathe. In deep and out slow." He watched as Laura's heaving chest calmed. "Again," he said.

Steve reached for a wet nap in the bedside table and cleaned his hands. Looming over her, he dropped to his elbows, his weight pressing her into the mattress and placed his forearms alongside her head. A slow kiss was her reward, her mouth so lovely, soft velvety lips he could taste forever. They kissed again, and once more. Drawing back he said, "You okay?"

"Yes, Sir," she whispered, her sweet breath on his face.

"How does it feel?"

"Strange, but nice. Different."

"Different is good." He gave her a quick kiss then left the bed. Seeing her open for him, beautifully wet, her glistening folds ready for him, so willingly submissive. His cock ached. If she were just any woman he'd take her now. Plunge his cock in deep and hard, making her come and then taking his pleasure. But this was Laura and she needed more. And she was going to get so fucking much more.

Gazing down at Laura, her skin luminescent in the candle-light, he realized he needed to catch up. He stripped and crept back onto the bed. She still clasped the headboard spindles and he reached up and released her grasp. "Give me a color."

"Green, Sir, very green."

Hmm, he wasn't so sure about that. He normally kept a woman on edge to heighten her orgasm, holding her back until she screamed for release. Maybe he needed to step it up.

Chapter 21

Apyre flamed low in Laura's belly, perhaps the reawakening of desire. Under Steve's caress her breast swelled and when his thumb circled the nipple her back arched for more. A shiver ran through her, again. His hands closed on her hair, pulling at the roots, and he smothered her gasp with his mouth. He possessed her, taunting her with his tongue, retreating to nibble and suck on her lips and kiss her neck before returning for more. Her fingers probed his hair, clutching him to her. Her eyes momentarily closed, she reminded herself: Steve, this is Steve.

The kiss ended and their eyes met. A hunger fueled Steve's gaze. And she wanted to feed it. She laid a palm on his solid chest and her heart skipped. Her hand closed on his biceps. Rock hard. She studied his handsome face: the blunt angle of his jaw, his five o'clock shadow, his demanding brown eyes and outlandishly long lashes.

Steve covered her with his body, her back sinking into the mattress. He took her hands and secured them above her head, holding them there. This would be the beginning of the end. The bad end. But for some reason her body relaxed under his.

"Give me a color?" Steve said.

"This would normally be yellow, but I'm still green."

"Good, girl."

Steve smiled broadly and Laura was glad he was pleased. Maybe hope existed this night, carnal ecstasy for them both. The possibility elated Laura. Could she be normal? Able to have sex with a man that would gratify both? Something that had escaped her, forever.

He kissed her, then crept down her body, kissing and nipping as he went. Spreading her legs wide he knelt between them, his erection standing large and proud.

Reflexively, Laura reached down and circled his dick with her small hand.

"Uh-uh, baby," he said.

"What about you? You're not getting any stuff."

Stuff? He thought back to the night everything went to shit and the morning after when Laura attempted a blowjob as a thank-you for enduring the botched sexcapade. Fucking adorable.

"No talking." He removed her hand from his dick, then sat her up, and placed her arms behind her, bending her elbows so her arms crossed at her lower back, and laid her back down. "Leave your hands under your ass."

Laura wanted to protest. Shouldn't she reciprocate in some fashion? "I'll take my pleasure last," he assured her. Laura liked it when Steve restrained her last time, and she guessed he was trying to avoid a repeat performance of that night, but she was equally controlled in this position. Being helpless was simultaneously devastating and wonderful.

Steve inched down to the foot of the bed and pushed her legs apart. He forced a finger inside, curling it forward, massaging, probing and awakening a whole new array of feelings. Her hips gave an involuntary wiggle and she closed her eyes as a tingle erupted. Steve laughed, then said, "Give me your eyes, baby."

She focused on Steve's dark sultry orbs, wanting more of his magic. "Stay with me, pet." He continued his assault on her vagina. One finger became two, gliding in and out, a punishing rhythm, but divine. His head fell between her legs and his tongue flicked her clit hard and fast. He twisted the plug in her ass and her toes curled in response. Her tissues were so sensitive, enflamed, engorged, she feared she'd burst. Pressure grew in her belly. This was it, or was it? Here's where she'd spiral into the dark abyss of her abuse. He continued to lick her clit, sucking, nipping. Laura gasped. Oh my God.

Everything stopped and Steve hovered over her. She was close to coming but he backed off. Again.

"Give me a color," he said.

"Is there a color for pissed off?"

Perfect. He had her where he wanted her. Distracted to the point where she was finally thinking about herself.

"You cannot come until I allow it, pet." It was time to drop the protocol and let her speak freely. "Tell me what you want?"

"I want you to fuck me. Fuck me hard."

"There'll be no fucking until you come. You ready to commit?"

"Hell yes."

One hand clasping a breast, he took her clit between his lips and sucked. His agile tongue tormented her flesh. His fingers plunged in and out, faster, harder, thrusting. He covered her with his body, his hand pinching her clit as he plunged his tongue past her supple lips. Laura squealed into this mouth. He wrenched back and gazed into her eyes at the crucial moment. "Let go, baby. Let it all go." The quake hit. Tremors pulsated through her being. She bore down on his fingers, her body jerking reflexively, wracked by the spasms that had set her free. "Oh God. Jesus fucking Christ!"

Steve chuckled. "Divine revelation."

Laura didn't respond. She squeezed her thighs around his hand, trembling, shaking, then curled into his body like a wounded creature. But she wasn't wounded any more. She was healed. At least he hoped so.

He held her tightly, his cock throbbing in anticipation.

Pleasure roared through Laura's body, every nerve burned so good. Falling, head first into a deep dark well. But wait, no darkness. Strobing lights enveloped her. Flying, upward, into the sky, piercing the clouds like a rocket to heaven. The dam finally broke and all her pain, shame and anger dissipated into exploding stars.

Her body went limp and tears surfaced in her eyes. Steve cradled her in his strong arms. Sobs heaved from her chest. She wrapped her arms around his neck and her tears drenched his shoulder.

"Shush, shush," Steve said, rubbing her back. "It's okay, you're safe. Intimate touch stirs up powerful emotions."

The sweetest serenity followed. She lay there for several

minutes, tiny hiccups punctuating the air. "Well," she finally muttered, "that was embarrassing. What a baby."

Steve ran his fingers through her hair, forcing her face up. A corner of his mouth lifted and a flush crept up her face. She wanted more. He handed her a tissue from the box on the nightstand.

"Nicely done, pet," he said and then kissed her. "Seeing you come is the most glorious thing I've ever seen."

"Can we do that again?" she whispered.

"I'm not done with you yet, pet."

First hurdle cleared, Steve intended to make sure her new enthusiasm extended to intercourse. Besides, he was about to explode. He held Laura at arm's length, securing her shoulders. He locked eyes with hers and said, "Same rules, eyes on me at all times and you will say my name when I ask."

"Yes, Sir."

"Do you want to be restrained?" he said. Normally he would never ask a submissive what she wanted but he was treading carefully. She was into it last time, but then things went south and he wasn't sure if repeating behaviors from that night was a good idea.

"On the bed or on *that thing*," she said, pointing to the black leather restraining bench.

"You're not ready for that thing. You need to be face down and I want your eyes on me tonight. Baby steps, we'll work our way up to that." And he couldn't wait to get her there either. Tempting, but not tonight.

"On the bed."

"Yes, please," Laura said, an impish grin pursing her lips.

Steve fastened her arms to the headboard.

"You must have been a boy scout," Laura said, scanning left and then right to assess Steve's handiwork.

"Not exactly," he corrected, "but I spent a lot of time on boats as a kid. Now, be quiet. No talking unless I allow it."

Laura pressed her lips into a straight line as if trying to suppress a smile, yet remained silent.

"Good girl." Steve briefly closed his eyes, savoring the moment, then focused on her stunning visage. "Fuck, you're so amazing. Restrained for my pleasure. I like knowing you can't move from where I put you." He pushed her knees apart and up, kneeling in the vacant space and plunged a finger inside her. "Still wet. I like that. I like it very much."

Moving up her body, he held her hair tightly in his grip as he plundered her mouth, their tongues dancing an erotic tango. Nose to nose, he whispered, "I'm going to finish inside you and I'm taking you hard with that goddamned plug still in you."

The fire between her legs blazed hotter and hotter. He pinched a nipple and her swollen clit throbbed as if it had a beating heart of its own. Hands in her hair, his tongue everywhere, sensitizing every inch of skin. He kissed her deeper, wetter, and a low moan erupted.

Steve propped himself on his elbows. "Give me a color."

"Green to the fucking power of infinity."

"Easy, pet. Patience. You may not come until I allow it."

Well, damn, she'd waited her entire life and now that she'd succeeded he dangled the prize just out of reach. She stayed silent and won herself another approving kiss, unsure of how much more exquisite torment she could endure.

Steve reached down and rammed two fingers into her wet folds. She gasped, clutching at the restraints. Every nerve shrieked. She hovered on the edge. What would happen if she came without permission?

The punishing rhythm of his fingers drove her higher and higher. He dropped down on top of her, his body heavy. She closed her eyes.

No. The rope inside her constricted.

"Laura!" Steve's booming voice pulled her from the brink. "Open your eyes. Say my name."

Her eyelids flew open to Steve's intense gaze. It wasn't *him*. It was Steve. "Steve. It's you, Steve."

He placed his strong hands on the sides of her face, fixing her with a stern stare. "Give me a color, baby."

"I'm okay. I was almost a yellow, but I'm green. Definitely green."

"Good girl. We're nearly there. You can finish this once and for all. Stay with me." He guided himself inside her, slowly, firmly, penetrating a few inches at a time before halting. "Still green?" Laura nodded. "Say the word," he prompted.

"Green, still green."

He drove in hard, once, twice and then a third time. His hands gripped her hips as he increased his speed. He rolled his hips in a circular motion, reaching every nerve inside her. His gaze pinned her as unyieldingly as his weight pinned her down. He stretched her, filled her, his erection hard and big, expanding.

Chapter 22

Steve prided himself on being able to last the extra mile, but he was at his limit, unable to avert his orgasm a second longer.

"Permission to come, pet. Let go!" Her whole center clamped down on him and he pulled up so he could watch her. She screamed her release. Him seeing past her flaws and into her soul. Clean and whole.

He clutched her bound hands, lacing his fingers through hers. He poured himself into her, his load blasting through him in uncontrolled fury, indescribable, the dazzling splendor. He growled his release and for a split-instant no space separated them. *One.*

Her body quivered beneath him, tiny aftershocks from her orgasm squeezing his dick. Until they lay still, their flesh melding in a final embrace.

Steve wanted to stay like this forever, her soft skin flush against his. He deftly released her from the restrains and rolled off her. He stroked her hair, moving the damp strands off her angelic face. "You okay?"

"Incredible."

Laura inhaled Steve's musky scent, his breath filling the space between them. They lay in a tender embrace for several minutes. Steve trailed his fingers up and down her spine.

"Time to go, pet," he whispered. His hand stroked her shoulder, then up and down her arm, his fingers finding hers. He laced them together and squeezed. "Ready?"

"Yes." Their hands separated and Laura placed her hand against Steve's face, lingering, then leaned in and kissed him. "Thank you."

"My pleasure, pet." He propped himself on his elbow and she rolled onto her back, pulling the sheet up to her neck.

"Give me a few minutes in the bathroom, then you can take your turn."

Steve rose and gathered his clothes, heading to the bathroom. That's one fine ass. She tugged the silky bed linen tighter, her mind summoning the images of other men she'd faked countless orgasms with. Sally—in the movie Harry Met Sally—an amateur compared to her. Pathetic, really. But she was done with that. She might actually be able to love a man wholly, the fear and shame banished from her psyche.

"Your turn," Steve said, pulling her from her musings. "There are warm, wet towels in the cabinet on the wall. Or you can shower if you prefer."

Laura extricated herself from the silky sheath, the cool air raising bumps on her skin. Steve gathered her garments and purse and handed them to her. She promised, "I won't be long."

Standing naked in front of the vanity mirror she assessed her image, thankful for waterproof mascara. Nothing worse than black smudges under your eyes, especially since she'd cried like a fucking baby. She leaned her hands on the cold gray marble. "The new me," she said aloud.

She freshened up and dressed, brushed the tangles from her hair, and dabbed her lips with a little gloss. It took a second for her eyes to adjust from the bathroom's bright bulbs to the dreamy bedchamber's candlelight. Steve sat on the bedside chair, legs splayed in front of him, his fingers steepled in front of his handsome face. He smiled seductively and her face flushed.

Steve rose and strode toward her. God, she wanted to fuck him all over again. "Come," he said, taking her hand. Warmth rose between her legs. Geez, don't say that word out loud.

They descended the spiral staircase, the bar directly in front of them. Colin poured drinks for a bulky leather-clad Dom with a diminutive male leashed to his wrist.

"Would you like a drink?" Steve asked Laura.

"No thank you, Sir," she said. Colin's eyes glinted with mischief. She turned to Steve. "I'd like to go."

Colin closed in on her, leaning his elbow on the bar, his legs crossed at the ankles. "Success?"

Laura blushed crimson, she didn't want to talk about this with Colin.

Steve answered. "All good."

"Did you need the vibrator?" he asked Steve, but his gaze stayed fixed on Laura.

"Nope. She did it all by herself."

Steve sensed Laura's uneasiness and hastened their departure. "See you next week," he said to Colin, tugging Laura toward the exit.

"Drive safe," Colin yelled after them.

Traveling along the expressway, Laura remained quiet and Steve worried what she was thinking. He didn't have to wait long. "I guess I can actually date a guy for real now. Maybe I won't be a lifelong relationship-phobe." The flicker of head-lights illuminated her features, like images in a timeworn movie.

Steve held his breath. That Laura might find love with someone, maybe even marry and have kids, hit him like a blow to the solar plexus. An interlude expired before he could speak. "It's what you deserve, what every woman deserves. To find her true self."

Laura chuckled. "I'm discovering lots of things." She paused, then said, "What did Colin mean about the vibrator?"

"A vibrator is sort of like training wheels. It's pretty much failsafe. I doubt there's a woman alive that won't climax with a vibrator on her clit."

"Huh, I didn't know that."

"But," Steve added, "it doesn't always translate to the real deal. Although, in a man's hands it can be quite satisfying."

Even in the near darkness he saw her lips curve into a smile. "Something to look forward to."

So many more things he wanted to show her, to do with her. He shouldn't overthink all of this. Their friendship with benefits, with exceptional and spectacular extras, could last forever. Maybe.

Steve unlocked his front door and deactivated the alarm. "You staying or going?"

In his foyer, Laura fiddled with the top button of her coat. "Do you want me to stay?"

"Of course. Why wouldn't I?"

Laura smiled weakly. "Maybe you're tired or—"

Steve came close and unbuttoned her coat. "I'm not tired. And if I was, then we'd sleep, just like last time." He slipped the garment off her shoulders and hung it in the closet. "It's only midnight," he said, "do you want a drink? Or something to eat?"

"I could munch on something."

"Me too. Let's get changed into something more comfortable and then we'll raid the kitchen." Laura followed him into the bedroom and he gave her a t-shirt and watched her strip as he donned a shirt himself and a pair of gray sweatpants over his expanding cock. Damn, he wanted to screw her into next Tuesday. Again.

Laura opened the refrigerator and surveyed the contents. She frowned. "Have an aversion to supermarkets?"

"Yeah, I don't shop much. I pretty much live on take-out and my mother's leftovers. Pathetic, I know."

Steve perused the contents of his pantry. "How about peanut butter sandwiches? I have jelly, honey, and I think the bread is still good."

Laura smiled, crossing her hands over her chest. "Score. I'm a peanut butter junkie."

"Jelly or honey?"

"Honey, *honey*," Laura said, yet regretted her use of the affectionate moniker. Perhaps Steve didn't notice. He did call her babe and sweetheart occasionally. She was being too analytical. A side effect of her FBI mentality.

Steve placed a loaf of whole wheat bread, plus the peanut butter and honey on the kitchen table while Laura rummaged through the cabinets securing plates and silverware.

"Milk?" she said.

"Definitely. It's sacrilege to eat a peanut butter bad boy without milk."

"Agreed."

Laura devoured her sandwich. Steve consumed two in the same amount of time. Their conversation veered toward Victor—they didn't even know his last name—and how the trail had grown cold, the chances of catching him more remote each day. "I admit my fantasy is that he screwed up enough that the organization disappeared him."

"I'd rather us nail the fucker." They loaded the dishes into the dishwasher and Steve returned the foodstuffs to the pantry. "Let's get in bed and watch bad TV. Do you watch *Cops*?"

"Sometimes, it's terrible."

"I know. I love it." Steve flicked off the lights in the kitchen and living room, set the alarm and Laura followed him into the bedroom. "I picked you up a toothbrush," Steve announced, heading toward the bathroom. "It's in the night-stand on your side of the bed," he said over his shoulder.

Her side of the bed?

Laura opened the drawer and rooted around for the plastic package. Steve shouted through the bathroom door, "I promise I'll move my socks out tomorrow." Her fingers bumped into something square, covered in velvet. She gazed at the ring box and, after a brief hesitation, opened the lid. A diamond solitaire ring stared back. Curiosity niggled at her like a bug crawling up her arm. Should she say something? She glanced over at Steve as he exited the washroom and deftly pulled down the bedcovers.

"What's this?" she finally said, offering the box and awaiting Steve's explanation.

Steve froze, his lips pursed. He ran his hands through his thick dark hair. "What does it look like?"

"Like an engagement ring. Whose is it?"

Steve lumbered to the end of the bed and sat down heavily. He leaned his head over his knees, elbows on his thighs, and stared at his feet.

Now she wished she'd kept her big mouth shut. The story had to be bad and he probably didn't want to talk about it. She had to make this easy for him. "Steve, we're good friends, right? You might even be my new best friend. We can tell each other anything."

"I bought it for Jillian."

She placed her hand on his back and gave a few sympathetic pats. Steve stayed silent. Best to get it out of his sight.

Laura returned the velvet-clad box to the drawer and shut it slowly. Steve was obviously in pain; why had she been compelled to confront him? And yet, the shock of finding the ring, when Steve had stated clearly that he had no interest in a relationship, and definitely not marriage, confused her. So perhaps he wasn't commitment phobic after all. Maybe... he'd had his heart broken.

She moseyed over and sat beside him again, leaning a shoulder into his. "And all this time I thought you were afraid of commitment."

Steve fell back onto the bed, his hands behind his head, his eyes focused on the ceiling. "I didn't used to be. I've been in several relationships but Jillian is the only one I considered marrying."

Laura crawled onto the bed alongside Steve, perched on her side, head resting on her hand. "You never told me much about what happened. I didn't know you were that serious about her."

Steve scrubbed his face with his hands, then fixed his gaze on Laura. "I've been dumped three times. I always get the same shit. I'm too controlling, my work hours suck and I'm oversexed."

Laura grimaced. "That's ridiculous, Steve. Those women are assholes. They obviously don't know a good catch."

Steve sighed, tucking his hands into his armpits. "Jillian left me for some actor guy. Didn't even leave a note."

"Did she ever go to the club with you?"

Steve harrumphed. "No. I wasn't honest with her about the lifestyle. I don't know why, I should have been. I guess it was because she wasn't that adventurous in the bedroom, and I thought I could change. I even stopped going to the club."

Laura edged her hand under Steve's shirt, his flesh threatening her undoing. "If you weren't honest with her, you weren't being your true self. Maybe she sensed it."

"I guess, same as you, right?"

Well, he had her there. "Seems as though we've both been liars, cowards actually. It's sad." Laura exhaled. "I think from here on out we promise to be truthful with ourselves and anyone we're intimate with. You taught me that you have to give yourself fully to another, to allow yourself to be vulnerable, to share your darkest secrets, your wishes and desires. Giving all of yourself."

Steve gave a wry smile. "Damn, woman. Look who's all grown up and taking me with her."

Laura laughed. "Come on, no more serious talk, where's that bad TV you promised?"

They snuggled beneath the covers and Steve surfed the channels, settling on an episode of *Lockup Special Investigation* on MSNBC: Tragic stories that unfolded in America's juvenile justice system.

───────

Steve stretched out his arm and Laura laid her head on his chest, his arm securing her in a loving embrace. She fit so perfect there. When she'd called him her new best friend, his heart soared. Could he be falling in love with her?

Chapter 23

Monday morning found Laura at her desk reviewing intel on her current cases, desperate for a lead on Viktor. Her phone rang and, seeing Steve's name, the corner of her mouth quirked up. "Hey, morning."

"How are you?"

Laura tried not to gush. "Feeling pretty good. Thanks again for this weekend. I had a great time."

"Me too. I want to do it again soon. I'd like to say this weekend but I think I owe Jack a shift."

"Whenever... I'm in."

"There's so much more to explore. I can't wait to get you on that restraining bench."

"Oh? Well, bring it on mister, or should I say, *Sir*"

"I'll get you into protocol yet."

"We'll see about that. No slave crap in my world. Not too sure about the kneeling either."

"We can tailor it to our needs. You might surprise yourself."

Now Laura laughed. "To be determined."

Another call blew up her screen. *Unknown caller*, a California area code. "Hey, I gotta go."

"Catch you later," Steve said.

She answered the new call. "Laura Logan."

"Hey Laura, this is Chris Donahue."

Her forehead crinkled. "Sorry?"

"From the convention in Chicago a while back? We had some drinks and a few laughs?"

Oh God. That guy she hooked up with, the agent from Sacramento. "Sure, Chris, so sorry. I didn't recognize your name at first." Laura tapped her pen on the desk in a staccato rhythm.

"I meant to call you the next day and thank you for a great night, but my flight left early and I had connection troubles and wound up in the airport all day. No excuse. I should have called. I apologize."

"No worries. There were no expectations."

"I'm glad that's over with. And I have news. I just got transferred to the New York office. I moved in to my apartment today and I'd love to see you again. Besides, you're my only friend in New York. Can I take you out to dinner Friday?"

Hmm. Chris was pretty easy on the eyes, and if memory served, his body was no slouch either. However, Alyx had invited her to dinner to celebrate her birthday on Friday. Steve said he probably had to work Saturday night so the club was out. "How about Saturday?"

"Great. You pick the restaurant and I'll meet you there."

"I'll be driving back from Long Island. I live in Nassau County and it would be a long day to drive back into the city. How do you feel about venturing out on the Long Island Railroad? We could eat some place near me."

"You don't live in the city?"

"I have an apartment in Chelsea for times when I can't get

home, but I have a house in the country. I try to get there as often as I can, especially on the weekend."

"I'm game."

"It's a date."

"See you Saturday. Looking forward to connecting again."

"Same here. Let's plan on around seven and I'll text you the details."

A date. Maybe there was a real relationship in her future.

Rich, the NAT still under her supervision, barged into her office. "This just came in." He put a paper in front of her and peered over her shoulder. "A tip on our perp. Allegedly sighted at a liquor store in Ridge."

Laura's pulse accelerated. She wanted that bastard so badly.

"Let's go." She grabbed her coat and purse off the back of her door. Rich followed like an obedient novice, taking his black pea coat from his chair back.

"Call Detective Moretti," Laura said. "He can get there faster."

"Roger that," Rich said.

Doing ninety, lights flashing, and the occasional siren when necessary had them in the vicinity in less than thirty-five minutes. "Try Moretti again," Laura instructed after three calls had gone unanswered. "Where the hell is he?"

Rich punched the redial button on his phone. Four beats passed. Felt almost like a miracle when Steve answered. "Detective, this is Special Agent Rich Ramsden, I'm with Agent Logan and we're about ten minutes away from Wayne's Liquors in Ridge. We've got a tip on Viktor. Agent Logan wants you to meet us there."

"Give me the phone," Laura barked. "Where have you been?"

"Working a domestic abuse case and I was at the scene."

Laura silently admonished herself. "Okay, sorry. I'm a little on edge."

"Not another word. I'm on my way."

Steve pulled up alongside Laura's vehicle outside Wayne's Liquors and exited, adrenaline fueling his mood. "Let's catch this fucker," he said.

Rich held the door open for Laura and Steve to enter. Behind the counter a lanky, baby-faced teen in desperate need of a dermatologist was ringing up a customer. The trio waited their turn, badges and IDs primed and ready for display. Steve thrummed his fingers on the glass countertop. The clerk glanced his way as he bundled two bottles of cabernet into a plastic bag.

"Thanks, Mr. Hornsby. Have a good day."

"FBI," "Suffolk County PD," Laura and Steve exclaimed at the same time. The clerk raised his eyebrows. Mr. Hornsby shuffled away.

Rich flashed his phone with the sketch of Viktor. "You seen this guy?"

The kid's eyes flitted from face to face, finally landing on Rich. "Ah, no, not me. It was Julian, he's in the back."

Leaning in, Steve ordered, "Get him."

"Yes, sir." The pimple-faced teen vanished behind the refrigerator stocked with wine.

"Isn't he a little young to be working at a liquor store?" Laura inquired.

"The least of our worries," Steve said.

The boy returned with a larger version of himself. "This is my brother, Julian."

"Hey," Julian said. "You guys got here quick. I called it in like an hour ago."

"This the guy?" Rich Ramsden said of the sketch.

"Yeah, that's him. His hair is darker and he has a beard but you can't mistake that scar. He was waiting outside when I opened up around ten."

"Any purchases?" Laura said.

"Two liters of Stoli."

"I don't suppose he paid with a card?"

"Nope. Cash. He had a wad of it."

"Did you recognize him right away?" Steve said.

"No, but my antenna was up. I don't often get customers that early. And he smelled bad, like he hadn't showered in weeks. I thought maybe he was some homeless dude, but not with that amount of cash. Then I noticed that scar. I remember the fellas at the Triangle Pub the other night talking about how that guy who kidnapped the nun and the girls hadn't been caught yet and he could still be in the area. They mentioned the scar." Julian paused to breathe.

"Did you notice what he was driving?" Rich said.

"I trailed him to the door and watched him walk down the street. He disappeared into the woods."

"Can you show us?" Steve said.

"Sure. Let me get my coat."

When Julian disappeared behind the wine cooler, Rich suggested, "Should we call in reinforcements? Search the woods?"

Steve nodded. "I can have my guys here in ten."

"Make the call," Laura said.

"You go ahead, I'll call dispatch."

Laura and Rich followed Julian to a small path between the coffee shop and the Post Office. "Thanks," Laura said to Julian. "We'll take it from here." They spread out, picking their way through tangled underbrush and low-lying branches. Laura wished snow had fallen again, footprints would be a plus. The trail ended at a road and they emerged to find a small strip mall across the street. They'd only traveled through a short wooded space, less than half an acre, essentially a dead end.

The crack of a twig behind her sent her defense training into high gear and she reached for her service revolver as she pivoted. Recognition dawned and she relaxed her grip on the weapon.

"You weren't going to shoot me, were you?" Steve said.

"Geez. Almost."

They walked to where Rich was talking to an employee sweeping leaves into a pile in front of a pizzeria. Laura said, "My guess is he had a car parked here and walked through the woods to the liquor store and he's long gone." Laura tucked her thumbs into the front pockets of her black trousers. "If you'd picked up the first time I'd called, you could've gotten here thirty minutes before me. He might've still been in the vicinity."

"Seriously? You're giving me shit over this?" His glower made her feel naked, not the good kind of naked either.

Laura put her hands up. "Okay, okay. I'm sorry. I'm just frustrated."

A line of police cruisers screeched into view, parking haphazardly on the street. The posse of eight officers surrounded Steve. He instructed them to show the sketch to everyone on both streets. They each summoned Viktor's image on their phones and set out on a perimeter search.

"Maybe we'll luck out and someone spotted a vehicle," Steve said.

Chapter 24

Two days passed and Steve hadn't spoken to Laura. Busy monitoring local tree-lighting ceremonies, his officers had experienced an easy few days. The highway patrol guys on the other hand had it rougher, handling DUI stops in abundance as the result of countless holiday celebrations. However, this was also domestic abuse season, those festering emotional blisters popping around the holidays, which kept him on edge. They were by far the most dangerous calls, the victims and perpetrators unpredictable and often whacked out on drugs or alcohol.

Arriving home Wednesday evening, Steve changed out of his work clothes, grabbed a beer and sat down for the evening news. He'd stowed his frustration at Laura's recent impatience. They both wanted this perp in handcuffs and it was obviously grating on Laura's nerves.

His phone rang. "Hey, Alyx, everything okay?"

"All good. I'm calling to see if you want to come over Friday night. I know it's short notice, but I'm having a little birthday party for Laura. Just me and Daniel, and Laura's partner and her husband."

Her birthday? How come Laura hadn't mentioned it? "Thanks, Alyx, I'd love to come. What time?"

"Seven, at our place in Hampton Shores."

"I'm there. Thanks for the invite."

"Oh, and don't mention it to Laura. She thinks it's just Daniel and me. She hates when I make a fuss over her birthday. If she found out she'd probably beg off."

"Sure, got it."

"Great, see you Friday. Oh, and by the way, everyone is staying over since it's such a long drive back and we'll be partying."

"Ah, thanks, that's very considerate."

"Later," she said.

"Later." Steve recalled that Daniel still had a playroom in his house. Hmm.

Thursday morning Steve woke to sleet pelting his bedroom windowpane. The winter weather on Long Island could be dreary, lots of cold rain, the occasional snowstorm but mostly just clouds and drizzle. He hated it. Maybe he should move to some place nicer, Colorado? He didn't mind snow as long as some sunshine showed up. He loved to ski and hadn't been since he and Colin celebrated their thirtieth birthdays together on a trip to Aspen.

The commute turned treacherous. Slips and slides from inexpert drivers going too fast had him on edge and he was relieved when he pulled into his parking space unscathed.

Completing his usual stack of paperwork and reviewing officer reports from the night shift, he handed everything off to Alice, when it struck him that if he was going to Laura's birthday party tomorrow he should probably bring a gift. He grabbed his coat off the back of his office door and told Alice, "Gotta run an errand. Call if you need me." And he disappeared before his secretary could respond. The freezing rain bombarded his windshield, the wipers making that horrid squeaking noise until they got lubed up.

A quick stop home to retrieve that friggin' ring and he was back in his car headed toward town. The bottom had fallen out of his gut when Laura had found the damnable thing. But it had turned out okay and actually brought them closer together.

The entry doorbell jingled and Steve spied his cousin Vinny behind the glass counter. The family tormented Vinny to no end after the well-liked movie hit the big screen and it continued to haunt him with interminable reruns. Alerted to a customer, Vinny removed the jeweler's loupe from his eye and glanced up. "Hey, cuz, how's it going?"

Steve leaned into the counter, staring at the velvet-lined tray of diamond rings as Vinny returned an overly large one to its slot. "Great, what's new with you?"

"Not much, we're having another baby." Vinny had three rug rats already, all under the age of five, and didn't seem overly thrilled with the announcement.

"Congratulations, when's it due?" Steve perused the array of gleaming diamond rings. The last time he'd been here he'd bought Jillian's engagement ring.

"June. So, you in the market for another engagement ring? I told you I'd take the other one back." Steve's eyes stayed focused on the items in the glass case while reaching into his pocket and silently placing the ring box on the counter. Vinny said, "I didn't know you were dating anyone."

"I'm not. I just need a birthday present for a friend."

"A *girl*friend?"

"A girl who is just a friend," Steve insisted.

"So, not a diamond ring then."

Steve glared at Vinny who swiftly put his hands up in defense.

"No diamond. I was thinking maybe something with her birthstone. It's tomorrow."

"Nothing like last minute," Vinny chided.

"Don't bust my balls, Vin; I just need something in a hurry. What can you suggest?"

"Well, for starters you're in the wrong case. Down here," he said moving left.

"December actually has three gemstones: tanzanite, turquoise, and zircon. Personally, I like tanzanite. I have these silver basket-set round studs, they're excellent quality. They retail at nine thirty-five but I'll give you the usual discount… yours for five hundred. I'll put the remainder of the cash back from the ring on account or write you a check. Whatever you want."

Steve fondled the lovely stones with his oversized fingers. They reminded him of Laura's vivid indigo-blue irises. "They're perfect, Vin. I'll take them."

"Excellent choice." He called over his shoulder, "Linda?" A slight brunette appeared from behind the backroom curtain. "Polish and wrap these for Steve." The salesgirl took the earrings and disappeared behind the red-and-white striped drape again.

Vinny flipped open the box on the counter and stared at the brilliant engagement ring. "So what happened with Jillian? I never got the deets."

Steve rested his hands on the glass top and drummed his fingers in a rat-a-tat rhythm. "She dumped me for some actor guy with long hair and a scrawny body."

"That sucks."

"I thought so for a long time but now I think I dodged a bullet."

Eyes focused again on the diamond ring, Vinny sighed. "Beautiful stone. I'll put it back in inventory and you let me know if and when you want the cash back."

The lovely chestnut-haired clerk reappeared and placed the square box, wrapped in pink rosebud paper and a satiny white ribbon, on the counter. She smiled at Steve, "Here you go, sir. They're beautiful. She's one lucky lady."

"Thank you." Steve tucked the giftwrapped treasure into his pocket. Turning to Vinny, he said, "Thanks Vin, I appreciate your help. And congrats on the new baby again."

"Any time. See you at Christmas. Your mom invited us for Christmas dinner."

"Great, it will be good to see Jenna and the kids again."

Laura and Rich sat in the conference room going over ship manifests, following up on a tip about more women arriving in cargo containers. Alyx entered, sipping a green drink. "Anything new on Viktor?"

"We followed up on a tip yesterday, a guy thought he saw him in a liquor store in Ridge. Dead end. Although Moretti has his guys canvasing the area hoping for another lead."

"Okay, well keep me in the loop. The higher-ups are asking."

The wipers were doing a shitty job stopping the ice from hardening on the windshield and Steve struggled to keep his eyes on the cars around him. The road had become slick as he crept along the highway on his return trip to the precinct. A large tractor-trailer crossed a few inches over the hard-to-see white dotted lines then quickly returned to its lane. Steve held his breath and gently pumped the brakes to avoid throwing his car into a skid.

A white SUV passed him on the left, its speed excessive for

the wintery conditions. Steve swore under his breath. Idiot. People driving these oversized vehicles thought they were invincible.

The SUV cut in front of the gray minivan ahead of him, causing the driver to slam on the brakes, sending the van into a skid. It narrowly missed the semi then crashed into the center guardrail, landing on its side. It slid a good hundred yards, sparks flying, and came to a stop on the center median.

Steve switched on his car's flashing red lights and navigated to the shoulder, then backed up to where the van lay motionless. Jumping from his car he ran toward the vehicle. Flames erupted, abruptly blocking his forward motion, and he covered his face with his arm. Damn.

But there was someone in that car. Maybe several someones. He needed to get them to safety. The engine flared but the fire hadn't spread to the cabin yet, if he moved fast he could save the driver. He hoisted himself up on the back tires and crept across the vehicle's side until he reached the driver's side door. He wrenched the door handle but it wouldn't budge. Inside, a woman slumped, her head pinned against the neck-rest by the air bag. Her nose bloodied, eyes closed. Two screaming toddlers were strapped into car seats in the back. Steve pulled the door handle again. Stuck.

"Here," yelled a man on the ground. "Try this." He pitched something at Steve who expertly caught the object, just like Colin used to catch his passes. It was a device used to break car windows. Steve hit the glass and it shattered instantly, allowing him to unlock and open the door. He used his penknife to puncture the air bag and cut the seatbelt. Lifting a dead weight proved challenging but he freed the woman and handed her down to good Samaritans waiting below. Thick black smoke, reeking of toxins, billowed into the frigid air, the acrid odor burning his nostrils.

Steve moved quickly, freeing both children, one under each arm, he perched himself on the edge of the vehicle and carefully handed them off to the men below.

"Hurry," someone shouted. "It's gonna blow!"

Steve positioned himself on the back tire again and gingerly climbed down to the bottom wheel, landing on the grassy median. He ran.

A loud explosion shattered the air, heat blasted his back and the force jolted him forward. He did a face plant on the slick road, the palms of his hands preventing him from breaking his nose, barely.

Two sets of hands grabbed his upper arms, lifted him and dragged him off the pavement. His head spun, dizziness making him queasy. "You okay, buddy?" Steve met the man's eyes. He wore a cap that said NYFD.

"I think so." He glanced at his abraded palms.

"Seriously," the guy said. "You're some kind of hero. Nice work."

"Glad you had that tool."

"I'm a firefighter and I've seen more than my share of accidents. I have one in all my cars."

Steve didn't feel like a hero. He was just doing his job. And if people drove more carefully this kind of shit could be avoided. "I need to call this in," he said, heading to his vehicle.

Ambulances, fire trucks, and additional police personnel arrived on the scene quickly. The EMTs assessed the mother and her two children and preliminarily announced them in good condition. A trip to the hospital to be sure, the general consensus being they'd surely have died if it weren't for Steve.

Drenched, dirty, and smelling of gas fumes, Steve left the on-site personnel to attend the scene and headed home to shower before returning to the precinct to fill out paperwork for the incident.

He wasn't home long when it hit the TV as a special bulletin. *Shit.* Of course, someone had taken video. Steve watched himself braving the flames and pulling the three victims from the crash site. Wait till his mother saw this. She'd never let him live it down, that's *after* she kicked his ass for putting himself in harm's way.

Chapter 25

Alyx burst into Laura's office, stopping Rich mid-sentence. "You need to see this," she said, grabbing the remote and turning on the TV in Laura's office.

Laura covered her mouth to hide her gasp as she witnessed Steve atop the burning vehicle, handing two babies down to a mob of men below. "Oh my God," she finally said. "When did this happen?"

"About an hour ago."

"Oh God, is Steve okay?"

"I don't know officially, but he looks like he survived." The video showed Steve being blown off his feet and landing face down on the pavement, then two onlookers pulling him to safety. "Maybe you should call him."

Laura already had her phone in hand and dialed Steve. "Don't give me any crap," he said, "I've just been reamed out by my mother."

Laura sighed, relieved. Steve often complained about how over-protective his family was. But she thought it wonderful to have people who cared that much for you.

"And hello to you too."

"Sorry. It's been a tough afternoon. I can't believe video is everywhere these days. You can't get away with anything."

"It's not like you were robbing a bank."

Steve exhaled loudly. "I know. I just don't like having my picture playing all over the television. It's embarrassing."

"Are you okay?"

"Yeah, a few scrapes and bruises. Nothing major."

"You sure? Don't play the tough guy with me. I'll come over and take care of you if you need me." Laura's eyes traveled between Alyx and Rich. She chewed on her bottom lip. Her comments sounded too personal for officers working a case together. Alyx would be okay with it, but Rich gave a fake smile then dropped his gaze. He probably wanted to crawl under the carpet.

"No, I'm fine. I'm headed back to the office to fill out the reports."

"Steve…" she said before he hung up, "Sorry I was so critical the other day. I didn't mean to snap at you."

"Forget it. We're both frustrated that the guy is still on the loose. At this point, the likelihood of finding him is practically nil."

Laura pinched the bridge of her nose. "I agree. I don't understand why he's still here though. If I was him I'd be long gone."

A few seconds lagged before he answered. "That's been bugging me too. Makes no sense. What's he still hanging around for?"

"You got me. Well, I'm glad you're okay. If you need me, promise you'll call."

"I will."

Laura switched the horrid images off the screen. To Alyx and Rich she said, "You know, I need a minute. If you don't mind."

"Of course," Alyx said. "Come on, Rich. Let me see what

you're working on." Rich dutifully followed Laura's boss out of the office, papers in hand.

Laura leaned back in her chair as the full impact of Steve's heroic actions hit. She couldn't catch her breath, her heart racing uncontrollably. He could have been killed. The image of him nearly being blown up constricted her throat and she swallowed hard. Tears welled and a sob heaved her chest. She hung her head in her hands and let the water run down her cheeks, a soft mewing in her throat. What would she have done if Steve died?

Maybe she should drive to his house, but he said he was going to his office. She was overreacting. She just needed to catch her breath and get back to work. Plucking a tissue from the box she mopped her face and headed to the bathroom to repair her makeup. But her heart still pounded, at the idea of Steve… dead.

Steve entered the precinct to a round of applause. He took a mock bow, then quickly paced to his office. Alice had her hands on his coat the second he passed through the doorway and hung it on the hook.

"You okay, boss?" Her blue eyes scanned him from head to toe. She stepped closer and took his hands, the palms scraped raw. "Let me take care of these for you."

Steve hated when women fussed over him. "It's fine, they'll heal in a few days."

"Nonsense. They'll heal faster if we clean and bandage them."

"Not necessary," Steve said to her back. "I'm a grown man. I can take care of myself." Gone barely a minute, she returned with first aid supplies. Alice spread the ointment on with a cotton swab, then placed sterile pads over the wounds and wrapped each hand with gauze.

"Jesus, Alice, I look like a mummy."

"Stop bitching. I'm the boss of this." Alice smiled. "Don't make me call your mother."

Steve laughed. "Okay, uncle. You win."

"The paperwork for the reports is on your desk. Why don't you let me help since I don't think your typing is up to speed. Not that it ever is." She narrowed her eyes at him.

They finished the required work in under an hour and Alice sent him packing, insisting he go home and take it easy for the rest of the night.

That evening he lay on the couch, drinking a scotch and fielding a ton of phone calls. His entire family, Colin and Jack, and at last his phone announced Laura Logan.

"How are you feeling?" she inquired.

"Like I just finished a heavy workout at the gym. Every muscle aches. I think I'm out of shape."

Laura chuckled. "From my perspective, you're in incredible shape. And I've seen every inch of you."

Steve thought of their spectacular night at the club, relieved and happy that Laura climaxed and more than once. "And I've seen every inch of you."

"Stay on topic, mister. This is about you."

"Yes, ma'am. But honestly, I've had enough. No more fawning over me. It's done."

"You should be happy that you have that many people in your life who care enough to worry about you. They love you."

Now Steve felt bad. Again. Every time he complained about people being concerned for his welfare, he remembered that Laura had no one. He best shut his trap. But then he considered her words. Could she be one of those people? One who cared? One who loved him?

"You're right," he finally said. "And I do appreciate everyone's concern."

"Well, I'll let you go. Get some sleep."

"Will do. Oh shit," he said with a sigh. "My landline is ringing. It's gotta be my mother. She's called three times already. Maybe I'll ignore it."

"Bad son, answer it and put her mind at ease."

Steve laughed. "Yes ma'am."

Laura stared at her phone long after the red dot vanished. She finally stuck it into the charger for the night and stripped out of her sweats and into a robe. Sitting at her vanity, she scrubbed the makeup from her face with a wipe and applied moisturizer, then dragged a brush through her hair in long slow strokes. She packed her overnight bag, intending to head to Alyx's house for the dreaded birthday dinner right after work. She gently chided herself for the habitual negative attitude about her birthday. She enjoyed having dinner with Alyx and Daniel. Their seaside abode was spectacular and she often crashed there in the summer, romping in the surf and sunning on the beach. Alyx had even given her a few surfing lessons. But she hated celebrating her birthday. Hated it with a passion. But it would just be the three of them and she could handle that.

Slipping into a pair of boy shorts and a cami, she slid between the cool sheets, shut off the bedside lamp and stared at the dark ceiling. "Happy birthday to me," she whispered in the dark.

Chapter 26

A strange sense of peace overtook Viktor. He was at the end. He'd finally have his reward. In his mind's eye, he envisioned his little slave strapped into submission, a spreader bar forcing her legs wide for his pleasure.

Viktor didn't even try to follow Laura that afternoon. She was probably going to that detective's house again. His attempt to obliterate the guy a dismal failure. Impatience making his judgment questionable. He needed to take a step back and plan more carefully.

Nothing left to do but wait her out. Whether she returned tonight, tomorrow, or Sunday didn't matter. This time however, he wouldn't leave without her. Abandoning his surveillance of the little Fed last night, he'd focused his efforts on securing a vehicle for his trip out west. Something he could imprison her in without attracting attention. He'd spent most of the day outfitting it with chains and shackles. Now all he had to do was clear out of the cabin. He intended to leave this godforsaken shack tonight, never to return.

Near the dead end by the creek, he maneuvered his newly

acquired vehicle onto the deserted dirt road. He parked in the space he'd cleared of brush and walked the fifty yards to his secret hideaway. The ramshackle hut had been a great find, although the conditions primitive. No heat or running water. He had to import his meager amenities and left his hygiene needs to the rest stop facilities on the Long Island Expressway. Years ago it had been discovered as a hook-up spot for the gay crowd, but after the newspapers exposed it, that practice ended. He actually thought people still avoided it because of its reputation. Nevertheless, its habitual vacancy proved convenient for his current situation.

He threw his toy bag over his shoulder, his cache of implements that he would use to inflict untold torture on the little Fed, when a flicker to the left caught his eye. He went to the cabin's small window and scanned the darkened woods. There it was again, a light, perhaps a flashlight. He best hurry, he couldn't risk being detected. Not now, when he was so close to claiming his prize. He'd been careful to leave no traces of himself, wearing gloves in the cold weather facilitated that, and besides he was pretty sure the Feds couldn't track him. Gathering his few personal belongings and his last bottle of vodka, he ran for the van.

Traveling the highway to Muttontown, he adhered to the speed limit, driving meticulously to avoid attracting attention. He was confident in the little Fed's routine. She'd go to that detective's house on Saturday and then they'd go out, not returning until after midnight. He'd simply wait. She had to come home eventually. And when she did, he'd be ready and waiting.

He parked the van on the next street and walked the dimly lit path to her house, rounding the side, he faced the keypad mounted on the garage molding. Punching in 0709, he entered through the garage. The house smelled so good: a fragrant mixture of fresh flowers, her perfume, and something he couldn't put his finger on. Perhaps she'd baked something.

He wandered through the downstairs rooms and selected the one with the luxurious couches and giant TV screen. He'd make himself at home: eat some decent food, lounge on her comfortable furniture and watch her oversized HD television. Weeks of living in that dump had taken its toll. Once he had her, and enjoyed some playtime, he'd stash her in the van and head west. His cousin had made arrangements for a place to live, something quiet and out of the way, where her screams would go undetected.

Viktor found a bottle of Grey Goose in the bar, he preferred Stoli, but this would do, and poured a double shot, throwing it back in one gulp. The warm elixir burned all the way down. Delicious torture and he exhaled with a loud, "Ahhh." He downed another, but warned himself not to consume too much since he needed to be sharp when she returned. He ran his hands over the bar top's cool dark granite, imagining himself living here: the Lord of the Manor with his enslaved handmaiden to do his bidding.

He ventured back into the kitchen and rummaged through the refrigerator. For a chick she didn't have much food, but he found cold cuts, cheese and bread and made himself a generous sandwich, slathered in copious amounts of hot mustard.

Settling on the long leather couch in front of the television, he flipped through the channels, eventually landing on a soccer match. He bit into his sandwich, laying the plate on his lap and crossed his feet at the ankles, resting them on the sandstone coffee table. He laughed. What was that fairytale his grandmother used to read to him at bedtime? Something about a fair-haired girl who wandered into a cottage where a family of bears lived. She eats their porridge and sleeps in their beds... He smirked, no way would he fall asleep and be discovered by that agent bitch. That tracker would alert him to her arrival.

———

Friday, Laura left work early and drove the sixty miles to Alyx and Daniel's house. She frowned, noting Molly's car parked in one of the guest spots in the circular driveway. She hadn't seen her partner in weeks, not since she'd stopped by after work one day to meet the new baby.

Damn you, Alyx. She'd been promised a quiet dinner, just the three of them, but apparently Alyx couldn't contain herself and invited Molly and probably her husband, Sam.

The door opened before she could knock and Alyx's beaming face welcomed her. "Happy birthday." Alyx threw her arms around Laura and hugged her tightly.

"Thanks," Laura mumbled into her shoulder.

Daniel stood behind Alyx and pulled her in for a similar embrace. "Happy birthday."

"Thanks," she said again.

Alyx tugged her hand and Daniel absconded with her overnight bag. "I'll put this in your room."

"Thanks," Laura said for the third time.

Entering the kitchen she faced Molly, spatula in hand, mixing bowl on the counter. Sam sat at the kitchen table but rose upon seeing her. The customary hugs and kisses ensued and Laura's chest expanded, still unaccustomed to physical expressions of affection. "You promised you wouldn't make a fuss over my birthday. It was supposed to be a quiet dinner with the three of us.

"I promised no such thing," Alyx said.

"And I'm insulted," Molly said. She smiled.

Laura shook her head. "Fine, celebrate away. A birthday hostage. Again."

"You're insufferable, you know that?" Alyx said.

Laura grinned. "Yeah, but you guys love me anyway."

"That we do," Molly said.

"So how's motherhood?" Laura inquired as they helped Alyx plate hors' d'oeuvres. The housekeeper, Lydia, had prepped for tonight's dinner party and Alyx often extolled Lydia's virtues. Alyx first encountered her when she arrived at Daniel's house to complete the training for her undercover assignment at the club. Lydia had quickly become a second mother to Alyx, especially since Alyx had lost her mother at three. Although, Alyx had never discovered any evidence of her mother's death, even with her FBI skills, and so Alyx wasn't entirely convinced her mother was deceased. But then, if she wasn't, why wouldn't she reach out to Alyx? What mother would willingly abandon her child?

"Motherhood is exhausting and wonderful," Molly said. "But I'm anxious to get back to work."

"Me too," her husband, Sam, said. "There are moments when I just have to shove her out of the house for some adult contact." Sam owned an investment firm and frequently worked from home.

The doorbell rang and Laura glanced up, a bacon-wrapped date in her hand. Who else could be coming? "I'll get it," Daniel said, popping the cork on an unfamiliar label of pinot noir as he exited the kitchen.

"Now that everyone is here we can make drinks," Alyx announced.

"Who else did you invite?" Laura said. Daniel spoke with a man as the door to the kitchen swung open. Steve stood alongside Daniel, one arm behind his back.

Laura blurted, "Steve? What are you doing here?"

Chapter 27

S teve frowned, a playful frown. "Maybe you could have told me it was your birthday."

Laura surveyed the room, as a bloom of heat crept up her face. "I... I didn't think it was important."

Alyx snorted. "Laura would never celebrate her birthday if it was up to her. So it's up to me or Molly, right, girlfriend?"

"Absolutely," Molly said. "Last year we practically had to handcuff and gag her to get her to that restaurant. It was like arresting a perp."

Hands on her hips, Laura exclaimed, "I'm not that bad. But it wouldn't have been so awful if the entire wait staff hadn't appeared with that flaming cake and sung a chorus or two of Happy Birthday!" Nobody confirmed her assessment and she went on, "It just doesn't seem necessary. It's only a birthday."

"Steve, I'm Molly, Laura's soon-to-be-returning partner and this is my husband, Sam."

"Pleasure," Steve said, displaying his palm. "Excuse me for not shaking hands." Everyone winced at the fresh scab. "Accident on the job."

"We saw the video. You're lucky you weren't hurt worse," Alyx said.

"That's right. Hero here. Nicely done, man," Daniel said.

Laura went to him and clasped his hand, studying the wound. "Looks like it's healing well." She gazed up at him. "You could have been killed."

"Well, I wasn't. So let's forget it."

"Let me see the other one."

"If you insist." He brought his hand from behind his back and presented the package wrapped in the pink-flowered paper with the perfect white bow. "Happy birthday, pet." He leaned in and gave her a peck on the lips.

Laura fretted over Steve's term of endearment, one used exclusively by Doms at the club. Would everyone know she'd played there? That Steve had been the Dom and she the submissive? Alyx knew, which meant Daniel probably did, but she didn't want her visit to the sex venue shared with Molly.

Cradling the petite box in her hand, she hesitated, her fingers poised over the silky white ribbon. "You shouldn't have, Steve. I mean it."

"She also hates getting presents," Alyx added. "This girl needs some serious retraining." She stared directly at Laura. "And you need to let someone do something nice for you now and again, to let someone take care of you for a change."

Laura had spent too many years at boarding school with no family to celebrate her birthday and most holidays. She usually made it home to her aunt's house for Christmas, but one year her aunt was overseas working some international human rights trial and she had been forced to stay at school with the other orphans.

"That's enough of beating up on Laura," Daniel said. "Open it."

Laura tugged the ribbon, releasing the bow, and ripped the

paper, exposing a square black box with 'Diamonds by Moretti' printed in gold letters. Her throat constricted. What had Steve bought? Sweat trickled down her spine.

Tentatively removing the cover, her eyes landed on the gleaming blue and silver studs. "Oh, Steve, thank you, they're beautiful. My birthstone? I've never gotten anything with my birthstone." Tears pooled in her eyes and she felt the fool. "I'm sorry," she said, dabbing at her eyes. "I'm being such a baby."

Steve came close and wrapped his arms around her, hugging her tight. "Happy birthday, baby," he whispered in her ear. "But I'd like to spank you right now for not revealing your imminent birthday."

"Shush," she said.

"Let's make drinks," Daniel said. "I can do martinis and manhattans, gimlets and pretty much anything else you fancy. And of course there's plenty of wine." Everyone agreed on martinis and Daniel invited Steve and Sam to accompany him to the bar.

Steve and Sam settled onto black leather stools as Daniel seized bottles from under the polished teak counter. "Are you and Laura dating?" Sam said. "Molly is light on details, which amazes me since details are vital in her job."

"Not exactly," Steve said. "We're more like friends with benefits. Maybe even my new best friend." As soon as the words left his mouth he regretted them. Perhaps Laura wouldn't want him revealing the specifics of their arrangement.

"How's the sex?" Daniel said.

"Exceptional."

"So, best friends and the sex is great?"

Sam smiled. "That's how Molly and I wound up together. She lived across the hall in my dorm sophomore year. We were both in the same computer class and studied together before a test. We were dating other people and one night I came to her room to ask her the most ridiculous question. Daniel knows this part: I went to an all boys' high school and hadn't had much experience with girls. In fact I was a virgin."

Steve regressed to his high school days. He lost his virginity as a freshman when a senior girl propositioned him on the school bus and she took him home and rocked his world.

"Well," Sam continued, "I'd been dating this girl for a while and I'd cleared the major hurdle but was too chicken to try oral sex. I could tell Molly anything and so I asked her advice." Sam laughed. "You know what she told me?"

"I wouldn't even venture a guess, but you've got my undivided attention," Steve said. Daniel pushed an icy martini toward Sam, adding a big green olive.

"Thanks," Sam said.

"Don't keep us hanging, I'm sitting on the edge of my seat," Steve said.

"She said, close your eyes, hold your breath and just go for it. You'll figure it out."

The three men chortled.

"And ask her how it was, she'll coach you."

"Good advice," Steve said. "You always ask a woman what she wants and what she likes."

"Yeah, but sometimes you need to give them what they need and they may not know what that is," Daniel added.

"Anyway," Sam said, "after I'd done the deed I needed to report to Molly and tell her how much I'd appreciated her advice. And that's when it happened. We started talking about sex and suddenly we were screwing on her bed. We both broke off our relationships and we've been together ever since."

"Funny how chemistry works," Daniel said. "I'd only been with Alyx a day and the attraction was so strong I couldn't imagine ever being without her. She had just gotten *out* of a bad relationship and I was *in* a bad one, although I didn't realize it at the time. But by the end of the week I think we both knew we would never be apart." Daniel placed Steve's martini in front of him. "So, Steve, you said Laura is your new best friend and the sex is great?"

Steve hoisted his drink toward his lips, pausing. "I did."

Daniel smiled broadly, placing both hands on the bar top, he leaned toward Steve. "Dude, I'm pretty sure that's the woman you marry."

"Abso-fucking-lutely," Sam said. "Tie that knot."

Steve gulped a mouthful of icy liquid. For a second there, he thought maybe his heart stopped.

The party congregated in the living room, the coffee table laden with a sumptuous array of appetizers. Steve sat beside Laura on the love seat and handed her a martini.

"Thanks," she said, taking a swallow. "Hmm, great martini, Daniel. Nothing like that first ice-cold mouthful."

Laura opened presents, an ivory cashmere scarf from Molly and Sam, and a powder blue leather Kate Spade handbag from Alyx and Daniel. Engaging chatter covered a bit of politics, some bitching about everyone's day job and even the annoying cold weather. Conversation continued amicably over Lydia's shrimp scampi with linguine and a green salad with pine nuts and shaved Asiago dressed in white balsamic vinaigrette. Crusty Italian bread sopped up the savory essences.

They cleared the table themselves. Lydia helped with

cooking and cleaning but she went home to her husband each evening. Mason had managed the house and grounds for Daniel long before Alyx arrived and he and Lydia inhabited a cottage at the far end of the property.

Coffee and tiramisu followed, bright with the glow of too many candles. They sang the traditional birthday ditty, much to Laura's chagrin. And yet, being part of this perfect sextet at a fabulous dinner party swelled Laura's chest. For once, she didn't feel like the odd one out.

The blaze in the fireplace dwindled and the partygoers along with it. "Shall we call it a night?" Alyx said, and a round of agreement had everyone heading upstairs. Arriving on the landing, Alyx said, "Molly and Sam have already taken the room at the end of the hall and Laura is here." She nodded to the door in front of her. "Laura, you take care of Steve's sleeping arrangements."

Alyx and Daniel disappeared to the right and Molly and Sam to the left, leaving Steve alone with Laura. "I meant to call you earlier. Jack said he's okay with me bringing you to the club and me doing part-time duty. You in?" Steve said.

"Oh, Steve. Sorry, I can't."

"Damn. How come?"

Laura shuffled her feet. "Well... I have a date."

For a split-second, Steve winced. He'd thought things were going splendidly and hadn't seen this coming.

Laura spoke but he had difficulty decoding the words. "This guy I met at a conference a while back got transferred to the New York office and called and invited me out to dinner. You said you probably had to work so I figured the club was a no-go."

"Is he the guy you hooked up with?"

"Yeah. I figured I owed him some honesty this time. Didn't we agree we were done being cowards? That we'd try and give our true self to someone?"

Queasiness roiled Steve's gut. Everything Laura said was correct and he needed to step back. "We did. And I wish you the best." He jammed his hands into his back pockets. "Tell me which room is empty. I'll sleep there."

Laura's chin darted up, the dark hallway casting her eyes in a blackish hue. "Steve, I thought this was casual. Besides, you have sex with women at the club all the time."

The realization that he'd forsaken all others since Laura entered his life slammed into Steve. His head was all messed up. Daniel and Sam had him thinking Laura might be more. And now she was ready to move on. "I haven't been with anyone since we met."

"Oh?" Laura grasped his arm, her fingers gently massaging his wrist. Then: "I still need to go on this date. It's not the guy. I don't really know him. I just feel like I shouldn't close myself off to any possibility. Don't be mad."

"I'm not mad, just… disappointed."

Steve entered a bedroom festooned in green and gold. He tried to close the door but Laura stood in the way. "Night," he said, shutting the door, forcing Laura backward. Through the paneled wood, he heard: "What have I done wrong?" He didn't answer.

He surveyed the room, then sat on the bed and kicked off his shoes and socks. He considered his fate. Laura was right, the agreement casual, no commitment, no ties. Both were free to do as they pleased and that included dating other people. He unbuttoned his shirt, ripping it free from his waistband, and tossed it on the bed, then ambled over and opened the double French doors leading to a small balcony. The ocean churned below and the bracing wind flagellated his bare chest. The balcony floor chilled his bare feet. He inhaled the briny, cold night air, gripping the railing and considered throwing himself into the ocean below. Not to kill himself but to knock some sense into his head. What was he doing? How had he gotten into this situation? He loved Laura.

Was it too late?

Chapter 28

Laura slipped out of her black patent leather heels and threw them across the room. "What the fuck?" she said aloud. Why did she feel like such a shit? She hadn't done anything wrong. Steve had adamantly stated that he wasn't interested in a relationship. Did this mean she and Steve were done? If this had been a female friend they could continue to be friends, to talk about her new dating experiences. But having sex with your friend was more complicated... *way* more. She'd never been emotionally involved with a sex partner and now, well, she loved Steve. Not like a boyfriend, just a boy who was a friend. Right?

Yet she wasn't so sure. The love for a friend was *platonic*.

She stripped out of her little black dress and underwear, walked into the bathroom and stood naked in front of the vanity mirror. A sigh escaped and she leaned heavily on the white marble and hung her head. Walking away from Steve might be more than she could bear.

The dark room blanketed her in silence, save for the crashing ocean waves on the beach. The wind howled its dismay and she felt one with turbulent Mother Nature. Sleep escaped her for most of the night, her nightmares real because they came to her awake.

The aroma of freshly brewed coffee finally brought Laura to her senses and she threw on jeans and a white angora sweater, gathered her hair into a ponytail, pulling it through the back opening of her tan baseball cap. The sparkling blue gems decorated her earlobes and she sighed, gazing at her reflection in the bathroom mirror. What was she going to do about Steve? Maybe she should give the earrings back.

She brushed her teeth and applied a touch of blush and a smidge of lip gloss, then packed her belongings into her duffle and headed to the kitchen for coffee. Molly and Sam sat at the table sipping the aromatic brew and munching on freshly baked cinnamon rolls, no doubt one of Lydia's delectable confections. Daniel had his head buried in the New York Times and Alyx stood at the coffeemaker pouring a fresh cup.

"Morning," Laura announced as enthusiastically as she could. "Is Steve up yet?"

Alyx poured coffee into a clear glass mug and handed it to Laura. "He left already. He said something about meeting his mother for lunch and doing some Christmas shopping."

"Oh," Laura said, slurping the hot liquid.

"The earrings are spectacular on you," Molly said. "They match your eyes perfectly."

Laura fingered one earring. "They are beautiful. But Steve shouldn't have. They're probably way too expensive."

"The man has excellent taste," Alyx added.

Laura hugged herself, wishing she could disappear.

Molly said, "You've got to have one of these cinnamon buns, they're amazing."

Relieved that Molly moved the conversation out of awkward mode, Laura sat beside her and selected one of the warm, gooey rolls. She scarfed down the scrumptious treat, partly because she was desperate to make an escape. Everyone in the room had probably mistaken her relationship with Steve for something it wasn't. And undoubtedly, they knew they'd slept apart last night and assumed some argument had occurred. A lover's spat. Wrong. So fucking wrong.

Viktor dozed several times Friday night, but he hadn't fretted, knowing the tracker alarm would alert him when Laura returned. He figured out how to make coffee, brewing it extra strong and scrambled up some eggs for breakfast. Dare he shower? He doubted the little bitch would be home this early, so he'd risk it. He'd hustle.

The hot water pleased him and he lathered himself with the vanilla shower gel twice, enjoying the well-appointed restroom. Abandoning his life of squalor had him stoked. His new life awaited him. Only another day or two and he'd be a man of indulgent pleasures.

It might be another twenty-four hours until she returned, but he didn't care, he savored her lavish home, content to wait in the lap of luxury.

Steve sped down the LI Expressway at an absurd speed, even for him. He couldn't get away from Laura fast enough. The dawning light cleared his head and he'd stuffed his emotions back where they belonged, buried with the bones of his other failed relationships. All considered, this one had been uncomplicated. No emotions surfaced and they both walked away unscathed.

Arriving at his parents' house, he shut off the ignition and took a moment to gather his wits. His mother's radar might not always be great at detecting his physical ailments, but when it came to his mood, her skills were flawless. Exiting the car, he turned his collar up to the frigid wind. Damn, way too cold for Long Island. The surrounding ocean ameliorated the frigid temps to a large degree, insulating them from winter's wrath, but to date, this winter had been uncharacteristically brutal.

He knocked twice on the front door, and then entered. "Mom?"

Andrea Moretti emerged from the kitchen, coffee cup in hand. "Morning, bunnie," she said. "From the looks of it we'll be having an old-fashioned Christmas this year. Even snow. I like the idea, but my old body isn't loving the temps."

Steve recalled his childhood when, to his delight, most winters brought snow, a white Christmas the norm rather than the exception. The golf course behind his house had spectacular hills and he and his buddies would go sleigh riding until darkness descended. And they'd skate on the manmade pond, the golf course their own winter wonderland. In the summer they'd retrieve balls from the same pond and sell them back to the golfers as range balls.

Steve pecked his mother's cheek. "It's friggin' cold out. Dress warm."

"You want coffee? There's a cup left."

"No thanks."

His mother disappeared into the kitchen while Steve stared out the front window. What was Laura doing? Was she still at Alyx's? Was she on the road back to her place? He probably should have stayed and acted pleasant, making sure Laura knew he was fine with her going on a date. He had no right to even have an opinion on her social life. He certainly hadn't hidden his feelings well when Laura announced she had a date and couldn't go to the club tonight. And, exactly what were his feelings?

"Steven Anthony Moretti," his mother said forcefully. Startled, he faced her. She only used his full name when she was angry. Dressed and ready to go, she had her leather-gloved hands on her hips. "What's wrong?"

"Nothing, why?"

"I called your name several times and you just kept staring out the window."

"I'm fine."

"You're not fine. I could tell the second you walked in the door."

Her emotional radar pinged Steve's chest. Damn. He didn't want to talk about Laura with his mother. She'd overreact, thinking another girlfriend had ditched him.

"It's just work. I'm desperate to catch the guy that got away. It's on my mind constantly." He pulled his mother in for a hug, kissing the top of her head. "But I promise to put it aside for the day." Setting her free, he said, "Where do you want to go for lunch?"

"Well, Steven, I don't believe you for one second, but in the interest of getting the rest of my Christmas shopping done I'll let it go for now." She poked a finger into his chest. "But I'll get it out of you eventually."

And Steve had no doubt she would.

Chapter 29

Laura entered her driveway and glanced at the car readout. Noon. She had plenty of time to primp for her date. A nap before she showered might be possible. However, she feared sleep might be elusive, like last night, her mind lingering on Steve's disappointment. She secured her car in the garage, entered through the kitchen, pausing a finger over the keypad adjacent to the door. The green light on. Had she forgotten to set the alarm? She must have, and she rearmed it.

She opened the fridge for a bottle of water and frowned, the contents askew. The hairs on her nape prickled. Could someone have been in her house? But how could they get past the alarm? No one knew the code. Although she apparently left it off yesterday.

Pulling her Glock from the duffle, she moved through the kitchen, her sneakered feet silent on the wooden floor. She crept down the hall, her back flush against the wall, and peeked around the corner into the den. Her breath hitched and her spine straightened, muscles rigid. He sat in the leather chair beside the blazing fireplace. A well-honed reflex seized her and she aimed the gun at him, two hands on the grip.

"What are you doing in my house?"

He didn't respond, as a grin revealed a chipped front tooth.

"I'm here for you," he finally said. The hand holding the gun in his lap rose and Laura considered her options. She had to kill him.

The sharp stab of pain in her neck threw her off balance. She fired, but the bullet hit the TV screen over the hearth, fissures in the plastic rendering it lifeless. The chemical surged in her bloodstream, her heart rate accelerated rapidly and her vision shimmered, as if blinded by fireworks. The sparkles faded to black as she slumped to the floor, her head slamming against the iron rendering of an owl her aunt had picked up on a trip to London.

Viktor knelt beside his prize. So beautiful, with her perfect body and sumptuous hair. He removed the cap from her head, releasing her long golden locks. A small amount of blood marred the back of her scalp. He hoped the injury was minor. He caressed her cheeks and smoothed her tangled tresses, then leaned down and rubbed his cheek against hers, soft as fine Asian silk. No time to dally, move fast.

Originally he had planned on dragging her back to the cabin, until the stranger with the flashlight threatened his discovery and the idea of bringing her back to the confines of the inhospitable bunker lost appeal. Why not stay here and enjoy the comforts of her home before he headed to Vegas, where his cousin had everything arranged for his new life. In the weeks he'd surveilled her, that detective had been her only visitor and just that once. She always traveled east to his house. Yeah, he'd be safe here to enjoy her magnificent body. The manse was huge, the neighbors on each side separated by a half acre. No one would hear her scream. He'd gag her and her muffled cries would die on her lips.

He slung her over his shoulder and marched up the stairs, depositing her unconscious body on her bed, then ran downstairs to retrieve his satchel. Inside he had the tools for abducting the bitch, slip ties, duct tape, but he'd left his toy bag in the van. Damn.

Working quickly, he secured her feet and hands to the bedframe with the vinyl zip ties, her body positioned in a perfect X, then duct-taped her mouth and blindfolded her with a gauzy white scarf he'd scrounged from her closet. That should keep her silent and in submission until he was ready to play.

Viktor studied her features, the face of a sleeping princess. She might be the most beautiful woman he'd ever fucked, maybe the most beautiful woman he'd ever seen. The tranquilizer drug would probably have her knocked out for several hours and he hoped the head bashing wouldn't prolong her unconsciousness. He made himself another sandwich and imbibed some more of her delicious vodka. Maybe he'd take a short nap until she woke.

Steve and his mother enjoyed lunch at Café Le Pain, known for their sweet and savory breads. The Kalamata olive bread was his favorite and he always took home a loaf. Thankfully, his mother avoided poking at his mood and he kept his unhappiness to himself.

The adults had stopped giving gifts to each other when the kids arrived so he only needed presents for his nieces and nephews. Steve detested shopping, yet his mother made the torturous chore palatable. Her engaging chatter and running commentary coupled with her unrelenting decisiveness got the job done in less than two hours. Everything wrapped. All he had to do was show up on Christmas day with the usual cache of booze and gift-wrapped goods.

He pulled into his parents' driveway and put the car in park. "Thanks for your help, Mom. I never would have been able to pull this off on my own."

"Don't mention it. It's a treat to have you to myself for the afternoon."

Steve smiled. He did enjoy spending time with his mother and he didn't do it enough. He often played golf with his dad in the warmer months but there wasn't anything similar he could do with his mom. Steve opened the trunk and retrieved his mother's packages, then followed her to the front door.

"Thank you, bunnie," his mother said as he deposited the purchases on the couch.

"Sure."

"Do you want to stay for dinner? I'm making Grandma Tina's sauce." The treasured family recipe produced a meat sauce, light on *the sauce*. It consisted of ground beef and tomato paste and the secret spice no one but Northern Italians would identify: ground cloves... but just a pinch, too much and the sauce would be distasteful. It resembled bean-less chili more than regular spaghetti sauce. Served over linguine and smothered in fresh grated Parmesan cheese, it was probably his favorite meal. Simple to make, Steve had cooked it for Jillian once. Maybe he'd make if for Laura someday. What? Yeah, no, that was never going to happen.

"No thanks, Mom. I've got to work tonight."

"Seriously, they don't give you Saturday night off? I mean, you're Chief of Detectives. Can't you work more reasonable hours? You need a life, Steven." And she was off! "Are you dating anyone? Are you bringing anyone to Christmas dinner?"

"Ma, let's not do this. I'm not dating anyone."

"Darling, you need someone in your life. You're not getting any younger."

"Ma."

She put both her hands up. "Okay, okay. I'm done."

"Good."

"What about Sunday dinner tomorrow? Can we expect you?"

"I'll let you know." He kissed his mother goodbye and made a quick escape. He'd lied to his mother. He didn't have to work tonight. Well, he did, but at the club, and going without Laura had him in a major funk.

The heavy metal music pounded Steve's ears painfully, intensifying the headache he'd been enduring after departing his parents' house. "Got any aspirin?" he asked Colin.

"Sure." Colin reached under the bar, handing over a white plastic bottle. "What's up? You look like shit." Colin offered a glass of water.

"Just a headache. I was shopping all day with my mother. You know how much I love shopping, plus she hammered me again about finding a *nice woman.*" Steve couldn't believe he'd just thrown his mother under the bus. She deserved better, but his foul mood affected his judgment. Maybe he should go home; he was not in the best frame of mind to be working with new submissives. His patience thinner than day-old ice on a pond.

He envisioned Laura dressed for her date, smelling good enough to eat, her sleek slender legs atop a pair of black patent leather heels. Her hair and make-up perfect, her smile wide, as she slipped her hand through some dude's arm. Steve palmed four blue gel-caps and popped them in his mouth, washing the medication down with the entire glass of water. "Thanks."

"Where's your lady?"

"On a date."

It took Colin a few seconds to respond. "Huh, so you two aren't an item?"

"No. Just friends."

"Friends with benefits?" Colin said with a smirk.

Steve suddenly hated that expression. A stupid term. It doesn't work. You can't be intimate with a woman and not have feelings. Maybe once, or twice, just as a hookup, but friendship and sex don't mix. It's a deadly combo.

Steve ignored Colin's remark and reached into the key cabinet, selected the one he wanted, then shut the door forcefully and headed up the spiral staircase. He unlocked the chamber and flung the key onto the king-sized bed.

Gazing at the silky comforter, he recalled Laura lying there, beautifully naked on the satin sheets. Her legs open, her glistening folds ready for him... so willingly submissive. She had her delicate hands clutching the headboard spindles, her lips pursed in anticipation of what he would do to her.

His cock ached.

Steve ambled over to the chair in the room's corner and sank heavily onto the seat. He perched his elbows on his knees, his chin resting on his steepled fingers. Shutting his eyes, he swore her scent lingered on the air, her soft moans and whimpers echoing in his brain.

"Talk to me, dude." Colin stood at the foot of the bed. Steve hadn't heard him enter. "This chick fucking with your head?"

Steve hesitated before answering. "She's not at fault. I was clear about keeping this casual. She took me at my word."

Colin perched on the bed's edge, leaning back on his hands, his feet splayed in front of him. "So you changed your mind. Fess up."

Steve rested his back against the chair, his eyes focused on the ceiling. He folded his arms over his chest. "I can't. She deserves someone better than me."

"You're an ass."

"I know."

Colin sighed. "How long have we known each other?"

"Since kindergarten." Colin was an only child and they'd been the brothers each didn't have. They were an unlikely pair in many ways. Colin's family had money, a lot of money, whereas Steve's family was clearly middle class. Steve's parents were college grads but they didn't run in the same circle as Colin's family. Steve's house could fit into Colin's seaside mansion three times. They spent summers entertaining girls on Colin's boat, showing off their waterskiing skills and hanging out on Fire Island where they drank too much and broke curfew on a regular basis.

But Colin's family treated Steve like one of their own, taking him on countless vacations to the Caribbean and even skiing in the Alps. Steve and Colin were football teammates, Steve the quarterback and Colin his favorite wide receiver. They were a dynamic duo and enjoyed a well-deserved reputation for putting countless points on the board during their high school career. Steve rode his football scholarship to Holy Cross whereas Colin went off to Harvard like his parents. Colin was the brains of the two whereas Steve provided the muscle when needed. However, Colin turned out to be a late bloomer and eventually the two sported similar physiques. Although still good friends, Colin resided in a Manhattan penthouse, the CEO of a billion-dollar software company. Mostly they saw each other at the club, the one exception being the Super Bowl, where Colin always procured prime tickets and Steve attended as his guest, complete with a ride on Colin's private jet.

"You know," Colin said, "you were always the outgoing one, confident around women and I had a hard time keeping up. What happened to that guy?"

"He got the shit kicked out of him too many times."

"That's bullshit. When did you turn into such a pussy?"

"Don't bust my balls, Colin."

Colin laughed. "That's my job, dude. You're a Dom, act like one."

Instantly on his feet, Steve stood before Colin. "I can't exactly tie her up and *order* her to love me."

Colin rose and they stood nose-to-nose. Colin pinched his chin. "Hmm, I suppose not. But seriously this connection you have with her won't go away just because you don't want it to be there. Get your shit together and tell the woman how you feel."

Steve sighed. "I don't know."

"It's obvious that you love her. The sooner you admit it to yourself and *her* the better."

Chapter 30

"Come on," Colin urged, "the subs are waiting for inspection. Let's go have a little fun."

Steve followed Colin out, securing the door behind him. In the locker room they faced a line of seven submissive trainees in the inspection position, awaiting permission to play.

Steve clasped his hands behind his back and paced back and forth, his laser focus on the women, their gazes cast downward, feet apart, hands in the same position as his. "Eyes on me," he ordered and they responded. "Looking fine tonight, ladies." He recognized Kate, and Lori—the sub who'd suffered abuse, as well as the rest, the exception being a tall redhead at the end of the line. He positioned himself directly in front of the new girl. "Name?"

"Michele, Sir."

"Michele what?"

"Michele Danford, Sir."

Colin interjected, "I interviewed her. The paperwork is in her file."

"Good," Steve said. "I'll review it after inspection. Is she ready to work with a Dom tonight or does she still require training wheels?"

"She's good to go."

"Fine." Steve worked the line, slipping a hand underneath a bevy of mini-skirts and over a hip to ensure they adhered to the no underwear rule, and running reassuring hands over shoulders and arms. "Any questions before I set you free?"

"No, Sir," several said, but Kate raised her hand like a schoolgirl.

"Yes, Kate."

"I was wondering if you would work with me tonight, Sir?"

Steve swallowed hard. He wasn't up to working with a sub tonight, but he'd been slacking lately. Jack might notice and then he'd have another friend breathing down his neck asking what was wrong with him. Maybe a little playtime would distract him from his misery.

He glanced at Colin who raised his eyebrows and tilted his head in encouragement. Steve finally said, "I have a few things to attend to. Wait in the submissives' pen and I'll come find you when I'm free."

"Oh, yes. Thank you, Sir. I'll be ready and waiting." Kate blushed. "Sorry, Sir, too many words, I know."

"It's fine, Kate. I appreciate your enthusiasm."

"Okay," Colin said, clapping his hands. "Come with me, ladies. I'll deposit each of you where you belong." The parade of submissives followed Colin out of the locker room leaving Steve alone. He slumped onto the nearby bench and gave himself a pep talk. Out loud. "This is your job. Buck up and find your Dom persona. Be the man you're supposed to be. The one you used to be." He inhaled deeply, pushing back his shoulders, and stood. "Let's do this."

Steve ambled into Jack's office, found Michele Danford's file and read it carefully. A veterinarian, recently divorced, and interested in experimenting. Steve chuckled at Colin's note in the margin, written in bold letters with three exclamation points. Something Michele said in her interview: "I've had so much unremarkable sex." Steve closed the file and pondered her words. Many women, and men too, could probably say this. He didn't consider himself to be one of those people, but since he'd been with Laura, well, his other sexual experiences paled. He sat a few moments longer, his hands pressed against his lips. Colin was right, he must tell Laura the truth and let the chips fall where they may.

He stowed the file and went to find Kate. She sat demurely in the gated space, her handcuffs attached to a chain bolted to the floor. "Ready, pet?" He released her from her tether and led her onto the club floor by her coupled manacles.

They reached the back wall where scenes were being played in the medical examining room, the office suite, and the Arabian Tent. Kate stayed in protocol, silent and obedient. Steve wrapped an arm around her delicate shoulders and whispered in her ear. "You may speak freely until I say we're in protocol. What would you like to try tonight?"

Her warm brown eyes peered up at him, like a young doe lost in the forest. "I—I—would—what would Sir like?"

"Kate, I'm not your real Dom. This is about you tonight. Name your pleasure and I will give it to you."

"I would like you to fuck me, Sir."

Steve gritted his teeth. "I'm not sure you have enough stamina for that, Kate. I'm quite demanding. Perhaps we can start with play that is more in the realm of foreplay. Then, we'll see."

"Yes, Sir. Whatever Sir wants. It's a privilege to be with you."

He tightened his arm around her shoulders, pulling her into his chest. "Thank you, pet. I appreciate the compliment."

They stood in front of the glass display window where a

burly silver-haired Dom flogged a woman so hard that welts bubbled up on her back and buttocks. He glanced at Kate, anxiety shivered through her. "Don't worry, pet. I wouldn't do that even if you wanted me to. I'm not into that level of pain."

"What level of pain are you into?"

"I enjoy spanking, and flogging is fine as long as the intensity is monitored closely." Kate remained silent. "Why don't we start on the restraining bench? Have you used that before?"

"No, Sir. I'm game."

"Good. Then I'll be spanking that pretty little ass of yours." He slipped a finger into a manacled wrist and led her left where a spanking bench sat unattended. Beside the bench stood an X-shaped cross where a Domme flagellated a young male with a deerskin flogger. The lashes elicited a moan with each crisp snap. "We're in protocol now so only answer when I ask for a response. You remember the safe words?"

Kate's large eyes met his. "Yes, Sir, green means I'm okay and continue, yellow means I'm not sure and I'm getting uncomfortable, either physically or emotionally, and red means I'm in trouble and stop."

"Excellent. But remember if you say red we're done. We'll discuss what happened and where your limits are but our time together tonight will end."

"Yes, Sir. Understood."

"Excellent," he said again. He gripped her shoulders firmly. "Time to lose the clothes."

She stared at him for a second, then glanced around and bit her lip. The bench faced a wall with a semi-circle of chairs for viewing. People were starting to gather. Like all the masters, his public displays garnered a sizable crowd.

Kate slowly removed her scant garments while Steve watched. Finally naked, he said, "Good girl. You're quite lovely, Kate."

She beamed.

"Kneel here while I get everything ready." He pressed downward on her bare shoulders and she sank willingly. "Slave position, please." Kate sat back on her knees, back straight, attention on the floor, hands resting palms-up on her thighs.

"Excellent, pet. You're doing well, Kate."

Steve readied the bench, unbuckling the restraints and laying the straps astride the soft tan leather. He retrieved a paddle from the shelf beneath and positioned it on the side table.

Squatting in front of her, he placed his hands on either side of her face her features augmented by a little too much make up. "Eyes on me," he ordered.

Kate peered upward through her incredibly long mascara-coated eyelashes. Give me a color."

"Green, Sir."

"Excellent. Now let's get you onto the bench." He released the buckle that linked her handcuffs and tugged her to her feet, guiding her to the end of the padded bench. "Face down position, pet." She put a knee on the low plank and swung her other leg over. He placed her right knee on the board, repeating the action on the other side. He gently stroked each leg as he drew a strap over the ankle and secured it. The bench forced her thighs apart into a wide V. Her forearms were restrained in the same manner and he tightened a strap around her middle.

Kate lifted her head and regarded her surroundings, noting the gathering of eager voyeurs.

Steve gripped her hips and pulled her toward him until the bench edge was at her pelvis. She attempted to wiggle back up the table but Steve swatted her backside. "Unh-uh, pet. Stay where I put you."

He ran his hands down her back, caressing, soothing. "Relax, pet. And breathe. I don't want you passing out on me."

But he was going through the motions, relying on a routine he'd delivered more times than he could remember. Tonight, however, he couldn't summon the enthusiasm.

He stroked Kate's ass gently, saying the rehearsed words. "You have a lovely ass, pet." He kneaded her cheeks then slapped her buttocks lightly, harder and harder again. Kate gasped. "Easy, pet," he said, rubbing a soothing hand over her reddened flesh. "I'm going to switch to the paddle. Give me a color."

Kate didn't answer. Steve squatted beside her and asked, "Are you okay? You may speak freely, Kate."

"Uh—um, I'm nervous. Will it hurt?"

He placed a reassuring hand on her shoulder. "Yes, it will hurt. But I will find your limit and then back off."

"Okay, Sir. I was thinking yellow but I'm still green. Go ahead."

He alternated, five swats, then his hand gently rubbed her enflamed pink buttocks. The crack of the paddle hitting flesh and the grunts coming from his little subbie usually excited him, but tonight it didn't even slightly stir him. He'd have to fake it.

Chapter 31

The sweet smell filling her nostrils made Laura queasy. Blindfolded and gagged, she struggled to discover her surroundings. Spread eagle, her hands and feet bound to metal, she yanked at the restraints, wiggling her torso, but her appendages wouldn't budge. At least she still had her clothes on.

She focused on slowing her breathing, inhaling deeply through her nose, then exhaling slowly. She remembered that monster in her house. Sitting in the same chair she sat in the night Steve came over. *Steve...* Damn, if she'd gone to the club with him as originally planned this never would have happened.

"Well, well, look who's finally awake. I must have over-dosed you." Viktor reached down and ripped the duct tape off her mouth. The sting burned her lips. "Scream if you want, no one will hear." He removed the blindfold and she blinked her eyes incessantly, struggling to focus on her captor. Her eyelids felt stuck together and she struggled to open them. Her vision blurry, she sensed daylight. What time was it? How long had she been out? Was it still Saturday? Probably not, the sun too bright, definitely daylight. She'd missed her date with Chris. Would he sound an alarm? Probably not, he'd most likely assume she stood him up. Who else might discover her abduction? The obvious answer? *No one.* Unlike Steve, she had no one who'd worry if they hadn't heard from her in a specific amount of time. Not until Monday morning when she was a no-show at the office.

The room came into view. What the fuck? Tied up in her own bedroom?

"You bastard." Laura growled. "I'm going to kill you." Her head pounded like she'd been belted with a sledgehammer. Oh, yeah, she kinda had, as she recalled slamming her head against that friggin' owl in the den. Maybe she had a concussion.

Viktor snorted. "Not likely," he said, sitting beside her on the bed. "I've been waiting for this moment for a long time. To have you all to myself to do with as I please." His hand landed on her stomach and he slid it under her sweater, tapping her flesh.

"Take your hands off me," she muttered.

"Oh, pet, I've only just begun. We are going to have so much fun and then we're taking a trip. Somewhere they'll never find you and you'll be mine to torture till the end of days."

Laura recoiled at the familiar moniker, one that she now realized was commonly used by the Doms at the club. Unfortunately, Viktor filled the bill. He was a Dom, only a sadistic and cruel one. He continued his assault, running his hand upward, rubbing her breast, seeking out a nipple. Laura grimaced, biting her tongue until she tasted blood, cringing at his vile touch. Her entire body clenched, her muscles taut, adrenaline fueling her rage. She wrenched her torso sideways in an attempt to escape his probing fingers. His crooked smile unnerved her as her mind drifted to the sordid possibilities of her captivity.

"I need a drink." A bottle of vodka sat on the bedside table. Viktor placed the opening against his lips and took a long swig, then wiped his mouth with the back of his hand. "I'd offer you some but I don't want your senses dulled for what I have in mind. I had intended on bringing you back to my little hideaway but then I figured why not enjoy your lovely body right here, in the comfort of your own home." Viktor sighed. He needed his toy bag. It was a short walk back to the van and he'd secure her tightly until he returned.

However, he'd start his torment now. "Lucky for you I just happen to have my toy bag." He sat beside her again and ran a hand over her breast. "I think a spreader bar is in order, to keep you open and ready for my use. And I want to whip you. The bloody stripes will be my signature on your perfect skin. Mmm, so many choices." He gulped more vodka then replaced the bottle on the table.

Laura was reasonably confident that was *her* vodka and remembered the bottle being full, not half empty. Hopefully, he was shitfaced.

She wasn't sure what a spreader bar was, but it didn't sound good. And whipping? A shudder wracked her and she closed her eyes. Stay in the moment. Focus.

"I've explored your house and I'm especially fond of your basement. So much like a dungeon."

The house was old and Laura spent little time in the dark and dreary cellar. Occasionally she had to accompany a repair man down there to service the furnace or water heater, but Viktor was right, the space was creepy, complete with cobwebs and a maze of overhead pipes and unsettling creaks and groans.

If he planned on taking her to the basement, then he'd have to untie her. That would be her chance. She'd have to be bold and quick, mustering all her strength to overpower him. If he kept drinking, he'd be right about dulled senses, only it would be *his*. The second he cut her loose she'd pounce and beat the living shit right out of him. But right now, her bladder was about to burst.

Steve slept late Sunday. He rolled over, reaching for Laura but his arm fell upon a cold pillow. She'd only slept here twice. Why did it feel like she'd been here forever? He'd treated her terribly Friday night. And then he'd sulked all day Saturday. She had every right to date someone. A real friend would call her and see how the date went. Listen, and not give any opinion or advice, just listen.

But then Colin had emotionally punched him in the gut and he promised to confess his feelings to Laura. Probably best to do it in person. Maybe he should drive to her house and throw himself at her feet. Hmm. That is the complete opposite of being a Dom. She should kneel at his feet. However, that felt wrong, too.

And what if she had a fabulous time on her date, and she slept with the guy and couldn't wait to see him again? "Oh God," Steve muttered, rubbing the back of his neck, his thoughts in a jumble.

Dragging himself from the warm covers he pulled on sweat pants, a tee, and hooded sweatshirt, then headed into the kitchen to make coffee. Six inches of snow blanketed his yard. He groaned. He hadn't expected snowfall overnight. How long would it take Cal to plow his driveway on a Sunday?

The whir of a snow blower turned his head and he went to the living room window to investigate. Seriously? Cal? And just when he'd badmouthed the guy. Cal waved a hearty hello and Steve returned it.

Steve watched impatiently as the coffeemaker dripped the dark roasted aromatic brew into his mug, his lackluster performance at the club last night a vivid memory. He'd made his best effort but feared he hadn't shown Kate a good time. He'd have to make it up to her when he got his head back in the game, maybe Kate would be there this evening. Although he wasn't sure he was up to it. He told Jack he'd work a shift tonight in lieu of the hours he'd blown off. The club was busy on Sundays, everyone's last chance before the workweek began anew.

Most Sunday mornings he'd drive to the local deli for an egg sandwich, but the idea of trudging out into the snow put him off, and he scarfed down two bowls of cereal instead.

Finishing his second cup of coffee he switched on the TV. The Giants were playing the Cowboys at one, this win important if they wanted to make the playoffs. He should break down and call Laura, unsure as to what he'd say. It would probably depend on what she said. He sucked in a breath, lowered the volume on the television, gulped the last swig of his coffee and dialed her.

Voicemail. He groaned. Was she still at the guy's house? The idea of Laura having sex with that guy, them languishing in bed on a cold snowy Sunday morning, threatened to be his undoing.

Several attempts later, interspersed with texts, he finally left a voice message. Could she please let him know she was okay?

Should he call Alyx to track her down? Again?

Oblivious to the game, he crossed and uncrossed his legs, fidgeting as if he sat on a pile of brambles. Although his protective instinct was probably unnecessary, she *was* an FBI agent and could take care of herself.

His phone rang, startling him out of his misery. He blurted, "Laura?"

"Ah no," a bewildered voice said. "Lieutenant? We just got a tip on a possible sighting of Victor. The guy says there's someone squatting in an old duck-hunting cabin in the back-woods on his property. Shall we send out an officer to take his statement? Look around?"

Steve sat up straight. "Have whoever is out on patrol meet me at the guy's house. No interviews until I get there."

"Yes, sir. Will do. I'll text you the guy's name and address."

Steve dialed Laura's number but it went to voicemail again. He cleared his throat in an effort to sound professional and left Laura a message about the tip on Viktor. Then he backed it up with a text: "Call me. It's work."

A police cruiser sat parked outside the small house, complete with front porch and two white rocking chairs. Snow drifts from the recent storm snuggled to the sides of the house, making it appear a cozy cottage you'd find on a Christmas card. Two officers exited the vehicle as Steve descended from his. "Afternoon, Lieutenant," the female officer said. The other tipped his cap.

"Jessica, Bob, thanks for meeting me here. So, the witness' name is Ralph Singer, correct?"

"Yes, sir," Jessica said, pulling a pad from her leather jacket. She consulted her notes: "According to the dispatcher, Mr. Singer reported that his daughter's cat got out two nights ago and he went looking for it. Apparently there's an old duck-hunting cabin about a half-mile into the woods. His grandfa-ther built it but since he's not a hunter it's fallen into ruin. He indicated that kids sometimes hang out there and drink or smoke pot. There's another way in from a lover's lane spot that connects to the road just east of here. It's a dead end, but if you walk in about fifty yards, there's a stream. If you follow the stream it leads directly to the cabin."

"Okay," Steve said, "let's talk to the guy."

Before they could knock, the door opened and a short, bald man met them, probably in his fifties. "Officers," he said. "Come on in."

A savory aroma reminded Steve that he'd skipped Sunday dinner again. And he hadn't even called to let his parents know he was a no-show. "Detective Lieutenant Steve Moretti," he said, displaying his badge and ID.

"Ralph Singer." Ralph offered his hand and they shook. A thin woman with graying hair emerged from the kitchen, wiping her hands on an apron. A young girl, hugging a black-and-brown-spotted white cat trailed her. A small feline, probably still a kitten.

"Jane Singer," the woman said, offering her hand as well.

"Detective Moretti," Steve said, shaking hands.

"Please, sit," Mrs. Singer said. The officers sat alongside Steve on the gray-and-white striped couch and the Singers descended into opposing black leather recliners. The girl sat on the floor, legs crossed, the kitten cuddled in her lap. "Can I get you something to drink? Coffee?"

"No, thank you, Mrs. Singer. We just came to take your statement and then we need to investigate."

"Of course," she said, resting her hands on her thighs.

Steve reiterated the information Jessica had offered. Ralph Singer confirmed the details, then added, "It was dark and I didn't have much hope of finding the cat but I took a flashlight and ventured into the woods. When I reached the cabin I noticed footprints in the snow. At first I figured it was probably the usual teenagers having some fun but then it seemed like someone had been camping there. I thought it odd since the weather has been so cold and snowy. A guy would freeze to death if he squatted there. There is a fireplace. When I saw the generator, it made me think somebody has settled in for a bit."

Mr. Singer inhaled before continuing, rubbing his hands on his baggy, well-worn jeans. "I didn't think much of it until I spoke to my wife. She reminded me that the guy who kidnapped those girls and that poor nun is still on the loose." He shook his head. "Sad day that someone could do that shit to a nun, and those teenagers too." He sighed. "Sorry about the language. It just makes me insane that there are perverts like that out there." His gaze fell to his daughter and Steve imagined Mr. Singer envisioning his daughter in the hands of a slave-trafficker.

"When exactly did you make this discovery?" Steve said.

"Friday night about 8:30. Sorry it took us so long to make the call. We just didn't put it together until this morning."

"Thank you for the information. We haven't had a lead in days and let's hope this pays off." Steve rose and his officers along with him.

"Let me get my coat and I'll show you where the path begins. It'll be tough going with the recent snow."

Chapter 32

The wait over, Victor needed to sample the goods now. After a little playtime, he'd pack his subbie into the stolen vehicle he'd parked on the adjacent street.

Checking to make sure Laura had no chance of escape, he was about to place another strip of duct tape across her lovely full lips. Laura jerked her head sideways and thrashed. "Stop, please, I need the bathroom."

She *had* been unconscious for many hours; but setting the well-trained agent free, even for a minute, was dangerous. However, something tugged at his emotions. Viktor thought of his mother and the filth she probably lived in, no one to attend to her personal needs in that decrepit institution. He hesitated then said, "One minute and no funny business."

Pulling the knife he had tucked into his waistband, he cut the ties binding her to the bed and yanked her up by her hair. He dragged her to the adjacent bathroom and shoved her inside. Laura fell forward her hands atop the toilet preventing a fall to the tiled floor. "Make it snappy," he said. "And the door stays open." He partially closed it, wedging his foot between the door and the jamb.

Relief. Laura surveyed the room, seeking out anything she could use as a weapon. This might be her only chance for escape. Her razor was one of those prepackaged jobs, no chance of getting the blade, her bath brush too flimsy. She tugged at the metal towel bar hoping to free it. Viktor pushed the door open and grabbed her by the upper arms, lifted her off her feet and threw her forcefully on the bed, pinning her with his knee to her chest. She struggled to free a limb, kicking and screaming but he sat on her, immobilizing her lower body and quickly bound a hand to the bed frame with a zip tie. She pummeled him with her other hand, but to no avail. He grabbed it and secured it with a second tie. He moved quickly restraining one ankle and the next, his weight and strength too great. Duct tape sealed her mouth shut, the blindfold plunged her back into darkness. She screamed, a guttural sound threatening to shatter the silver gag.

Viktor laughed. "Patience, my pet. You'll have plenty to scream about when I get back." He caressed the side of her face, his hand drifting downward, stopping at her belly, he reached under her shirt again and slid a hand into her bra. The warmth of her flesh excited him. He'd spent so many nights these past weeks thwarting the cold, but now he would devour her heat, his desire for her a force that threatened to consume him.

"Back soon, my pet. You just lie here and think about what delectable torture awaits you." He left her tied to her bed, locked the doors and got behind the wheel of her government issued sedan. It gave him a perverse pleasure to be driving an FBI vehicle. Stupid Feds, if they only knew that he'd captured one of their prize agents and what he'd do to her to exact his revenge. He fondled his cock with satisfaction.

"Sunset is in about forty minutes, we'll need light," Steve said. "Let's load up." Steve and the officers each pulled .388 caliber sniper rifles from their car trunks and attached SureFire X300 weapon lights to the sights, then grabbed their tactical flashlights with high beam strobes. They slipped into their Kevlar vests. "Let's go," Steve ordered.

Ralph Singer stood at the forest's edge and the officers approached. "Start here and head due east. The path is cleared so you should be able to stay on it if you keep track of the underbrush."

"Thanks again," Steve said.

"Good luck."

The crusty snow under their boots made walking difficult and low-hanging boughs forced them to duck often. They trod down the covered trail and about fifteen minutes in, Jessica said, "There, I see it."

The silhouette of a shack came into view. Bob said, "Don't hear a generator or see any smoke. He's probably not here."

"Let's spread out. Jessica, you go left and Bob, right. Circle around back. I'll come in from this direction." Both officers nodded and fanned out. Steve wished Laura was here. Where the hell was she?

Steve approached the small four-paned window from the side and ventured a peek. A one-room structure, about the size of a small studio apartment in the city. He spied a table with two wooden chairs and a cot with a sleeping bag atop. Jessica faced him in the opposite window and he gave a wave to indicate they should enter.

Inside, they found a small gas generator. Bob reached down and touched it. "Cold." They searched the primitive cabinetry and found some canned foodstuffs, along with a one-burner propane stove.

"There's an old latrine out back," Jessica said. "Not much in the way of plumbing. It would've been a rough go out here these past few weeks."

Steve nodded. "It's obvious he hasn't been here today, the snow is undisturbed except for animal tracks."

"Should we call in CSI?" Bob said.

"No," Steve said. "Don't think we'll get much evidence to help us find him. Let's head toward that lover's lane access. Maybe we can find evidence of the car."

Jessica rubbed her chin. "What I don't get is why the guy is still in the area? What's he hanging around for? If I was him I'd be long gone."

Steve had to admit he'd had the same thought. Viktor had to know they were on the hunt for him. What was so important that he'd risk being spotted and eventually captured?

"Singer said to follow the stream to the left and we'd arrive at the dead-end. Let's go," Steve ordered.

They continued their trek in the darkened snow-covered woods, the light from a full moon aiding in navigating the terrain. Twenty minutes later they stood in front of the octagonal yellow sign that announced 'DEAD END'. No vehicle, and the snow nixed any possibility of finding tire tracks.

The fall of footsteps on the stairs alerted Laura to Viktor's return. It couldn't have been more than a half hour. Her futile attempt to wriggle free had tired her, her wrists burned raw from the struggle. She sensed him looming over her.

"Time for some fun," he exclaimed. "I've waited so long to hear your shrieks as I take my pleasure in your pain."

Desperation frenzied her. Was there anyone who would deduce that she had been kidnapped? It was Sunday and she had no commitments that would arouse anyone's suspicions.

Not until she failed to show for work and by then Viktor had threatened to have her long gone. Probably taking her across state lines, or worse, out of the country. If he had arranged to transport her back to Russia, the chances of her being freed proved dismal.

Viktor removed Laura's blindfold and once again she struggled to regain her vision. When his face came into view, her stomach roiled at the sadistic grin.

He held a metal bar with shackles attached. What the hell was that for? He sat on the bed then reached for her jean zipper, sliding it down. He pulled the knife from his back pocket and slit the denim down both legs and yanked the shredded garment out from under her and threw it on the floor. He snaked his index finger inside the leg of her panties and gave a tug. "I'll rip these off you last."

Oh God. She had to focus on overpowering him. Don't succumb to the fear. Like she had with her stepfather. She wouldn't be a victim again. Never.

Viktor rested the metal bar between her legs then slit the right zip tie binding her leg. She kicked and wriggled, hoping to land a blow to his head. His strength surprised and over-whelmed her, threatening her confidence at the idea of taking him out. He buckled her ankle into the manacle, doing the same with the other leg. Her ankles were chained about twelve inches apart, yet she could see that one end of the bar inserted into the other, which meant he could lengthen it to a wider breadth.

"Off to the dungeon, my pet," he said. He unbound her hands but quickly restrained her wrists with duct tape, then secured her upper arms against her chest with more tape.

He threw her over his shoulder, but stumbled, righting himself with a hand against the wall. Drunk, she hoped. He quickly straightened and marched down the stairs.

Laura's optimism faded fast. Steve… where are you?

Chapter 33

Another dead end… at an *actual* dead end. Steve's patience was gone. Not a good mood to be in for his shift at the club tonight. Where the hell was Laura? He called her for about the hundredth time, still no response. Frustration creased his brow and he called Alyx next, punching the speakerphone icon, while he shed his clothes. He needed to redress quickly if he was going to make it to the club on time.

"Hi, Steve. What's up?"

"Alyx, sorry to bother you at home again, but I've been trying to reach Laura."

"I haven't talked to her since she left yesterday and she was going out on a—"

He imagined Alyx biting her fingernail on the other side of the call. "It's okay. I know about the date."

"Oh. Honestly, I'm not sure what's going on with you two and I don't think either of you do either."

Alyx was probably right in her assessment. He needed to talk with Laura and explain that he had feelings for her. Be his 'true self' as Laura said. "I've been phoning her all day and left like ten texts but I haven't heard back. It's not like her not to answer my calls. If I didn't know she was out with an FBI dude, I'd be worried."

"It is odd that she hasn't responded. Let me try her and I'll get right back to you."

"Thanks. I appreciate it, Alyx."

Steve drove too fast, even for a cop, determined to arrive at the club on time. The place was packed, hardly a space left on the dance floor. He wove his way through the mob of scantily clad patrons, the overwhelming musky scent like a fetid invisible cloud stealing away his breath. He made a beeline for the bar. Glancing at the clientele hanging on the bar top, he prayed Kate wasn't here. He'd make it up to her, just not tonight.

Steve headed into the office to stow his weapon and check paperwork for new clients, wishing he had a scotch in hand. Drinking was probably a bad idea, his patience on a hair trigger, stringently coiled like a cobra ready to strike. He penciled some notes on a new file, then moved to the next.

The office door opened. "Hey, buddy," Colin said. He slumped into the seat in front of the desk and folded his arms on the desktop. "You talk to Laura yet?"

"No," Steve said without looking up.

"Why not?"

"Because I can't fucking find her, that's why."

"What do you mean, you can't find her? You're a cop."

"What the fuck do you think it means? I've called her like fifty times and she won't pick up."

"Whoa, don't take it out on me, man." Colin sat back in his chair and crossed one brown wing-tipped clad foot over a thigh.

"Sorry. I don't know whether she's just blowing me off or if there's something wrong."

"Why would she blow you off?"

Steve picked up the stack of folders and straightened them on the desktop. "Maybe she had a great time on her date and she's still with the guy. I'm just a memory."

"Trust me, dude, women have long memories. I doubt she's forgotten you already."

Steve rose, stowing the files in the allotted cabinet, then shrugged out of his holstered weapon and walked toward the safe. He punched in the code and opened the green metal door, placing his weapon on the shelf.

"On the other hand, maybe she is in trouble. You've always had that sixth sense. Remember the time that kid on your street got lost? What was his name?"

"Billy."

"Yeah, and it was like you had ESP or something. You knew right where to look for him. Back in that old quarry, the one where they took the sand to build the Verrazano Bridge."

"Not much ESP involved. All the kids used to build ramps there and jump their bikes."

"Yeah, but still, the sight of you with him in your arms melted every mother's heart that night. You were a friggin' hero. Made the cops look bad."

Steve didn't say anything. Hero was way too big a word.

"And that's not the only rescue you've pulled off. Should I recite them for you?"

"No. I'm just concerned with Laura and where she could be."

His phone rang, startling him. *Laura?*

His shoulders slumped when Alyx's name appeared on the screen. "Did you get her?"

"I didn't, and I even went as far as calling her date." Silence, too long a silence.

"And?"

"He said she stood him up."

Steve gripped the back of the office chair with one hand,

hard enough to turn his knuckles white. "Now I'm seriously worried. Where the hell could she be?"

"That makes two of us. I'm sending the locals over to check her house."

"News?" Colin said.

"Laura never made it to her date last night." Steve dragged his hands down his face and sighed heavily. His temper flared and he kicked the chair hard enough that it sailed into the sidewall, denting the sheetrock.

Colin stood. "Whoa, buddy, get a grip. You won't be any good to her if you lose your shit."

The office door opened. "What the hell is going on?" Jack said.

Colin brought Jack up to speed, ending with, "Steve, maybe you should leave. You're not going to be any good working with subs tonight."

"I agree," Jack said. "Go do whatever detectives do and find her."

"She lives in Muttontown. It'll take me two hours to drive to her house."

"Take my chopper," Colin said. Colin used his private helicopter to travel back and forth between the club and his Manhattan penthouse. Steve had ridden in it twice, both times on leisure outings. "My driver is in the lot and the chopper is at the East Hampton heliport. The pilot is on standby. He'll get you there in under thirty minutes."

Unsure if he was overreacting, Steve hesitated. He should probably wait for Alyx's call before jumping into panic mode. Who was he kidding? He was already there. Dread choked his throat. Something was wrong, terribly wrong. And he needed to find Laura now.

"Okay," he finally said. "Thanks, Colin. I'll take you up on your offer."

Viktor slung Laura over his shoulder, hands and feet bound, on his way to the basement for some playtime before they ventured out. He wasn't stupid enough to make her mobile. Although not a large woman, he had no doubt she could be lethal and he wouldn't give her the opportunity to get the upper hand. At the bottom of the stairs he stopped. Gravel crunching in the driveway caught his attention and he glimpsed oncoming headlights through the front windows. "Shit," he said. "Motherfucking cops."

Hiding in the cellar was his only option. Luckily he'd scoped it out in anticipation of using it in lieu of a dungeon. Having been at her house for so many hours he'd had plenty of time to explore the nooks and crannies and to his delight he'd discovered an old wine cellar. It had a secret door that no one would notice if they hadn't taken the time to study the layout. The square footage of the basement was under represented if you took the first floor into consideration. It meant that half the house would have no basement and that didn't ring true. His curiosity piqued, it took some time, but eventually he found the hidden latch. She had a good stash of wine in there, but the layers of dust told him that she didn't venture inside often.

He flicked the light switch on and hustled down the rickety cellar staircase, the toy bag on one shoulder, his captive wriggling and twisting on the other. He faltered, but quickly righted himself with the aid of the handrail. Traveling the length of the floor, he hit the latch and entered the musty chamber, shutting the door behind him. The pitch black forced him to feel his way deeper inside until he found the string that illuminated a series of three dangling bulbs. He pulled a zip tie from his pocket, propping his little subbie against the wall, he used his penknife to cut the duct tape binding her upper arms to her chest, then secured her arms over her head to the ceiling pipe with the plastic tie.

Laura noticed Viktor's abrupt stop at the bottom of the first floor stairs. Although immobilized and nearly mute, her hearing worked just fine and she swore a car was coming up the driveway. Judging by Viktor's outburst, she must be right. But how in the hell had he found the wine cellar? The hidden entrance invisible to the naked eye. Lots of these old houses had them, leftover from prohibition, when rich people had secret alcohol stockpiles, but how would he know that? Maybe he'd spent enough time in her house waiting for her that he'd discovered it. Unlikely that someone making a precursory search would uncover it.

She screamed as best she could behind the silver tape binding her mouth. Viktor pressed his blade against her neck. "Not a peep, or I'll slit your throat."

Laura despaired, help might be here but they'd never locate her. She had to overpower him. Rescue herself. Tears welled and the salty water dripped down her cheeks. Who was here? Alyx? Steve?

Steve, please let it be you.

Chapter 34

Settled into the back seat of Colin's chauffeured Mercedes, Steve gripped his phone tightly, his hand resting on his thigh. The ringer signaled a call. "Alyx."

"Steve, something's happened. A Detective Sergeant Jackson is at the house. The TV in the den is shattered. They retrieved a bullet. It's a 9 millimeter."

"Fuck," Steve said. Laura's gun used that ammo.

"There's also blood, and what looks like some strands of Laura's hair, on a metal statue near the bar. There's also blood on a pillow in the master bedroom. She may be injured."

"On my way," Steve said. "Be there in less than a half-hour."

"Got it. Meet you there."

After the helicopter touched down, James, another of Colin's drivers picked Steve up in a gleaming black Escalade. He dropped him off in front of Laura's house. "I'll wait right here," James said.

"I might be a while."

"No problem. Mr. Mackenzie has me on retainer."

"Thanks."

A half-dozen cruisers from Nassau County PD crowded the driveway and Steve maneuvered the serpentine path to Laura's front door, which stood ajar.

Several uniformed officers met him as he stepped onto the foyer's black marble floor. He displayed his credentials, introducing himself.

"You'll be wanting to speak to Detective Jackson," a uniformed officer said. "He's in the den with the FBI." Good, Alyx had arrived.

A tall black man, in a green hooded puffer jacket, had his back to him, engaged in conversation with Alyx. The spotlights over the fireplace highlighted his shiny bald head. Alyx caught sight of Steve and waved him over. "How'd you get here so fast?" she said.

"Colin's helicopter."

Alyx's forehead furrowed. "You can pilot a helicopter?"

Steve frowned. "No, of course not. He had a pilot on standby."

"Oh," Alyx said.

The detective had an evidence bag in hand containing a 9-millimeter slug, definitely ammo for a Glock. Steve introduced himself to Sergeant Jackson, informing him that he and Laura had been working a sex-trafficking case together. "That Russian mob case," Detective Jackson said. "Having a bitch of a time finding that perp that got away."

"We've had several leads but nothing's panned out," Steve said. "About at my wit's end."

"I hear you," Detective Jackson said. "The ones that get away haunt you forever."

"This has to be Viktor," Alyx said. "I can't imagine who else it could be."

"Could just be a robbery, or a kidnapping for ransom," Detective Jackson said.

"There's nobody to pay ransom," Steve explained. "She has no relatives."

Detective Jackson waved his hand around the room. "It's obvious she's got money. Nobody lives on this street without serious wealth."

"Understood," Alyx said, "but she'd have to get the funds herself. No one else has access to her money."

"I'll have some guys check her account, see about any large withdrawals or if she's been spotted at her bank," Detective Jackson said.

"Good idea," Steve said. His head pounded and he pinched the bridge of his nose. "You know... for weeks now, I've been asking myself why the perp is still in the area. What's keeping him here? What does he want? I figured he'd be long gone by now." Steve exhaled slowly, his hands on his hips. "I think it's Laura he's been after all along."

"Damn," Alyx said "He's targeting her in revenge for stealing his merchandise."

"Yeah, I think so."

"If that's the case then he's intent on taking out his anger on her. Physically. Oh God. He'll torture her and then kill her." Alyx put a hand over her mouth.

Steve had the details of Alyx's capture and the torment she'd endured at the hands of her kidnappers. The perverted motherfuckers had caned her. He paled at what this guy would do to Laura.

"Have you searched the entire house?" Steve asked Detective Jackson.

"Top to bottom. Nothing askew outside of this room and the blood on the pillow in the master bedroom."

"Her car?"

"In the garage. Engine warm. Tire tracks in the snow showing the vehicle left and reentered the garage fairly recently. Which means she drove it in the last hour or so."

"That doesn't jive. No one's been able to reach her in over twenty-four hours. She'd have answered her phone if she was out and about."

"Maybe she lost her phone," Detective Jackson said.

"Something feels wrong." Steve rubbed the back of his neck. "There are no physical signs of a break-in?"

"No, either the perp knew the alarm code or she let him in."

"I'm gonna take a look around," Steve said to the detective.

"Have at it," Detective Jackson said.

Steve wandered the first floor but Jackson was right, other than the den, everything seemed in order. He climbed the stairs and entered her bedroom. The bedcovers were askew, a bloodstain on the pillow. The room wasn't feminine, a navy and white motif, nothing frilly, and without the annoying pile of throw pillows on a woman's bed. The oak furniture gave the room warmth, antique for sure, adorned with carved inlays and shiny brass handles. He went to her closet and surveyed the contents, the scent of her fragrance in the air. The closet appeared full, not like someone had packed to go somewhere. He briefly rummaged through the contents of her armoire and remaining bedroom furniture, her nightstands, and found nothing unusual. The lacy undergarments in her top dresser drawer caught his attention but he didn't touch anything. That felt wrong. He surveyed her bathroom, neat and tidy, no signs of trouble.

Steve roamed the other rooms, eight additional bedrooms with adjoining baths, but again nothing appeared disturbed.

Alyx and the detective were in the same place he left them. "What about the basement? Somebody checked it?" Steve said.

"Yeah, it's a typical basement for an old house. Lots of cobwebs, exposed pipes, water heater, furnace. An old work bench." Detective Jackson appeared weary. Steve figured he wasn't all that thrilled at being called out this late on a Sunday. "Anything else I can do for either of you?"

Alyx shook her head.

"No," Steve said. "Let us know if your forensics team finds anything useful."

"Will do," Detective Sergeant Jackson said. "They're just about finished."

All police personnel having left the scene, Alyx and Steve were alone. They stared at each other. Alyx said, rubbing her forehead, "I don't know what else we can do."

Steve stared out the bay window; the snow sparkled in the moonlight. "She could be anywhere by now. If there's no contact at the bank, I'm at a loss."

"I set up roadblocks at all exit points off Long Island and insisted every vehicle be searched, trunks and cargo. Also, the ferry terminals at Orient Point and Port Jeff."

"Good thinking," Steve said. "But if she was taken when she arrived home from your place yesterday, it's already too late."

"I know," Alyx said, "but then who drove her car?"

"I'm stumped."

Alyx sighed. "If I find that bastard I'll kill him."

"You're preaching to the choir."

Alyx put a reassuring hand on Steve's arm. "I'm heading back to the office. Maybe something will come in. I'll be there all night. Keep in touch."

"I will." Steve watched Alyx walk down the long driveway to her car parked near the roadway. He sat on the living room couch and hung his head in his hands. He didn't know where to go, what to do, but doing nothing wasn't an option. Eventually he rose and made his way to the waiting Escalade. He reached for the handle, then froze. His chest tightened, his pulse accelerated rapidly. If he lost Laura, he'd lose his mind. He'd gone into clinical depression when Tony got killed.

That night had been hot and humid and Steve almost didn't wear his vest. They'd been tracking a major dealer, a gang member and one nasty dude. Tony called him and said one of his informants told him a major buy was going down at the abandoned headquarters for the old Grumman Corporation in Calverton, the same place where Alyx cracked her trafficking case. The campus had several large buildings, airplane hangars and enormous warehouses where they'd manufactured jet engines. Located in an isolated area it had been the site of several unsavory dealings over the years. Steve wished someone would raze the skeleton site.

His heart pounded as if it would burst out of his chest, and he leaned over, trying to get his equilibrium. When Tony got shot, it was like the bullet traveled in slow motion. The round had hit him in the neck, pierced his carotid artery. Blood exploded, a geyser spewing Tony's lifeblood onto the cracked pavement. The suspects ran and he drew his weapon and fired, reasonably sure he hit one of them. He chased after the small posse but they outran him and escaped in a waiting car. He returned to Tony's side and used his shirt to put pressure on the wound, yet the life force drained out of him in less than a minute.

An arm touched his shoulder. "You okay, sir?" James said. He reached under Steve's arm and supported his weight before he slumped to the ground.

"Yeah, just need a minute."

James opened the back door of the car and eased Steve into the seat. "Put your head between your knees."

Steve complied. But now he felt like an ass. The flashback of Tony's death terrified him. If Laura was dead, he didn't know how he'd cope. He'd never gotten the chance to confess his love. Or know what a life with her would be like.

He straightened his back and inhaled deeply. "I'm okay," he told James. "Give me a few minutes and we can leave."

"Sure thing, sir."

Where could Laura be? Where would Viktor take her if he wanted to exact his pound of flesh? It wouldn't be the cabin. Maybe a local motel. Or— Steve was on his feet and jogging up the driveway. He'd searched every inch of the house himself, except for *the basement.*

Chapter 35

Voices and footsteps, gone. Alone with Viktor. Fight or flight, fight or flight. Not much time. If he put her in the trunk of the car, escape would be tricky, although she knew where the release lever was. If he stopped the car for any reason, she might be able to make a run for it.

The knife still against her neck, a prick of pain, blood trickled down her throat. She worried that the close call could amplify Viktor's psychotic tendencies. He'd need relief and she'd be the object.

His breath on her nape, he whispered, "Close call, little pet. I bet you thought you'd be rescued. Probably that cop you've been screwing."

Steve was on this maniac's radar? *Holy shit!* Viktor had targeted Steve on the highway that day. He'd nearly killed him.

"The detective won't be fucking you again, or riding in on a horse to save the day."

He'd been following her, and Steve. All those times when she'd had the feeling someone was watching her, well, *wow*. If only, but too late, she was on her own. "I'm taking you down, sicko, even if it's with my last breath."

Viktor licked his lips. "You overestimate yourself, pet."

Her arms stretched high, Laura's bare feet stood on tiptoes. Viktor reached between her legs and opened the nut on the bolt, spreading the ankle bar to a length of about two feet. "Time for new experiences before our little trip."

He dragged his dagger across her collarbone, then over the white angora covering her torso. The blade grazed the skin on her belly, lingering over her navel, then pierced the soft fabric. He forced the knife upward and slit her sweater to the neck. Cutting and ripping, the garment fell to the ground, leaving her clad in underwear.

Oh God. At the end of her tether.

Calloused fingers stroked her skin, his mouth landed on her shoulder and he bit down hard. Laura clenched her teeth, unwilling to give him any satisfaction. "Good enough to eat," he said. His crooked smile reminded her of a monster in some sordid fairytale. She shut her eyes to banish the horrid image and sucked in a deep breath, slowly exhaling. Focus. Think.

Opening her eyes she spied Viktor on his knees. He unzipped his bag and pulled out a cat-of-nine tails. He removed a string of beads from his neck, kissed them and tucked them into the bag. Rosary beads? He prayed?

He rose and faced her, his back only inches from the wooden shelving laden with wine. "We need to release some tension." He cracked the whip several times. "I know how."

Laura flinched.

This was it.

Now or never.

If she didn't immobilize him, his retaliation would prove violent and probably lethal.

She gripped the overhead pipe with both hands and did a chin-up. Knees into her chest, she thrust her heels out. The metal ankle bar slammed into his windpipe, smashing him against the wine racks.

He grunted and dropped the whip, eyes bulging like a giant toad. His fist slammed into her nose, snapping her head back, her ears ringing, her skull thundering with terror. His massive hands circled her neck, squeezing, choking. His thumb on her jugular meant she had only five seconds before unconsciousness hit. Sparks dotted her vision. Pressure built inside her face. A circle of light in her mind grew small, smaller.

Underwater… drifting toward the bottom of an ocean.

Viktor slapped her face. She surfaced, her eyes shot open. Her gaze locked to his. "Don't pass out on me, bitch. This is just part of the fun."

Laura tried to breathe, but air wouldn't enter or leave her lungs, and yet adrenaline flooded her veins. She wheezed in a breath. Uttering a primal scream, she heaved her shoulder into his chest using all her weight. The shelf's edge forced his head forward, bones cracked.

In a rasp, she said, "Take that, you bastard."

A sickly gurgle crossed his lips and blood oozed from his mouth. She pressed with all her might and more bones crunched. His head tilted left and fell forward, his chin resting on his chest. She held it in place for what seemed an eternity, until she'd convinced herself he was finally burning in Hell.

Slowly releasing the bar, she pulled back and his limp body slumped to the floor.

She closed her eyes, and dropped her chin, exhausted, fire zigzagging through every muscle.

Tears flowed freely, traveling down her face and onto her chest. A sob erupted, followed by a keening she'd never made before.

"Laura? Laur-r-r-a!"

Steve? "In here, in here!" she screamed. "To the left, there's a latch at the end of the wall. Behind the light fixture."

The door creaked and a familiar hand yanked it fully open. Steve's handsome face appeared in the entranceway, marred by fright.

"Jesus! Laura!" Steve moved quickly, giving Viktor a cursory glance, using the discarded knife to free her hands from the overhead pipe. He eased her to the ground, her legs still trapped by the bar. "Damn, a spreader bar?"

"Is that what it's called?"

"Where are the keys?"

"Check the bag."

He picked up the whip. "He didn't get a chance to use this, did he?"

"Almost, but no."

Steve threw the torture implement to the ground as if it'd suddenly burst into flames, then rooted around and came up with a set of small keys. He released her ankles and stood her upright. "You're bleeding."

"Asshole punched me in the face," she said. Touching her nose, her fingers came back red.

Steve hugged her so tightly she feared she'd break. She wrapped her arms around his neck and buried her face in his shoulder, crying her fucking heart out. Her body shook and shivered as the panic slowly dissipated. He whispered, "I thought I'd lost you."

"I thought I was a goner," she sputtered.

Movement. A groan. A hand clutched her ankle.

"Son-of-a-bitch!" she spat.

Steve pivoted but Viktor bolted upward and smashed a wine bottle over his head, hurtling him into the wall. Steve's knees buckled, falling forward. Viktor wielded the knife, his devil-crazed eyes yellowed and bloodshot. Laura seized his blade-laden hand and leveled a right hook to Viktor's jaw. He careened backward, lost his balance, collapsed. Laura sprang on him, straddling his hips, pinning him. Frenzied, blinded by rage, she punched his face over and over, pummeling him until his own mother wouldn't recognize his mangled features. The vodka bottle lay on the floor, just within reach. Laura snatched it and cracked him in the head. Fragments flew but the largest lodged in Viktor's forehead.

Steve gripped her wrist. "Enough," he shouted. She wrenched her hand to free it, but he held her fast. "He's down, he's dead."

Queasiness roiled her gut and bile spewed into her throat. Laura struggled to back off, panting. "He's not! Not!"

Steve placed two fingers at Viktor's neck. "No pulse. It's over. Promise."

Laura sat her full weight on Viktor's body, her shoulders sagging, her raw and bloodied hands at her side. Her dead stepfather's face flickered behind her eyes, an old worn-out picture. "They never die inside my head. They always come back."

"I'm here now," Steve assured her, slipping his hands under her armpits and heaving her up. He removed his coat and eased Laura into it, hugging her close. "You're not alone."

They stayed like that for several shaky interludes, until Steve gently pushed her back, holding her at arm's length. He studied her. "I'm serious. I've got you. And it's probably insane for me to bring this up but... I've been trying to find you for two fucking days to tell you that I lost my mind when you said you were going on a date."

Steve's sad eyes pricked her heart. "I know. I felt terrible. But I thought that's what you wanted."

"I thought I did, originally, but I want you all to myself."

Laura narrowed her eyes. "What are you saying?"

"I love you. I love you with all my heart and I never want to be without you ever again."

Steve's heart pounded, but this time it wasn't terror. It was love. He put Laura's arm around his neck then scooped her up by the back of her knees. He carried her upstairs and rested her on the couch. He called Detective Jackson to report the dead body, and Alyx as well, then handed the crime scene over to the Nassau County PD.

He wrapped her bloodied knuckles in kitchen towels. "I'm taking you to the hospital to get checked out."

"I'm fine. Not necessary. How's *your* head?"

"Don't change the subject." Steve chucked a finger under her jaw and turned her head. Blood. "Is this why there's blood on that owl statue in the den? Did you hit your head on it?"

Laura reached up and touched the crusty wound. She winced. "Maybe."

He tucked Laura into the back of the black Escalade and checked her into the emergency room. The nurse made him wait outside and he paced. How long did it take to confirm that she was all right?

"Steve." He looked up as Alyx and Daniel entered the waiting room.

"Hey, guys, thanks for coming." Alyx bundled him into a hug and Daniel did too.

Alyx inquired, "How is she? Have you heard anything?"

"No and the waiting is killing me."

"I'll go see what I can find out," Daniel said and disappeared through the swinging doors.

"Why don't we sit," Alyx said, pulling Steve toward a two-seater chair. Steve felt like he'd been awake for a forty-eight-hour shift. He was dog-tired and massaged the back of his neck to ease a sudden crick. Alyx patted his back, then pressed her shoulder into his. "I can't believe we didn't find her in the house. What made you go back in?"

"I'm not sure. Just a feeling. I flashed back to when my partner was killed and, honestly, I lost my shit at the idea of losing Laura. And then I was running up the driveway. I hadn't searched the basement myself and I—I don't know, I just needed to."

"There was a secret door? How did you find it? And more importantly, how did the perp find it?"

"I heard voices but couldn't figure out where they were coming from. I called her name and she answered, telling me where the latch was to the old wine cellar. Laura said that the guy had been in her house long enough to figure out the floor plan upstairs didn't match the basement. He discovered the wine cellar."

"And Viktor was dead when you found her?"

"Not exactly. She was suspended from the ceiling and he had her ankles bound in a spreader bar. She slammed the guy against the wall, crushed his windpipe with the bar. We both thought he was down for the count. But he came to, knocked me over the head with a wine bottle and went on the attack. Laura punched the living shit out of him, literally."

"Damn," Alyx said. "I'm glad the fucker is dead."

"I'll second that."

Daniel emerged and stood in front of them. Steve rose. "What's the verdict?"

"She's in pretty good shape. A concussion, bruises and contusions, mostly around her ankles and wrists from being bound. Some swelling on her face. Nose not broken. They're going to keep her overnight for observation but she should be released tomorrow."

"Thank God," Alyx said.

Steve let out a slow breath and sunk back into his seat.

Daniel said, "Thank Steve, not God."

Chapter 36

"Can I see her?" Steve asked Daniel.

"Sure, come on."

Steve trailed Daniel through the swinging doors. They arrived at a curtain and Daniel opened it to reveal Laura lying on a gurney. She sat propped on pillows, her face wan, her hair a messy tousle. Dark circles underscored her normally vibrant eyes, unhappiness clouding her features. Neither of them had gotten much sleep in the last two days. He guessed Laura didn't sleep much Friday night either.

"Hey, baby, how are you?" Steve neared the bedside and took her hand. The red burn marks on her wrists turned his stomach. Her knuckles bruised and swollen. Her flesh cool, he wanted to gather her in his arms and warm her.

"I think I'll live."

"Glad to hear that. I wasn't so sure a few hours ago," Steve said.

"Me either." Her tears welled and flowed.

Steve wiped them away with his thumb, then bent down and kissed her.

Alyx said, "Why don't we let them have some time?"

"I'm taking her home with me tomorrow," Steve assured them.

"Good," Alyx said. "I'll stop by her house and get some things."

Laura opened her mouth and Steve anticipated resistance to his suggestion, yet no way he'd let her out of his sight. She could protest until the sun came up but he wouldn't give in.

"Don't give me any shit, Laura. You're coming home with me so I can take care of you. We'll figure things out from there."

Laura shut her mouth. Good. Obedient and compliant just like a good little subbie. He laughed.

"What's so funny?" she said.

"Nothing. If I told you, you'd probably kick my ass."

Daniel and Alyx said their goodbyes and Alyx told Laura she'd drop off her things tomorrow on her way home from work.

Steve kept Laura company until she was moved into a room and they both finally agreed that sleep was the order of the night. "I'll be here in the morning to take you home."

"All right. Thanks."

Steve squeezed her hand. "I love you." He leaned in and kissed her, an extended, passionate kiss. Every atom in him wanted to make love to her. He savored the moment when they'd be together again. To relish her soft curves, to caress her delicious skin, to be inside her wet, warm folds.

The kiss ended too soon. Every nerve in Laura's body tingled. She probed Steve's enormous brown eyes with hers, his exceptionally long lashes enhancing his sultry gaze. She loved Steve too but the words sat frozen on her lips.

"You make me happy, Steve. I've never been so happy."

They kissed again, when a voice said, "Time for Agent Logan to get some sleep." A nurse stood at the foot of the bed, arms crossed over her chest.

"Right," Steve said. "I'm going." He gave her a quick peck before exiting.

"That's one fine-looking man," the nurse said, checking Laura's monitor and writing something in her chart.

Laura couldn't help but grin. Even finer without his clothes.

The following morning Steve appeared as promised and shepherded Laura to his home. Each time she'd been here it was on the way to the club and then in the morning, having slept over twice. Laura recalled the night they ate peanut butter sandwiches in the kitchen and snuggled in bed watching bad TV. She gritted her teeth, and the night she'd confronted him about the ring. Ugh. Why hadn't she kept her lips glued together? Had she already been in love with him then? Had the stab of jealousy pierced her, knowing he'd bought a ring for another woman? That he wasn't commitment phobic after all, it's just that he didn't want a relationship with her. But all of that was in the past, they hadn't been truthful with each other and now they could share their raw feelings, be honest enough... to love. No cowards here anymore.

Steve's family saw the news report regarding Viktor's death and he'd fessed up about his feelings for Laura. Both his sisters and his mother offered to drop off food when he indicated Laura would be convalescing at his place, but he told Laura he wasn't about to subject her to his family's onslaught, not yet.

"My mother insists you come for Christmas," Steve said as he cleaned up the dinner dishes. They'd heated up canned chicken soup and made toast, Laura vowing that a trip to the supermarket was in order so she could cook them a proper meal.

Laura kept silent. She loved Steve, but she wasn't sure she

was ready to meet the entire Moretti family. What if they didn't like her? She had no idea how to be a member of a big family. She wasn't much of a hugger, and she imagined the Morettis were a big affectionate clan.

"What's the matter?" Steve asked as he loaded the dishwasher.

"I'm terrified of meeting your family. I've got no skills in that regard."

Steve laughed. "Not to worry, pet. You just jump in with both feet and let the tide take you. You'll see."

Laura leaned her chin on her hands atop the kitchen table. "If you say so."

"I do. And remember, I'm the Dom."

"I like the sound of that. When do you think we can go to the club again?"

Just the notion of taking Laura to the club again gave him a hard-on. "We could go Saturday night if you're feeling up to it."

"I feel fine. I'd like to go and try that *thing*, that restraining thing." Laura's face flushed and Steve's pulse quickened. They hadn't had sex since he'd brought her home.

"But right now I need a shower."

"Excellent, I'll join you."

"Okay," she said, rising.

Steve followed her into his bathroom, excited to show her the pleasures of his exceptionally equipped shower. He turned on the water, setting the jets to moderate.

"Wow, what is this, some kind of water torture?"

"You have no idea, my pet. I will show no mercy until you scream your release."

"Oh my, Sir. Please do."

They stripped out of their clothes and Steve took both her hands in his, rubbing his thumbs over the scrapes on her wrists. She had a matching pair on her ankles. "Do they hurt?"

"Not really."

He kissed her bruised knuckles, one at a time. "We need to get you a set of brass knuckles."

"Very funny. They're illegal."

"Okay, but just thinking about what could have happened is tearing my guts out."

"Well it didn't so let's put all that in the rearview mirror."

"I'm trying." Steve opened the shower door, but froze, his gaze focused on Laura's shoulder. He touched the mark. "Jesus, he bit you?"

Laura fixed her attention on Steve's big brown irises. "Rearview mirror."

Steve steered Laura inside. She squealed as the hot rivulets pelted her body. Steve lathered the loofa with gel and spread the soapy foam over Laura's back. She purred and moaned softly. "This is divine. You're spoiling me."

"I haven't even gotten to the good part yet."

"Mmm."

Appropriately lathered and rinsed, he told Laura, "Sit." He applied gentle pressure on her shoulders guiding her down to the shower bench. "Pull your knees up and apart, your heels on the seat."

Laura gazed up through her wet lashes. "What will you do?"

"No talking, pet, we're in protocol."

"Yes, Sir." She licked her lips and Steve almost put his cock in her mouth.

He unhooked the handheld attachment and pressed the button, releasing a stream of water. "I'm going to make you come with this."

Laura blinked her eyes several times, yet remained silent.

Kneeling in front of her, he aimed the jet between her legs, moving the stream in a circular motion. Laura gasped and moaned, her hands tightly gripping the bench. She thrust her chest out and her head fell back against the black marbled tile. Her body responded to the water pressure with little wiggles. He switched the button so the stream pulsed in little spurts, keeping the pressure on her clit.

Laura's moans became louder and her back arched. Almost there. He was intent on making her climax without touching her. But there would be touching… soon. Laura closed her eyes and a momentary panic seized him. Would eyes closed lead to a panic attack? Hopefully she wouldn't go there again, ever.

He continued the assault on her vagina until she finally screamed her release. The most beautiful sound in the universe. She grabbed his hand forcing the stream away from her body.

"Oh God. That's enough. I can't take any more."

Steve rose and returned his torture implement to its bracket. "Well done, pet."

"Damn. How did you do that?"

"Skill, my dear. I'm a pro, remember?"

"I'll say. But now it's my turn and I don't want any resistance this time."

Steve was unsure what she meant. Laura placed both hands on his buttocks and pulled him forward. Her lips touched the tip of his cock and he groaned with pleasure. She circled the head with her tongue, teasing, taunting, then took him into her mouth.

"Jesus, baby, that's so good." He threaded his fingers through her wet tresses, holding her head in place. She sucked hard and he feared he wouldn't be able to hold out long. "Oh God," he murmured. She alternated, flicking her tongue over the tip with a sucking motion, building a rhythm that hurled him toward ecstasy. His cock hit the back of her throat and he couldn't hold back, but he didn't want to come in her mouth. Not this time.

He pulled her to her feet, pinned her against the wall and yanked up a knee, resting it on his arm. His mouth melded with hers and he plunged his cock in deep. Laura moaned into his mouth. The kiss was deep, passionate, all-consuming. He pressed his chest against hers, then grabbed a breast and pinched the nipple. Laura wrapped her hands around his neck and hugged him tightly, then slid her hands down his back and clasped his ass. She pulled him in deeper, the rhythm building to a crescendo, a song he planned to sing forever.

Reaching down, he pressed her clit with two fingers, pinching, rubbing. Laura screamed, her back arched and her chin thrust upward. "Now," he said, ordering her orgasm. He thrust in one more time, smashing her against the wall. His release, a tsunami of epic proportions. His growl startled him as he poured himself into her. They breathed in perfect harmony, their breaths finally slowing.

They gazed at each other, water dripping down their faces. Laura chuckled and Steve smiled, reveling in her pleasure. "I missed that," she said.

"Me too." They kissed once more, long and languorous.

They settled into bed. More sleep was still needed.

Steve surfed the channels but then Laura reached over and took the remote from his hand. She sat tall and faced him. "I don't want to go home again. I want to sell the house."

Chapter 37

S teve turned off the TV and faced Laura. "You want to live here?"

Laura hesitated. "Maybe I could buy a beach house near Alyx and Daniel. Something for the weekends and vacation days. I have the apartment in Chelsea that I can stay in during the week."

"I won't see you except on the weekends?"

"I don't know. Do you think we're moving too fast?"

"No, I don't." Steve secured both of Laura's hands in his. "I think you love me but you haven't actually said the words."

Laura gulped. All the air got sucked out of the room. "I... I..." She'd never said those words to anyone and never imagined saying it to any man, this man. "Um…"

"It's easy," Steve said. "Just three little words." He raised his eyebrows.

Laura held her breath and on the exhale said, "I do. I love you."

"Then I'm not going to wait another minute to start the rest of my life."

"What are you saying?"

"Marry me."

Oh God. Sure, Steve had said he wanted to be with her forever and that they'd work things out when they got back to his house, but marriage?

"Steve, I love you with all my heart, yet I'm not sure I'm equipped to be a wife. I have no family experience; I don't even know what a family is like. A normal family."

"Somehow, I think you'll be a quick study. And I'll be with you, for every step."

"What about kids? Do you want kids?"

"Yeah, I think I do. I didn't for a long while."

"But I don't know how to be a mother, a good one."

"I disagree. You'll be a wonderful mother, probably one of the best because you know the things *not* to do."

"To hell with caution." Laura laughed. "Yes, yes! My answer is yes!"

Steve circled his arms around her and kissed her until her breath had evaporated. Her chest swelled, filled with his love for her.

"We'll go get a ring tomorrow. My cousin owns a jewelry store."

"Is that the one where you bought the earrings for my birthday?" And probably where he got that other ring. Ouch.

"The same."

"And maybe we can do some shopping. I should bring presents if I'm going to your parents' house for Christmas."

"Deal. We'll stop at Vinny's first thing tomorrow then head to the mall."

For someone who'd committed to eternal bachelorhood just a few short weeks ago, Steve couldn't believe how happy he felt. The love he had for Laura was something he couldn't have imagined, a love so big it filled him up. The world seemed a wonderful place, full of possibilities and amazing adventures. He pictured endless nights with Laura snuggled in his arms, her breath warm on his neck, her legs intertwined with his as they drifted off to dreamland. Jesus, he was turning into a sap, and he loved every second.

"I haven't slept till noon since I was a teenager and Colin and I partied all night on Fire Island," Steve said as they got into his car.

"Well, I've never slept that late, ever. I think you're a bad influence." She punched his shoulder.

"Ow," Steve said, rubbing his arm in mock distress. They both laughed.

They arrived at the jewelry store at two. Vinny stared, wide-eyed, as Steve approached with Laura on his arm. "Hey, Vin, this is Laura."

"Nice to meet you." Vinny's eyes darted back and forth between Laura and Steve. "And she's your...?"

"We're getting married," Steve said.

Vinny's jaw dropped. "I thought you weren't dating anybody."

"I didn't think I was." Steve slinked his arm around Laura's shoulders and hugged her close.

"Judging from her eye color, I'm guessing she's the one you bought those earrings for."

"And you'd be right."

Vinny drummed his fingers on the glass countertop. "And you're here because?"

"We want to pick out a ring. Whatever she wants."

"Nothing too expensive," Laura said.

"Trust me, Steve can afford it." Vinny removed several

trays from the case Steve didn't want to get near last time he was in Vinny's shop. Vinny queried Laura as to what her taste was: white, yellow, or rose gold, whether she wanted a high setting, a solitaire or something more old-fashioned. He had an array of antique rings he'd acquired from countless estate sales and Laura picked one from the middle row. "This is lovely," she exclaimed.

"Excellent taste," Vinny said. "14k white gold with an open lace pave, a halo diamond. Quite spectacular."

Steve took it and slid it up her ring finger, gently pushing past her swollen knuckle. Laura held her hand up and turned it right and left. The overhead lights shot a sparkling ray into Steve's eye. Igniting a flame that would never be extinguished.

Steve waited as Laura scanned the tray, but nothing else caught her eye. "I like this one. But is it expensive? I don't need anything too extravagant."

"If you like it, it's not too expensive. I want you to be sure. Nothing else interests you?"

Ogling the gem adorning her finger, she said, "I love this one."

"We'll take it," Steve said. "Do you want me to get down on one knee?"

Laura laughed. "No."

No fuss, no muss. Laura was a practical woman and it just added to his love for her.

⸻

They traveled the thirty miles to the mall and Laura purchased gifts for his parents, his sisters and their children and some clothing to wear Christmas Day, she only had casual attire at Steve's.

Steve was no help at all, and Laura chastised him for being so inept at shopping.

"Trust me, your gifts won't be as important as the gift I'm giving them."

Laura frowned. What had Steve purchased for his family that could be of such import?

"Don't look so disappointed," Steve said, apparently sensing her unease. "It's you. The gift I'm giving them is *you*."

Speechless, she simply slipped an arm through his package-ladened arms and pressed her cheek into his shoulder.

Saturday night had Laura on edge, the good kind of anxiety. The club held special meaning for her, the place where she'd let all her pain go, where she'd become whole again, unburdened by the trauma of her abuse. However, the snap of a whip followed by a loud almost inhuman shriek turned her head, and suddenly she wasn't so sure. Steve put an arm around her. "Remember everything that goes on here is safe, sane and consensual, even if it doesn't seem that way."

"If you say so," Laura said, searching the room for a possible victim.

Everyone acted happy to see them, especially Jack and Colin.

Colin kept slapping Steve on the back. "You scared the living shit of out me last time I saw you. Glad it's all good in the neighborhood now."

"Same here," Jack said. "You had me worried."

Steve smiled. "Meet my fiancée," he said, taking Laura's hand so they could eye the engagement ring.

"Congratulations, buddy," Colin said with additional back-slapping. "Come here, pet," he said pulling Laura in for a hug. "He's a lucky man."

Jack partook in the hugs and congratulations and ordered drinks on the club. The contagion of celebration spread like wildfire and Laura found herself embraced by an endless line of leather-clad Doms, Dommes and submissives. Protocol was suspended for a brief period and she could have been at any bar in any city, people just happy and celebrating with friends.

***

As much as Steve was enjoying the congratulatory festivities, he was desperate to get Laura upstairs and on *that thing,* her pet name for the restraining bench.

Tugging Laura away from the arm of an older Dom, a sadist as he recalled, he whispered in her ear, "I want you upstairs. Now."

Laura fixed her indigo eyes on him. "I thought you'd never ask. Let's go."

Steve spirited her away through the partying crowd, snatched the key he wanted from the cabinet and led Laura up the spiral staircase. He opened the door and pulled her inside, shutting and locking the door behind them.

"At last," he said, hugging her to his chest. "I thought I'd never get you alone."

They kissed and he slipped a hand under her crisp white shirt. The warmth of her skin threatened his undoing. Again. "Do you have any idea what I'm going to do to you tonight?"

"No," she whispered near his ear. "And that's half the fun. Not knowing."

Steve moved his fingers down the line of shirt buttons, lingering on each as he anticipated the vision of her nakedness. His hands settled on her shoulders as he pushed the fabric down and over her arms. The garment landed on the floor. "You're so beautiful. I love looking at you."

Laura smiled and opened her mouth to respond. Steve put his fingers on her lips. "No, talking. You are to remain silent and obedient. Understood?"

"Yes, Sir."

"You get that the restraining bench is used for spanking or anything else I'd like to do to your ass?" Her cool flesh alerted him to the need for warmth. He slid his hands up and down her arms, massaging, soothing, stimulating.

Laura nodded, her eyes cast downward. He nudged her chin with his knuckle. "You want that?" But Laura remained silent. He worried that she could regress into the well of her abuse if he didn't keep her focused on him. "You may speak. Tell me what you want."

"I want to try this."

"You remember the safe words?"

"Yes, and I know if I get to yellow I must tell you. I don't want to get to red."

"Excellent, and remember it is me here with you. You'll be face down so it will be difficult for you to keep eye contact. I'll prompt you to say my name. Focus on my voice. My scent. Smell is a factor that people don't often notice."

"I can do this. I can," Laura said, bolstering his confidence. The fact that she wanted it should help her stay in the moment.

"Then let's begin. Off with the clothes." Laura obeyed and stood *au naturel* next to the black leather bench. "Let me see if you remember the inspection position." She clasped her hands behind her back, feet apart and gaze downward. "Excellent. Now this will be an erotic spanking, not a punishment spanking." Laura stayed silent and in protocol. "If it was a punishment spanking I'd make you count, but in erotic spanking I will stop when I choose." Steve was playing a part and he hoped Laura was into it. He'd never spank her as punishment. There'd be no punishments in their relationship. Never ever.

"Good girl." He touched her cheek, then guided her to the end of the bench. He lifted a knee. "One foot on the step," he said, "then swing your other leg over and settle on the opposite one." Laura complied. "See, just like riding a horse." She smiled wanly. "Now bend over and lay your upper body on the bench." Again she complied and he knelt and buckled her right hand against the bottom post and repeated with the other. "You okay?" he said.

"Yes, Sir."

"Super job. You're doing great." He stood and stroked her hair then ran his hand up and down her back several times. His attention drifted to her soft round buttocks and he massaged the firm skin, warming it. "You have a spectacular ass, my pet."

He knelt again and strapped both legs against the stanchions, then grabbed her hips and pulled her toward the bench's edge. "Stay where I put you, pet."

Laura watched Steve strip, the taut muscles of his thighs, his corded arms and neck, and his rock-hard pecs heightened her arousal before he even laid a finger on her. Or in her, for that matter. The problem with this restraining stuff was: no mutual touching. Not yet, but when she did get her hands on him, and her mouth, well… yum. Stretched across the smooth leather, a throbbing ache between her thighs threatened her undoing.

Chapter 38

Steve's hand stroked Laura's bare butt and she found herself clenching her thighs against the bench. Longing rushed into her loins, so raw it winded her. She couldn't believe she wanted this so badly. Desire was making her bold.

"I will be spanking that adorable round ass until you're begging me to quit," Steve said, trailing a finger down her ass crack. "But first I think we'll add a plug."

He disappeared briefly and then the cool lube hit her anus. A shudder shivered through her at the anticipation of his finger inside her, followed by the plug. She glanced sideways, the plug in Steve's hand glistened with lubricant. He spread her cheeks and his finger circled the tight rim of muscle. "Relax and push back," he said, and a second later the hard cold plug slid into her. She gasped and squeaked, clutching the bench legs.

The first slap stung and she jolted in response. "What's my name," Steve said, keeping her in the now.

She focused on his voice. "Steve, Sir."

Another slap, the sound echoing in the room, the burning on her bottom intensified.

"Give me a color."

"Green," she said, panting.

The third and fourth came almost together, rough and fast. Then slower, alternating cheeks, by eight she feared she might explode. She lingered on the precipice of pain, the heat, the pleasure.

The spanks subsided and he slowly stroked her flaming flesh.

"Give me a color."

"Blissfully green, Sir."

"Excellent. Now you get a reward for enduring your first real spanking."

Steve inserted a finger into her soft folds, swirling over her clitoris. She was so wet and he added two more fingers. He twisted the plug and Laura moaned and squirmed under his ministrations. He chuckled, gazing at the hot pink skin of her delectable ass. The way Laura wriggled and made those little squeaking noises when he played with her ass, sent him soaring into the carnal stratosphere. He continued the rhythmic thrusts into her wet center, while his thumb kneaded her swollen clit.

"You with me, pet?"

"Yes, Sir. I don't think I can hold out much longer," she sputtered.

"You will wait until I give you permission to come."

"Steve, I'm not sure I—"

"Not yet," he commanded. "I'm taking you so much higher." He flipped the plug's vibrator switch on.

Laura gave an operatic shriek. "Oh God! What's that?"

"Quiet," he barked. "No talking, just feeling." He traced a finger through her wetness then probed deeper, thrusting rhythmically as his thumb circled her clit. He pinched it hard and said, "Now, come now, Laura." She stiffened, every muscle taut, she hung on the precipice. Her breathing stopped.

He thrust three fingers in and out, "Let go, baby. Let it all go."

Laura's heart hammered. Her body flamed. A ripple began low in her groin, like a wave rushing shoreward. Her thighs, her belly, her whole body tightened and she sucked in a sobbing breath and finally yelled her release. Her vagina convulsed around his fingers. Her mind splintered, her world went white, hurtling her into oblivion, like a stone skipping across a boundless lake.

Her stepfather: a demon banished to hell.

"You okay, pet?" Steve knelt beside her, deftly unbuckling the arm restraints. He kissed her gently. "You were amazing. I'm so proud."

He moved to the other end of the bench and unbuckled the leg restraints, then picked her up and turned her into his embrace, handling her as if she were weightless. He took her mouth gently and sweetly as he carried her to the bed, laying her on the satin coverlet. Reaching underneath her, he pulled the covers down and lay alongside her, holding her close. "So, do you like *that thing*?"

Laura laughed. "Which one?"

"The spanking bench."

"Well, that vibrating thing was pretty spectacular also."

"Then I've achieved my objective. Amazing how much fun a good spanking can be."

Heat flooded her cheeks. "Well done, Sir. You've got some skills, mister."

Steve roared a laugh and Laura's heart swelled with love for him. "But," he said. I'm not done with you yet."

"Lucky me," she said, laying a hand against his cheek. "I love you."

His mouth quirked up. "I love you too, with every atom of my being."

They lay still for a while but the yearning returned. Her body ached for him. Would it always be like this? She wanted Steve inside her and reached down and circled his cock with her hand. Steve involuntarily jerked and a moan escaped his lips. He rolled toward her, his palm cupping a breast, his thumb pressing on her nipple. His tongue probed her mouth, the kiss wet, deep, as their tongues danced an erotic tango.

Steve took a nipple in his mouth and sucked hard as Laura worked his cock up and down, creating a rhythm that drove him wild. He could barely tear himself away from her lush and responsive breasts. He concentrated his attention on her nipples until her muffled whimpers became audible. She gasped as he plunged a finger into her vagina, moving it against the swollen sensitive walls.

"That's enough, baby," he said, pulling her hand off his cock. "Let's slow this down."

He knelt between her legs, pushing her knees up and spreading them wide. "I'd like to tie you down but I don't think I can wait that long." His fingers pulled back her folds, exposing her engorged clit. He licked up and over the nub, and she bucked his grip on her hips as his tongue probed and laved. She panted as he plunged a finger inside her again and she moaned. He added another digit, moving slowly in and out, circling the wall of her vagina. His tongue flicked over her clit mercilessly. Her vagina constricted on his fingers. She was close. He pulled back and his fingers stopped. "Not yet, pet. You don't have permission to come."

Laura simpered.

Unable to wait any longer himself, he took her mouth hard. Her full breasts cushioned his chest, her soft thighs cradling his hips. He snuck his palms underneath her and grabbed her buttocks and thrust into her.

Laura constricted every muscle she could, it was like trying to hold lightning in a bottle. Her hips lifted off the bed as waves of increasing ecstasy traveled through her. She gritted her teeth at the raw animal feeling. Rocking her pelvis in time to the thrusts of his cock, she almost climaxed. She held her breath and arched her body toward him.

"Not yet."

He flipped the switch on the plug again, sending sweet vibrations coursing through her. Every nerve between her thighs throbbed.

She was close, so close.

Chuckling, he pushed himself up and plunged in deep, impaling her so forcefully she screamed. His thick cock pressed against the vibrating plug and she shuddered with sheer ecstasy. His fingers dug into her hips, holding her immobile as he hammered into her. "Now, pet," he said. "Come now." His soft growl signaled his release and he jerked inside her, making her buck and shiver. Everything inside her contracted and exploded, her nerves singing a vibrant melody. The after-shocks lingered, until their breathing calmed.

Steve pulled out the plug and shut it off, tossing it in the bedside trashcan. He returned to lie atop her. He wrapped his arms around her neck, hugging her tight. "Am I crushing you?" he whispered near her ear. "Because I like it here."

"No," she whispered with what little breath she could find. Her nails raked over his back in gentle strokes. "I want to stay like this forever."

Chapter 39

L aura changed clothing three times. "Is this okay?" she said, sporting a pair of skinny-fit black pants and a green velvet top with long sleeves and a sweetheart neckline. She toed into black suede booties with a princess heel.

"You look great, but you looked great in the last two outfits." Steve sat in the bedroom chair watching Laura dress and undress, the latter being his favorite part. "If you take your clothes off one more time I'm going to have to fuck you."

"We fucked this morning and twice last night." They'd spent a quiet Christmas Eve, drinking champagne after a dinner of cheese fondue, followed by chocolate fondue. No presents. Laura insisted she had the best present of her life in her engagement ring and Steve said *she* was his present. They agreed they sounded pathetic, two lovesick teenagers, but were happy to be so damn annoying.

"Yeah, well, I'm two seconds away from doing it again. I'm not keeping count."

"You're an ass."

"I know, but I'm your ass. Speaking of which, I love your ass. I want to play with it right now."

"Steve!"

He smiled and rose, taking her hand, "Let's go. I can't wait to see my mother's reaction when I finally bring a girl home for Christmas dinner. She's going to have a stroke. It just might kill her."

"That's a terrible thing to say."

He put her neck in a chokehold and dragged her from the bedroom. "We're outta here."

They arrived fashionably late, arms laden with packages and wine, the driveway lined with cars. By Steve's count, his sisters and their families, plus Vinny and his, had already landed. His mother's wish had come true as another four inches of snow blanketed the front lawn. Long Island was experiencing a bumper snow crop this year.

Steve grabbed the screen door handle, but Laura stopped him. "I need a minute."

"Stop. You're overthinking this. They're going to love you. Promise."

Laura's indigo eyes found his, she inhaled deeply and let it out. "Okay. Ready."

However, Steve underestimated the reception that awaited them. Kisses, hugs, voices talking over each other, children clutching at him and Laura, fussing over the ring—everyone politely ignoring her bruised knuckles. He feared she might freak. He gave a loud whistle and the room quieted. "Okay, everybody, let's give Laura a breather. We don't want to scare her off."

Andrea Moretti came to his rescue. "Come, darling. Why don't you help me in the kitchen?" and she whisked his fiancée away. Steve's mother was a pro when it came to toning things down. Her years as a high school principal in a large Long Island school district boasted a constant stream of teens, parents, and teachers who never came to her office unless they were pissed. Her talent for smoothing things over—so well honed by now, meant she could probably end a war. The State Department should recruit her.

Steve helped his father and brothers-in-law make and distribute drinks, confident that his mother and sisters had Laura well in hand.

Vinny patted him on the back. "Welcome to domestic life, cuz."

Steve smirked. "Thanks, and thanks for helping with the ring."

"No problem. Any time." Vinny winced. "That didn't come out right. This is the *last* time. Right?"

Steve placed a hand on Vinny's shoulder. "You're so right, man."

The savory aromas filled the house and although he often balked at having to attend these family gatherings he had to admit that there was nothing like the holidays to bring you peace. The love of friends and family.

And soon, perhaps a new family of his own.

Laura plated warm bacon cream cheese squares onto a Santa Clause-faced platter. Christmas music and the friendly banter of Steve's mother and sisters filled the space that had so often been vast and silent in holidays past. She smiled, lost in a Christmas card daydream, the way she always fantasized a holiday should be.

Andrea Moretti stood beside her. "I've never seen Steven so happy. Content, to be exact. And it makes me happy."

Laura stayed mute, not knowing what an appropriate response would be.

Andrea Moretti placed a hand on her wrist, the rope burn from her ordeal exposed, not to mention her prizefighter knuckles. Laura tugged her sleeve down reflexively. "It's okay. Steve explained what happened. You're quite brave."

Laura wasn't sure how she felt about the fact that Steve shared the details of her abduction and torment. Did his mother know she killed Viktor?

"I'd like to say I was just doing my job, but this was a little off the grid. If I let myself think about it, I should've been more on my game and figured out he was targeting me."

"Nevertheless, being an FBI agent is impressive. You're a woman I think we all wish we could be. I'd never have the guts to do your job."

Dinner of grilled filet mignon—Steve's father manned the grill on the snow-laden deck—and potatoes stuffed with ham and onions, homemade biscuits, butternut squash, green beans with almonds and Caesar Salad proved to be more food than Laura had ever seen at one meal. She sat to Steve's right, next to his father at the head of the table. Antonio Moretti squeezed her hand as he poured her a glass of pinot noir. "I'm so glad you're going to be part of our family."

"Thank you, I'm privileged to be here and you've given me such a warm and loving welcome."

He smiled and it was Steve's expression. Laura wondered, did she have *her* father's smile? A hand on her thigh pulled her from her musings. The love on Steve's face overwhelmed her.

Presents were exchanged, desserts wolfed down, and children soon drifted off to sleep in any place they could find: the couch, floor, the coveted beanbag chair. Goodbyes followed, hugs and kisses and promises to get together soon. Laura was reminded about the weekly Sunday dinner and vowed to attend as often as possible.

Home, snuggled under the covers, Steve still in the bath-room, Laura surfed the channels. She lingered on an old flick, hitting the info button: *Boys Town* 1938 starring Spencer Tracy as Father Flanagan and Mickey Rooney as the recalcitrant teen. "Steve," she yelled. "Look what's on TV."

Steve rushed from the bathroom and jumped onto the bed like an oversized kid, gaping at the screen. "You're kidding?"

"Can you believe it? The movie you mentioned when we met at the teen rehab place, the day of the kidnapping."

"Yup. This is it."

"By the way did you hear back from *our* Father Flanagan?"

"I did. He'd be honored to perform our nuptials."

"Awesome. Let's watch it," Laura said as Steve nestled under the blanket, offering his arm as a pillow.

Let me savor this time, Laura thought, let me capture the moment…

As the credits ran, they both remained silent. Laura switched off the TV and sat cross-legged facing Steve.

"I have something to tell you."

Steve sat opposite her in the identical pose. "Okay. Shoot."

"I have money."

Steve smiled. "I know. To quote Detective Jackson, 'nobody lives on that street without serious wealth'."

"I have a lot of money."

"Okay, I'll bite. What's *a lot*?"

"A little over five-hundred million."

Steve gulped. "Jesus. Then you'll want a prenup?"

"What? No, absolutely not."

"I don't mind. It's your money."

"Technically, it's my aunt's money. I didn't earn it. And that's not why I brought it up." Laura scrunched up her face as if decoding a complicated calculus. "The guy who manages it does a stellar job. It grows exponentially every year."

"I think the expression is: it takes money to make money."

"Well, I haven't spent any, other than the fund that pays the bills on the house, it's just sitting there collecting interest. I want to do something with it."

"Like what?"

"We both know that there are a lot of needy and abused children right here in the U.S. Remember that night we watched the program about the kids in juvie? We've both witnessed it firsthand. They're hungry, they have no opportunity to get an education. I'd like to start a foundation for children who are victims of sexual abuse." Laura fidgeted with the leg of her pajama pants, a gift from Steve's nieces—green flannel with imprinted candy canes.

"Fucking spectacular. I'll help any way I can."

"Selling the house will just add to the fund. There'd be plenty of money left and we can still buy a beach house."

Steve took Laura's hands in his, his thumbs stroking. "Laura, here's what I meant about you being a wonderful mother. You're ready to mother the world."

Laura smiled, but it vanished. "If my aunt hadn't rescued me I might be in jail right now. I'd have had a different life, no education, no career. I'd be a convicted felon instead of an FBI agent." She paused, gripping his hands tightly. "And I never would have met you."

"And that would have been a travesty of justice right there." Steve leaned in and gently kissed her lips. He whispered, "I'm all in."

Steve's words from the first night he tried to make love to her, the night when it all went horribly wrong, came back. 'Bad things happen to good people and good things happen to bad people. You can't control what happens, only how you react.' Her abuse no longer had power over her.

She was worthy of love.

"I'm hopelessly in love with you, Steven Anthony Moretti. I know that now and I can actually say the words."

Steve took her into his arms and kissed her senseless, stealing her breath away.

Laura lay back on the pillows and slipped off her pajama bottoms. She snuggled under the covers and gave an impish grin. "Speaking of *all in…*"

Chapter 40

One Year Later

Laura and Alyx stretched out on the crimson loungers, matching baby bumps prominent and proud. Laura snickered.

Alyx lifted her sunglasses and turned her head toward Laura. "What?" she said.

"I still can't believe we have the exact same due date," Laura said. "What are the chances?"

"Actually, I think Daniel figured it out, you know, being a science geek and all. I can't remember the number but it was astronomical."

"Do you think they were conceived the same day?" Laura smirked. "We never did compare notes on that little tidbit."

"Ha, funny," Alyx said. "But it's not an exact science, so who knows. I still have to pinch myself sometimes. I honestly never imagined I'd have a kid. Daniel didn't want kids either, but one day we just arrived at the same place and well, here we are."

Laura turned on her side to face Alyx and not without

considerable effort. "Well, neither of us had a normal childhood, or mothers who'd win any awards. No Mrs. Brady in our lives."

"True that," Alyx said. "Although Daniel's childhood was stellar. And his mother is awesome. I'm lucky to have her in my life. Lydia too. I had no mother when I was little but as an adult, I have two. Who'd-a-thunk?"

"Same here," Laura agreed. "Steve's mom is a true gem. She treats me like her own daughter and I can always go to her, talk to her, about anything. His sisters are great too."

"A corona and a virgin Pina Colada," Steve said.

"Same here," Daniel added.

"Lime with the Coronas?" the bartender asked.

"Yes," Steve said and Daniel nodded. "Pretty stupid name," Steve said. "Couldn't they have come up with something better?"

"Yeah," Daniel agreed. "Two virgin Pina Coladas for two obviously *not-virgins.*" They fist bumped.

Steve gave Daniel a slap on the back. "This was a great idea and thanks for the jaunt on the private jet."

Daniel folded a cocktail napkin into triangles. "My mother's idea. I'd never heard of a *baby moon.* And since we had our honeymoon before the wedding I figured maybe this time we'd go with the norm."

"On your room?" the bartender said, placing the frosty drinks and bottles of beer in front of them.

"On my tab," Steve said. "4525."

"Thanks," Daniel said.

The bartender handed Steve the ticket. He signed and they returned to find their wives sprawled under the colossal red umbrella.

"Thanks," both wives said, accepting the icy drinks. Steve and Daniel settled into the loungers on either side of the women.

"You'll never guess who I ran into the other day," Alyx said to Laura. "Jamie Gallagher."

"No kidding," Laura said. "Wasn't she stationed in D.C., assigned to the Secret Service?"

"Yup. She's back at the New York office. She'll be working with my old boss, Rob Scarborough."

"Cool. Didn't she graduate at the top of our class?"

"That she did. And she's been on top often, high school valedictorian, number one at UVA and don't forget she was an Olympian."

"Geez, yeah, I forgot about that."

The men perked up. "Olympian?" Steve said.

Laura tapped a finger against her forehead. "I think it was that skiing and rifle shooting event, I forget the official title. Seriously, that woman is lethal."

"Hmm. What did we call her, again?" Alyx asked Laura

"Martin, for Martin Riggs in the movie *Lethal Weapon*."

"Yeah, that's right. Remember how she kicked ass in TEVOC?"

Laura laughed. "I do. When that car comes out of nowhere and slams into the side door of your vehicle, you accelerate, and they catch up, then the driver rolls down his window, pulls a gun, and fires. Shit, I nearly died without the aid of real ammo."

Alyx sipped her drink, then said, "Yeah, those SIM bullets hurt like a son of a bitch. And it took me two days to wash that red paint out of my hair."

Laura placed a hand on Steve's thigh. "Most of us peed

our pants, but not Jamie. That woman has nerves of steel." She turned to Alyx. "Didn't she do the two extra weeks for intelligence training?"

"She did. That's how she wound up working tandem with Secret Service. I told her we'd meet for lunch when we got back."

"Great," Laura said. "I'd love to see her again." Laura removed her sunglasses and adjusted her lounge chair, flatter. A nap perhaps.

Steve placed his hand on her round belly. "Happy?" he said, sliding his sunglasses down the bridge of his nose.

Laura's pulse accelerated just like it did every time he looked at her with that intensity. "Yes. And I understand now that happiness is a choice. Bad things happen, but holding onto unpleasant memories is contrary to happiness. It's your choice whether you let it affect you or not."

"That's my girl," he said, rubbing her baby bump. He leaned over and kissed her.

The End

Kendra Greenwood

Kendra Greenwood has always been a storyteller. She often told stories to her kids at bedtime in lieu of reading to them. A serious daydreamer, she used to think it the complete opposite of her education and work in the sciences, but now realizes scientists are the ultimate daydreamers. Fantasy has always been an escape for Kendra. Weaving a thrilling romantic tale around her favorite TV and film characters, her favorite way to fall asleep at night. Eventually she wrote them down and found a place to share her stories.

Kendra grew up on the beaches of Long Island's bucolic east end, but recently relocated to Virginia. When she's not writing you can find her in the kitchen whipping up something scrumptious or in the studio fusing glass into decorative dishes.

Follow her on:
Twitter @k51greenwcod
Facebook Kendra Greenwood
Email kendra51greenwood@gmail.com

Don't miss these exciting titles by Kendra Greenwood and Blushing Books!

Steel and Desire Series
UnSub
UnBound
Unguarded
Unsaddened

Blushing Books

Blushing Books is the oldest eBook publisher on the web. We've been running websites that publish steamy romance and erotica since 1999, and we have been selling eBooks since 2003. We have free and promotional offerings that change weekly, so please do visit us at http://www.blushingbooks.com/free.

Blushing Books Newsletter

Please join the Blushing Books newsletter
to receive updates & special promotional offers.
You can also join by using your mobile phone:
Just text **BLUSHING** to 22828.

Every month, one new sign up via text messaging will receive
a $25.00 Amazon gift card, so sign up today!